IF HE'S DANGEROUS

He grasped her by her shoulders, intending to scold her about foolishly risking her good name. Touching her immediately proved to be a mistake. The warmth of her beneath his hands rapidly entered his blood. The way her sweet face was turned up toward his, her soft mouth but a breath away, proved that he was right to think he had lost all control over his lusts. The lecture he had planned fled his head as rapidly as a buck did a hunter's party. He lowered his mouth to hers, hungry to taste her again.

The moment his lips touched hers, Lorelei flung her arms around his neck and held on tight. His kisses were intoxicating. When she was near him, kissing him was about all she could think of. The memory of his kisses haunted her for most of the time she was not with him as well. He tasted good, smelled delicious, and the hunger his first kiss had stirred within her just kept growing stronger . . .

Books by Hannah Howell

ONLY FOR YOU * MY VALIANT KNIGHT *
UNCONQUERED * WILD ROSES * A TASTE OF
FIRE * HIGHLAND DESTINY * HIGHLAND
HONOR * HIGHLAND PROMISE *
A STOCKINGFUL OF JOY * HIGHLAND VOW *
HIGHLAND KNIGHT * HIGHLAND HEARTS *
HIGHLAND BRIDE * HIGHLAND ANGEL *
HIGHLAND GROOM * HIGHLAND WARRIOR *
RECKLESS * HIGHLAND CONQUEROR *
HIGHLAND CHAMPION * HIGHLAND LOVER *
HIGHLAND VAMPIRE * THE ETERNAL
HIGHLANDER * MY IMMORTAL HIGHLANDER *
CONQUEROR'S KISS * HIGHLAND
BARBARIAN * BEAUTY AND THE BEAST *
HIGHLAND SAVAGE * HIGHLAND THIRST *
HIGHLAND WEDDING * HIGHLAND WOLF *
SILVER FLAME * HIGHLAND FIRE * NATURE
OF THE BEAST * HIGHLAND CAPTIVE *
HIGHLAND SINNER * MY LADY CAPTOR *
IF HE'S WICKED * WILD CONQUEST *
IF HE'S SINFUL * KENTUCKY BRIDE *
IF HE'S WILD * YOURS FOR ETERNITY *
COMPROMISED HEARTS * HIGHLAND
PROTECTOR * STOLEN ECSTASY *
IF HE'S DANGEROUS * HIGHLAND HERO *
HIGHLAND HUNGER

Published by Kensington Publishing Corporation

IF HE'S DANGEROUS

HANNAH HOWELL

ZEBRA BOOKS
KENSINGTON PUBLISHING CORP.
http://www.kensingtonbooks.com

ZEBRA BOOKS are published by

Kensington Publishing Corp.
119 West 40th Street
New York, NY 10018

All Kensington titles, imprints and distributed lines are available at special quantity discounts for bulk purchases for sales promotion, premiums, fund-raising, educational or institutional use.

Special book excerpts or customized printings can also be created to fit specific needs. For details, write or phone the office of the Kensington Special Sales Manager: Attn. Special Sales Department. Kensington Publishing Corp., 119 West 40th Street, New York, NY 10018. Phone: 1-800-221-2647.

Zebra Books and the Z logo Reg. U.S. Pat. & TM Off.

ISBN-13: 978-1-4201-1878-0
ISBN-10: 1-4201-1878-1

First Printing: June 2011
10 9 8 7 6 5 4 3 2 1

Printed in the United States of America

Chapter 1

England—Summer, 1790

There was a naked man in her father's rose garden.

Lorelei Sundun blinked her eyes several times, but the man was still there. She wondered why he was staring at her in astonishment. She was not the one standing naked in a garden, a fat white rose the only thing protecting her modesty. Lorelei was certain she should be the one doing the gaping. In fact, she mused as she allowed her gaze to travel the long length of his lean body, she should be on her feet and racing toward the manor, perhaps even screaming for help. Loudly. Instead, she was utterly fascinated.

For a moment she wondered if she had been sitting in the sun contemplating her lack of a husband for too long. She was not wearing a hat. Could one get a brain fever from sitting hatless in the sun? Lorelei was not sure that even a brain fever would cause her to see a naked man. Certainly not one with a big, fat white rose hiding his manly parts, the part of a man she was most curious about. Lorelei was certain that the drawings in a book she had found hidden in her father's massive library could not be accurate concerning those parts of a man. A man could never hide something that large in his breeches. She doubted a man could even walk properly with such an appendage and suspected the looks on the faces of the women in those drawings were not ones of ecstasy but excruciating pain.

He was, she decided, a very handsome man. It might be why she found it impossible to look away as any woman of sense would do. His hair was thick, hanging far past his broad shoulders, and a black so deep and true the sunlight caused it to glint with faintly blue highlights. His features were harsh, almost predatory, but there was no fear in her heart. His eyes were dark and she was tempted to move closer to see what color they really were. He was tall and lean, but she could see the firm muscles beneath his smooth, swarthy skin. There appeared to be the remnants of bruises marring his fine body. Lorelei clasped her hands together in her lap to quell the sudden, and startling, urge to touch that sun-kissed skin, to soothe those hurts. He had good teeth, straight and white, she mused even as he shut his mouth and revealed lips that had a seductive hint of fullness to them. Those lips and his enviably long lashes were the only soft features on his hard face.

"Who are you?" he asked, his deep voice holding such a strong note of command she could feel it tug at her mind, and had to quell the instinctive urge to immediately refuse to answer him.

"Lady Lorelei Sundun, seventh child of the Duke of Sundunmoor," she replied, thinking that she ought to be the one making demands. "And you are?"

"Sir Argus Wherlocke." He scowled at her. "This is not where I wished to be."

"I suppose it is somewhat awkward to find oneself standing unclothed in a duke's garden."

"And you should not be able to see me."

"Why not?"

"You have no Wherlocke or Vaughn blood, do you?"

That was no answer to her question, she thought, but swallowed a flare of annoyance. "Neither name appears in the family lineage."

Lorelei decided she could not leave the man unclothed any longer. His state of undress was stirring an unwelcome curiosity within her. She stood up, walked over to him, and handed him her fine shawl made of Italian lace. His eyes widened as he took it in his hand and she could see that those eyes were the dark blue of the night sky. When she realized how close she stood to him, how her palm itched to touch his skin, she took a step back. She briefly averted her eyes as he tied her shawl around his waist, for he had to step back from the shelter of the rose. Before looking away, however, she had noticed that the look of utter astonishment on his face had begun to lessen.

"This is most strange," he muttered and frowned at her. "You should not be seeing me. You most assuredly should not be able to hand me this shawl nor should I be able to hold it."

"And you should not be standing unclothed in my father's rose garden," she said. "Yet here you are. Where did you wish to find yourself?"

"I sought out one of my family." He cursed softly. "I am being pulled back."

"Pulled back where?" Lorelei knew her eyes were widening as the man appeared to be slowly losing all substance, the roses behind him beginning to show through his body. "You appear to be fading away, sir. Are you a ghost then?"

"No, not a ghost. Heed me now, for I have little time left. You must find someone in my family, a Wherlocke or a Vaughn. Tell them that I am in need of help. A man who calls himself Charles Cornick is holding me captive. He seeks knowledge of our gifts."

"Your gifts?" The man was so faded now that she could see right through him and had to clench her hands tightly against the urge to grab hold of him and try to hold him in place.

"He seeks a way to steal them, to take them into himself. You must contact my family so they can help me. Soon. I need help soon."

"Where are you? Where does this man hold you?"

"In the country. I know not where. I smell lavender and sweet peas."

Between one blink and the next, he was gone. Lorelei stepped up to the rosebush he had stood behind, but there was no sign that he had ever been there, not even a footprint left behind in the soft dirt. He could have been standing on one of the rune-marked stones her father had surrounded with his roses, but there should have been footprints leading to the stone.

Lorelei was just convincing herself that she had dreamt the whole incident when she reached to tug her shawl more closely around her shoulders. It was gone. A chill that had nothing to do with the late-afternoon breeze went straight through her. Her shawl had been tied around the man's waist. That small fact proved that something had happened, something she could not explain but could not deny.

"But what?" she muttered and lightly rubbed at her temples to push away the faint ache of an approaching headache. "A man simply cannot appear and disappear like that. Nor should a spirit be able to hold fast to a shawl and disappear with it."

It *had* to have been a dream, she firmly told herself. Lorelei started toward the manor house only to stop and look back at the place where the man had stood. She was certain she was awake. She pinched herself just to be sure and cursed at the pain. There was no doubt that she was awake, yet it was difficult to believe all that had just happened. It would be so much easier to believe that she had left her shawl in her room and had just had a little dream while sitting in the sun.

Soon. I need help soon.

Lorelei hurried into the house. This matter needed looking into. If it had not been some delusion brought on by sitting too long in the sun, then there was a man in trouble somewhere. She needed to know more about the family he wanted her to summon to his aid. Her father and his extensive library was a good place to start.

Roland Sundun, Eighth Duke of Sundunmoor, looked up from his book as his youngest daughter burst into his library. "M'dear, is something wrong? Have the twins misbehaved again?"

"No, Papa, Axel and Wolfgang are with their tutor," Lorelei replied.

She stood still for a moment to catch her breath, surprised that she had actually run all the way to the library. Her tall, almost too thin father looked a little startled and she could not blame him. Her impetuous entrance must have made him think there was some emergency. In truth there might be, but she would keep that knowledge to herself for now.

"Papa, do you know anything about a family named Wherlocke or Vaughn?" she asked.

"Oh, yes, m'dear." He stood up and carefully set his book aside. "I have studied them for years. Why do you ask?"

"Just some gossip I heard. Something about them being, well, a bit strange."

"Not strange. Gifted. Wondrously gifted. Fascinating people. Utterly fascinating."

Lorelei watched her father stride over to a set of shelves that reached up a full two stories. It held papers and books about a subject dear to his heart. Dissertations on ghosts, magic, witchcraft, and all manner of strange happenings filled the shelves to overflowing. She sighed even as she experienced a surge of interest. The answers she sought would be a long time in coming, but the very fact that her father went straight to that shelf told her that what she had seen in the garden could well have been real.

Argus grimaced as he fought the nausea and cold sweats he always suffered when he sent his spirit out from his body. It was wrong that he should suffer so only to have failed in his mission, he thought crossly. He moved a hand down his body to rub at his roiling belly and tensed as his fingers brushed against soft lace. Opening his eyes, he looked down at the delicate shawl tied around his waist.

"Damn my eyes, she was real," he whispered.

Hope surged in his heart, easing his discomfort.

She had called herself Lorelei, seventh child of the Duke of Sundunmoor. Argus sorted through his vast knowledge of the aristocracy until he dredged up a few scraps about the duke. Wealthy, powerful, eccentric, three wives, a widower who preferred books to people, and a small army of children. As far as he knew there never was and never had been any connection between his family and the Sunduns, yet she had seen him, nearly touched him. Unless she was gifted as those in his family were, she should not have seen him at all.

What he could not be certain of was that she had believed what she had seen and would now act upon his request for help. He could see her clearly in his mind, her big, dark green eyes holding a glint of curiosity and no fear. She had looked small, delicate yet fulsome, her breasts lushly rounded and her hips nicely curved. A delightful armful, he mused, with thick dark red hair tumbling wildly over her slender shoulders. What she did not look like, however, was someone who could help free him.

The scrape of a boot on the stairs leading down to his prison pulled him from his thoughts. He quickly undid the shawl and stuffed it beneath the thin, straw-filled mattress that made up his bed. Once assured it was completely hidden, he crossed his arms beneath his head and waited. His calm was a hard-won façade, but he was determined to reveal no fear to his captors. After a fortnight of scant food and water, torture, and lying naked and chained to a bed by the ankle, that façade was getting harder to cling to.

Charles Cornick strode into the room, two thick-necked men right behind him, all three wearing

tinted spectacles. Light came with him as all three
carried lanterns that they hung from the hooks on
the walls of his prison. Argus struggled to hide the
furious hatred that surged through him at the sight
of his captor. The air of arrogant calm he maintained
annoyed Charles and, for that pleasure alone, Argus
meant to hold fast to it. The fury and hate that
gnawed at his innards grew stronger every day, however. Argus knew it was born of his helplessness.

"You are looking surprisingly hale, Argus," said
Charles as he sat in a chair just beyond Argus's reach.
"Mayhap we are treating you too kindly."

Argus wished he had the gift of being able to move
things with his mind. He would like to slam Charles
against the hard stone walls a few times.

"Your hospitality has been all I could have expected of you." Charles's muddy brown eyes narrowed
and Argus suspected his words had been a little
too heavily weighted with sarcasm, but he inwardly
shrugged. "I am not sure stripping a man and chain-
ing him to a bed will become de rigueur, however."

"A shame. I can think of many who would benefit
from such treatment." Charles smiled. "Ones who
would be far more cooperative than you are."

Yet another threat to my family, Argus thought. He
fought to hide his anger over those continued
threats, to hide his aching wish to wrap his hands
around Charles's throat. The man constantly threatened his family and Argus knew it was no empty
threat. Charles refused to believe that the gifts the
Wherlockes and Vaughns had were not things that
could be taught, given away, or stolen.

"Are those scratches on your stomach?" Charles

asked, staring hard at the lower half of Argus's body.
"How did you come by such wounds?"

It was on the tip of Argus's tongue to say rosebushes,
but he bit the words back. Charles was a believer. The
man did not understand how one gained such *gifts*,
but he did believe in them, respect them, and covet
them. Charles would not be angered by what he
would see as impertinence, or shocked, or confused,
as many another would be. The man would be curious. There would be questions, demands for an explanation that would grow increasingly brutal.

"Small injuries incurred while attempting to un-
chain myself," Argus replied.

"Unchaining yourself would do you no good.
There is no way out of this room. Your talent does not
allow you to open locked doors or break down walls.
I believe one of the younger members of your very
large family has that gift."

The man knew far too much about his family. It
was one reason Argus had risked sending his spirit
out to seek help despite the growing weakness captivity and repeated beatings had inflicted on him. His
family needed to know that Charles had learned far
too many of their secrets and that the man might not
be working on his own.

"You have put too much faith in rumor," Argus
said, filling his voice with the demand that Charles
believe him.

Yet again he tried to use his gift, but none of the
men fell under his spell. The tinted glasses they wore
blocked the power of his gaze. The small bits of cotton
each man tucked into his ears muffled the power of
his voice to bend them to his will. From the moment

he had seen the glasses and the cotton, Argus had known that Charles was aware of his gift and believed in it. It did not stop Argus from trying every time Charles and his brutes came to visit, however.

"I would think you would weary of that game. Your gift does not work on us." Charles rested his left ankle on his right knee and idly rubbed at a smudge on his boot. "And, please, do not deny, yet again, that you have any gift. That, too, has grown tiresome after a fortnight. Are you not bored with this game yet?"

"'Tis no game. Even if I had a gift, as you claim, I doubt I could but hand it to you."

"Perhaps not, but you could share it."

"As one shares the gift of writing music or poetry? You cannot truly believe that is possible."

"Why not? You have a skill, and skills can be taught, shared, learned about. The ability to make people tell you all they know, to pull the truth from a person even when they do not want to tell you it, is a very useful skill. I can think of many ways to make use of it."

"There is no skill I can give you."

"So tiresome. So stubborn. You bring this discomfort upon yourself."

"Do I? And what would happen if I had the skill you claim I do and gave it to you as you ask? Am I to believe that you would then kindly set me free?"

It did not surprise Argus when Charles did not answer, just smiled and signaled his men to begin their work. Argus put up a fight as he always did. The chain holding him to the bed, a fortnight of beatings, and a lack of enough food and water to keep a man healthy and strong made it impossible to hold his own against Charles's two brutes. The few injuries he did inflict before they subdued him gave him some pleasure, however. He would have felt more except that he suspected Charles enjoyed watching the uneven match and that was why he had never fully restrained Argus.

By the time the two men finished pounding him, Argus was hanging on to consciousness by a very thin thread. There was not a part of him that was not crying out in pain. When Charles leaned over him, Argus glared at the man even though he suspected Charles could see little of it due to Argus's rapidly swelling eyelids.

"As I have said, this grows tiresome," said Charles. "Very tiresome indeed."

"So sorry to bore you," replied Argus, not surprised to hear how slurred his words were for his mouth was bruised, bleeding, and swelling up as fast as his eyes were.

"This may end soon. We think we have found a way to get what we want."

Alarm swept through Argus, pushing aside the rapidly approaching dark of unconsciousness, as he feared Charles was about to use one of his family to try and break him. "I have told you that, if I had a gift, it would not be something that can be taught or given away."

"So we begin to think, but there may be a way to steal it." Charles straightened up and fussily tugged at the lace around his wrists. "I am uneasy about what has been proposed, but one can always be rid of a witch when her usefulness passes." He smiled at Argus and then started out of the room. "Be sure to rest well, Sir Argus. We want you strong when next we visit."

Argus stared at the door as it shut behind the men, wincing at the sound of the lock turning. A witch? Despite all the strange gifts his family had been blessed with, Argus was not sure he believed in witches. The abilities his family had could be explained logically. Magic, potions, and spells often defied logic. Yet, he could not fully dismiss the possibility that such things existed. And, if they did, there just might be a way to steal his gifts from him. The thought of a man like Charles Cornick possessing his gift, going after others in his family to steal theirs, made Argus's blood run cold.

We. The man had said *we.* Argus knew he would have to consider the importance of that once he recovered from this beating enough to think clearly. If there was some conspiracy against his family, they could all be in a lot more danger than he had first thought.

"Lorelei, seventh child of the Duke of Sundunmoor," he whispered as unconsciousness tightened its grip on him, "I pray you are stronger than you look. It appears more than my own fate rests in your small hands." Even as he fell into the beckoning blackness, he slipped his hand beneath the thin mattress to touch her shawl.

Lorelei frowned at her father as he paused in his long dissertation concerning the Wherlockes and the Vaughns. "So they are magic?" she asked.

"No, child," he replied and smiled at her, revealing the sweet handsomeness that had gained him three beautiful wives. "They have God-given gifts. I believe we all have a touch of them, but some people have a much stronger dose, something they can actually make use of. We have all had that faint warning of danger, that moment of unease that saved us from some accident or threat. The gifted ones can actually see that danger coming in a dream or a vision."

He took a breath, and, knowing he was about to launch into yet another long lecture, Lorelei quickly asked, "Can a person send his spirit out from his body?"

"Is that the rumor you heard?"

"Amongst others," she murmured and hoped she looked as innocently curious as she was trying to.

"I have heard something of that. A man goes into a trance and sends his spirit, his soul, out to wander the world. It is not written of as much as the other gifts are, the ones such as seeing ghosts and having visions."

"I see. So, you do not think it is possible to do that?"

"Oh, I cannot see why it cannot be done, just that it must be difficult. After all, we all believe we have a soul that leaves the body when we die. Why can we not find a way to send it on a little trip now and then while we are still alive?"

Lorelei let her father ramble on for a while longer before excusing herself to dress for dinner. As she made her way to her bedchamber, she thought on all he had told her. It appeared that the Wherlockes and the Vaughns might truly be gifted, that the rumors whispered about them might all be true. Her father certainly thought so and, although he did seem to be lost in his books most of the time, he was a very intelligent man. And, she mused, enough others believed in it, too, or there would not be so many papers and books written about such gifts.

That meant that Sir Argus Wherlocke could have actually sent his spirit into her father's garden. The man could actually be in danger. Her heart pounded at the thought and she told herself it was from excitement and not fear for a man with dark eyes and smooth skin. The question now was, did she write to his family telling them what had happened and risk being thought a mad woman? Or, did she just ignore the whole matter, decry it as the product of a fevered brain, and risk leaving a man in captivity?

The moment she entered her bedchamber she went to her writing desk. It would be easier on her mind to be thought a fool or mad than to think she had left a man in mortal danger when she could have helped him. She quickly penned three letters, certain that their butler, Max, could find the addresses for the three Wherlocke names she recalled from her father's lengthy, and somewhat rambling, talk.

Letters that would take time to get where they were being sent, she thought. If the people she had chosen were not at home it could be even longer before they learned of the trouble Sir Argus was in. Lorelei decided she could not just sit by like some delicate flower of womanhood and wait for others to rush to the man's rescue, especially when she could have no certainty that they would rush, or even be able to do so. She needed to begin the search for him herself, immediately.

Setting the letters aside to be addressed, franked, and sent out in the morning, she began her preparations for dinner. She needed to make a few plans, but was confident she would be able to decide on the best place to search if she just thought about it for a while. Lorelei knew there was an added spring to her step as she headed down to dinner. She was looking forward to being a heroine.

Chapter 2

"I have no idea why we are trudging around after you on this mad quest."

Lorelei ignored her cousin Cyrus's grumbled complaint as she studied the house below them. Since arriving at her cousins' home, Dunn Manor, it had taken three long days to find it. She idly scratched her arm, the grass she was sprawled in irritating her skin. Every instinct she had told her this was the house she had been searching for, but, although it was in relatively good repair, it looked empty. Nestled in a shallow valley, surrounded by low hills and trees, it looked utterly devoid of life. Yet, there were the lavender and sweet pea, both growing luxuriously without the tempering touch of a gardener. And there were the distinct small barred windows running along the bottom of the house that she had briefly glimpsed through Sir Argus's rapidly fading form. He was behind one of them; she was sure of it.

"You are here because you know I can find anything I go looking for," Lorelei said.

"True," agreed Cyrus as he cautiously sat up,

glancing all around to make certain no one was near. "That is, of course, if we believe that you truly saw some man in your garden asking for help and had not just cooked your head too much in the sun."

"If you did not believe me, why did you come with me?" Since no one had sounded an alarm when her cousins sat up, Lorelei quickly did the same.

"Nothing else to do and there was always the chance you could be right. I fancy myself a hero." Peter grinned, giving his square face a touch of true handsomeness. "House appears deserted. Do we go hunting for the prisoner now?"

"We might as well," Lorelei replied.

"You sound disappointed."

"I rather envisioned us creeping up to the place, hiding in the shadows of a moonless night, dressed all in black. Perhaps even masked so as to hide our true identities." She grinned when her cousins laughed, and then she stood up. "However, we have seen no sign of occupancy in the hour we have lain here watching the house. Best we set about the matter of rescuing the man now." She brushed off her skirts and headed down the small hill.

"What about Vale?"

Lorelei stopped to look back at where her maid still sprawled in the grass, obviously sound asleep. "We could just leave her here to sleep. She looks quite comfortable."

Peter shook his head, his dun-colored curls bouncing with the movement. "She will get upset if she wakes to find herself alone."

Upset was a mild term for what Vale would be if she woke up alone with no knowledge of where her mistress had gone. Vale was very prone to loud dramatics. Lorelei walked up to her maid and gently woke the woman.

"Are we returning home now, m'lady?" Vale asked as she stood up and brushed off her skirts.

Before Lorelei could reply, Peter and Cyrus yanked her and Vale back down to the ground. Her complaint over such rough treatment lodged in her throat when Peter silently pointed to three approaching horsemen. She patted his arm in gratitude for his quick thinking and studied the men now reining in before the house.

One gentleman and two ruffians, she decided. No one came out to tend to their horses. No one appeared to even open the door for them. That confirmed her opinion that the house was deserted. All except for Sir Argus Wherlocke. Lorelei was even more certain now that her garden visitor was in that house and that the three men who had just arrived meant Sir Argus harm. She had to clench her hands tight on the long grass shielding her from view to stop herself from leaping up and running down the hillside in a vain attempt to stop the men from entering the house. They were all well armed and would probably just shoot her and go on about their work.

"Now, just why are three men entering an abandoned house?" whispered Peter. "No one to escort them, to tend the horses, or open the door for them. They have guns and I cannot think why you need weapons to go into an empty house. And two of them look like dockside rogues."

"That they do," agreed Lorelei, tense with fear for the man she knew in her heart was a captive inside that house. Was she too late to help him? "I was just thinking the same."

"You might be right about this house, but we cannot go in there now."

"No. We will just watch for now and try to slip in there tonight."

"Are you certain that will be safe?" asked Cyrus.

"As certain as I can be," she replied. "There is nothing here to show that these men reside here. As Peter and I have said, there is not one servant, no fire to welcome them, and they have left their mounts saddled."

Cyrus nodded. "So if they are here tonight when we return we will know, for we will see their horses. Are we waiting now to see if they leave?"

Lorelei nodded, her gaze fixed upon the house and her stomach clenching with fear. The men were here only to hurt Sir Argus and the knowledge churned her insides. Time crawled by as she waited for the three men to come back out. When they finally reappeared, the way one of the gentleman's thick-necked lackeys rubbed the knuckles of one hand made her shudder. She watched them ride away and beat down the urge to immediately storm the house.

"Something is most certainly going on in there," muttered Cyrus as, several tense moments after the men were gone, he sat up. "I did not like the look of those men. Up to no good. One dresses like a gentleman, but he keeps damned poor company."

"True." Lorelei sat up, unable to look away from the house. "I doubt those men are his servants. And the man I saw in our garden was covered in barely faded bruises."

"So you think this little visit was made to deliver even more bruises?"

"I do." The need to run into the house, find Sir Argus, and nurse his wounds gripped her with surprising strength. "They believe he has a gift, one he can just hand over to them, and these visits are made in an attempt to persuade him to do that." She finally looked at her cousins, not surprised to find them frowning at her, their doubt clear to read on their faces. "I know you find all this difficult to understand and believe, but Papa believes in such things and the vast number of books and papers he has collected on the subject means many others do as well."

As her cousins considered her words, she continued, "But it does not really matter what you and I believe. The gentleman who just left does believe Sir Argus Wherlocke has a gift, and he wants it. I *did* see a man in the garden. The loss of my shawl is proof enough of that. I understand how difficult it is to believe that as I barely believe it all myself, yet my shawl disappeared with him. I also feel certain that this is where Sir Argus Wherlocke is being held prisoner and that those men certainly did not come here to share a cup of tea with him."

"That is certain," said Peter as he stood up and then helped Vale to her feet. "No matter what else I believe concerning your man in the garden, I *am* certain that something bad is going on in that house. So, why do we not go right down there now?"

"Because we cannot be sure the men have left for good. If they have done what I believe they have, we will also have to deal with a man beaten hard and we did not bring what was needed for that. Best to be sure they have gone and come readied for a man who cannot aid us much in his own escape."

"Agreed. So, tonight we shall return and see

exactly what is going on in that house. Seems you will
get your chance to creep up to the house, hide in the
shadows, and wear black. But it will not be a moonless night and I am not wearing any mask."

"Oh, m'lady," protested Vale as Cyrus helped
Lorelei to her feet, moving to assist her in brushing
off her skirts, "I wish you would forget this business.
It could be dangerous. I did not like the look of any
of those men—not even the gentleman. You wrote to
Sir Argus Wherlocke's family. Can you not wait for
them to come to his aid?"

"Vale"—Lorelei stepped away from her maid's fret-
ful attentions—"those men beat Sir Argus. I am certain that is why they were just here. To beat him
again. I doubt they then paused to tend to the
wounds they gave him. I cannot wait knowing that
each day he is so abused."

Her cousins murmured their agreement, but Vale
argued against taking any action all the way back to
Dunn Manor. Lorelei finally shooed the woman away
and went to the bedchamber she always used when
visiting her cousins. She needed to make plans for
the rescue of Sir Argus and could not do that with
Vale fluttering about the room wringing her plump
hands. As Lorelei readied the clothes she intended to
wear, she grinned. Vale might just swoon when she
saw what her mistress intended to wear as she slipped
through the night to rescue a stranger.

"You stole my clothes!"

Lorelei grinned at her cousin Peter, ignoring Vale's
gasps of shock. "You did not expect me to creep about
rescuing a man hampered by skirts, did you?" She

idly brushed her hands over the black breeches she wore. "I will need to be quick and nimble. Skirts do not allow that."

"Vale is dressed in skirts."

"Vale is staying here."

"M'lady, I . . ." Vale began to protest.

"Vale, you need to make sure no one discovers that we are gone and that the room I chose is readied for Sir Argus." Lorelei kissed Vale on the cheek and gently pushed her maid from the room.

"But . . ." Vale tried to argue as Lorelei nudged her out into the hall.

"We need someone to keep watch here and help us when we return." Lorelei quietly closed the door on a muttering Vale, waited until she heard her maid walk away, and then turned to her cousins. "You know I am right about this. I will be better able to keep pace with you while dressed as a lad." She ignored the way her cousins stared up at the ceiling as if looking for heavenly aid. "Shall we go?" She started to walk away from them, smiling a little as she heard them stumble to catch up to her.

"You do realize that, if anyone sees you in those clothes, you will be utterly ruined," said Cyrus.

"Considering that we are about to snatch a man from the cruel grasp of some kidnappers who beat him regularly, I believe that ruination is the very least thing I need to concern myself with."

"Ah, good point."

"Thank you."

Lorelei moved along a little faster, nearly running to the stable to get the horses. She did not want her cousins to have too much time to think or they would realize that she was spouting utter nonsense. No matter what the reason, even a matter of life or death, she would indeed be utterly ruined if anyone caught sight of her in male clothing. There was a chance some people might understand, might even find it amusing and hold silent. However, her luck was such that, if she were seen, it would be by someone who could not wait to tell the world and its mother of the scandalous behavior of the duke's daughter.

Just as they reached the rise above the house, the moon came out from behind the clouds. Lorelei scowled up at the full, brilliant moon. Shadows would have been better and safer, but that moon made those few and far between. She could only pray that no one came to see the prisoner or, at the very least, the clouds returned before they had to make a run for safety.

"Peter will stay with the horses," Cyrus said as he moved to stand beside Lorelei. "And act as a guard for us."

"Lost the coin toss, did he?" She shook her head when Cyrus just grinned, and then she looked at Peter. "Watch for a signal from us. We may need some help with the man." When he nodded she started down the slope, eager to find some shadows to shelter them from view.

Cyrus kept watch as Lorelei worked to unlock the door. The sound of the lock releasing after many failed attempts nearly made her cheer. Her brother Tudor had shown her the trick several years ago, but she had not practiced it in a long time and had feared, for a moment, that she had lost the knack. The loud creak of the door as it opened made her wince, but no outcry followed the sound. Then Cyrus lit the lamp he carried and she knew she had been right. The house was no longer lived in, no longer even tended to. The only disturbance in the thick layers of dust and cobwebs coating everything in sight was a neat path made by the men who had come to the house.

"Nice of them to point the way," muttered Cyrus. "But to what?"

"Sir Argus Wherlocke," Lorelei replied as she followed the trail left by the three men.

"Or smuggled goods. Or some thieves' lair. Or a dead body or two."

"They need Sir Argus alive. A dead man cannot give them anything. He is here. I am certain of it."

"I am not sure I wish you to be proven right. The thought of someone being able to send their soul out for a little journey gives me a chill down my spine."

"I do not see why it should. 'Tis not as if he would go about spying on everyone. A man cannot wish to be appearing naked all about the country at odd times."

"True, but I suspect you were not supposed to see him."

"Ah, no, I do not think I was. He was most surprised that I could. I can also see why his enemies might wish to learn such a trick, but I suspect it is not something one wishes to do very often."

"Why not? Think of all you could learn, all the secrets you could uncover."

"True, but your body must be very vulnerable to attack while your spirit is floating about elsewhere. And what happens to your spirit if they kill your body?"

"Oh. Of course. Not a good thing."

She frowned down at the footprints that came to a halt before a door in the kitchen. Marks in the dust revealed that the door opened outward. Lorelei realized she was afraid to open the door, but not because she feared she was wrong. She did not wish to discover that she was too late to help Sir Argus Wherlocke. Cyrus's talk of dead bodies was preying on her mind.

"Lolly?" Cyrus whispered the pet name from her childhood. "Do you wish me to go in first?"

Lorelei quickly stiffened her spine and, shaking her head, reached for the door latch. It opened to reveal only darkness. Cyrus held the lamp just inside the door, revealing narrow steps that went down into that blackness. Either there was another door at the bottom of the steps or the men had left their prisoner with no source of light at all. She was briefly relieved to find a door at the bottom of the stairs, but annoyance quickly pushed it aside as she had to struggle to unlock the door.

Argus heard a soft scratching noise at the door and tried to open his swollen eyes. Although the newest beating had come a lot sooner than he had expected, he could not believe that Charles would be back so soon. The man did not want him dead, just in constant pain. Another harsh beating on top of the one he had just received would almost surely kill him.

Death might not be so far away now, he mused as he shifted his body on the narrow bed and bit back a cry of agony. There was not one small part of him that did not ache or throb. The fact that he was kept on starvation rations only increased the chances that he would succumb to the next beating. The cold and damp as well as the lack of water to cleanse his wounds also tempted infection to set in. Argus doubted he could survive another fortnight of such continual abuse.

He was just thinking that it was taking Charles a long time to unlock the door when he heard the familiar sound of the lock releasing. A soft *aha* followed it and he frowned. That voice was a feminine one. Had Charles actually brought a witch with him? Argus could almost hope the man had found a real one. If it were just some foolish woman who thought to trick the man, she would soon end up dead.

Light entered first and Argus discerned two shapes, one tall, and one short. The hulking forms of Charles's bully men did not appear as the two people approached him. They stood right next to his bed before he could see them clearly through the narrow slits his eyes had become.

"Damn my eyes, Lolly! The man is naked!"

Argus heard a sigh blended with a distinctly feminine annoyance. "I believe I have already mentioned that, Cyrus. Is that not why I had us bring some clothing? Sir? Are you awake?"

A small, soft hand lightly brushed across his shoulder and Argus wanted to hold it against his skin, but he was too weak to give in to that strange urge. "More or less."

"Sir, do you recall visiting me in the garden?" asked the female leaning over him, her clean womanly scent filling his nose.

"Lady Lorelei Sundun. My family?"

"They have not yet replied to my letters. I felt it was necessary to act now and wait no longer for their aid." Even in the shadow-streaked light from the lantern she could see that he had been badly beaten.

"Do you think you can move at all? We brought some clothing and have some horses waiting."

"I can move enough for that." Argus began to sit up and quickly placed a hand against the damp stone wall to steady himself as pain, hunger, and exhaustion threatened to send him into unconsciousness. "May need some help."

"You shall have it."

Argus fought to clear the fog from his mind when the youth called Cyrus set down his lantern, retrieved some clothing from a sack, and began to dress him in a fine linen shirt. Lady Lorelei gingerly knelt on the bed and worked to unlock the chain on his ankle. Despite his pain, Argus's curiosity was roused when he realized she was attempting to pick the lock, and had probably done so on the door to his prison. Another soft *aha* sounded as the shackle fell from his ankle. *One step closer to freedom*, he thought, and experienced a brief surge of strength and determination that cut through his pain.

"Turn your back, Lolly," said Cyrus. "Need to finish dressing him."

Lorelei turned her back, ignoring the sharp pinch of disappointment that rippled through her over not being allowed to see exactly what Sir Argus hid beneath the filthy blanket he held over his lap. She set her mind to deciding the best, and quickest, way to get the man out of the house. He was so badly beaten that she doubted he would be able to even stumble along without aid. Once they reached the horses the burden of moving him would ease, but, until then, she and Cyrus would have to give the man a great deal of support even as they tried to move along as quickly as possible.

"Ready," said Cyrus.

Cyrus stood with one of Sir Argus's arms wrapped around his shoulder and his own arm wrapped around the bigger man's waist. Years of working in the fields at harvest time had made Cyrus a strong young man, but Lorelei was not sure that her cousin was strong enough to hold Sir Argus upright all the way back to the horses. Part of that journey would be uphill. She said nothing, however, for she was accustomed to how easily a young man's pride could be stung. She simply picked up the lantern, ready to lead the way out of the dank prison.

"Your shawl," said Sir Argus, his voice weak and hoarse. "Under the mattress."

Calling the hay-stuffed rag a mattress was doing it too great a compliment, Lorelei mused as she reached under it. She tied her shawl around her shoulders, picked up the lantern again, and led the way up the stairs, careful to make sure her cousin and Sir Argus had enough light to see their way up. She ignored the grunts and soft curses she heard behind her. By the time they reached the foot of the slope, both Cyrus and Sir Argus were panting heavily. Lorelei was just about to offer some help when Peter came running down the slope.

"By damn, there really was a prisoner in the house," said Peter as he slung Sir Argus's other arm around his shoulders.

"If neither of you ever believed what I told you, just why have you helped me search for him?" she demanded as she held up the lamp to light their path as the three of them staggered ever so slowly up the hill.

"Not much else to do. A shame the man you have rescued is not a bit smaller."

"I believe I am lighter by a stone or more than I was a fortnight ago," said Sir Argus.

There was a faint tremor in his voice that told Lorelei the man was very close to collapse despite his efforts to make a jest. She tensed as the hairs on the back of her neck suddenly rose. It was not something that happened to her often, but she recognized the sign of something about to happen, something wrong.

"Move quickly," she said. "I have a bad feeling."

"Bloody hell," muttered Peter. "It cannot be those bastards returning to pound on this poor sod again. You said they wanted him alive. By the look of him, he would not be if they beat him again so soon."

The sound of approaching horses was easy to hear by the time her cousins got Sir Argus to the top of the slope. Lorelei knew Sir Argus heard it as well. He revealed a brief surge of strength, moving on his feet more steadily. It helped her cousins get him to the horses and slung up into a saddle with a greater ease.

Despite that burst of speed the riders were in view by the time Lorelei extinguished the lantern. Moonlight replaced its glow and Lorelei knew she could easily be seen. She darted into the shadows of the trees, her heart pounding in fear. The lead rider had looked her way. She doubted he had seen her clearly, but it could mean that she and her cousins would be chased. They needed to flee as swiftly and as quietly as possible. She mounted her horse, glanced briefly at Cyrus to be sure he had a firm grip on Sir Argus, and then led their retreat back to Dunn Manor.

"Did you see that?" Charles squinted up the hill in an attempt to discern some movement.

"See what?" asked Tucker, idly scratching his wide chest.

"I thought I saw someone up there."

Tucker also squinted as he looked up the hill. "Nothing there. Deer?"

"No. I thought I saw a woman dressed in male attire."

"If she was dressed as a man, how'd you know it was a woman?"

"A long braid that shone red in the moonlight and a nicely rounded arse. And what appeared to be a pale shawl wrapped around her shoulders. Odd thing for a man to wear."

"Want me and Jones to go take a look?"

Charles shook his head. "It may have been nothing or just some foolish girl slipping home from a tryst with her lover. We do not have the time to go and make certain. We have business to attend to." Reining in before the house, Charles quickly dismounted. "Tucker, Jones, go drag that fool up into the parlor. The old woman needs room and light to do what she has to do."

As the two men hurried to obey, Charles turned to help the woman from her horse. He fought down his distaste as he hastily set her down on her feet and stepped away from her. Charles was not sure she was the witch she claimed to be, but she was certainly the homeliest, dirtiest woman he had ever seen. In his opinion she was a fraud, just some old crone who knew what herbs did what, but no one had asked his opinion. He waved her ahead of him into the house and then led her into the parlor, trying to stay as far away from her as possible.

Charles was pulling his flint from his pocket to

light a fire when Jones and Tucker stumbled into the room, without the prisoner.

"Where is Wherlocke?"

"Gone," replied Tucker.

"It seems I did see someone then," Charles murmured as he fought the rage surging through his body. "Was the door locked?"

"Nay. Door to the cell was unlocked too and someone had unlocked his chains."

"Just 'cause you done lost the man, best not be trying to cheat me of what I'm due," said the woman, the wrinkles on her face prominent as she glared at him. "I want what is due me now."

"And so you shall have it." Charles pulled his pistol from his pocket and shot her right between the eyes.

"Bloody hell!" Tucker looked down at the dead woman. "Now we have to get rid of the mess."

"No. Leave her where she lies." Charles started toward the door. "Hurry, we have work to do."

"What? Wherlocke's gone. Doubt he will be falling back into our hands again."

"He will. We just need to find out who freed him."

"And how do we do that? We got no idea who got him out of here."

"Oh, yes, we do. It is someone close to here and it is a woman with a very fine arse and long red hair. Find her and we find Wherlocke."

Chapter 3

Argus woke to pain and could not silence the groan that escaped him. He did not think anything was broken inside him, but he doubted there was a place on his body that was not bruised. There was a tightness around his ribs and he suspected someone had wrapped them, for, although he was certain none of them were broken, he would not be surprised if they had been cracked. Something cool and damp rested on his eyes and then it was gone. Cautious, unsure of how swollen his eyes were, he opened them and found himself staring into a pair of wide, dark green eyes. Beautiful eyes, set beneath gently arched brows and rimmed with long lashes tipped with copper. Eyes soft with concern.

"Lady Lorelei," he said, and winced when just speaking those two words hurt his throat.

"Yes." Lorelei slid her hand beneath his head, easing it up just enough so that he could drink some broth without drooling. "I think the sleep has done you some good. Your face is not as swollen as it was."

"How long have I been asleep?"

"Last night and most of this day."

"Ah. And just where am I?"

"At Dunn Manor. My cousins' home. Only Cyrus, Peter, and my maid know you are here. Cyrus and Peter tended most of your injuries, including wrapping your ribs for they were certain some were cracked, so you must be careful how you move. We have placed you in a room at the far end of the wing used only for guests. It will not even get its next round of cleaning for a week. As soon as you regain some of your strength, we will take you to Sundunmoor. You can finish healing in the gatehouse there. It is also only used for guests, being cleaned and aired out only twice a year or when some visitors are expected, and none are expected for months yet, so you should be quite safe there."

All the while she spoke, she urged more broth down his throat. It was surprisingly tasty and well seasoned, but he knew he would soon want more substantial food. He also suspected that some of the herbs he tasted were added not just for the flavoring, but to help in healing his wounds or in aiding him to sleep well. Argus was not sure lying in a bed being tended to by a pretty green-eyed woman was what he ought to be doing, however. Charles would not take the loss of his prisoner well. His presence here could well put this woman in danger.

"My family?" he managed to ask between swallows.

"Still no word from them. The ones I sent letters to may have left for the country as so many do at this time of the year. It will take some time for my letters to reach them. Unless, do you happen to know exactly where some of your family are now? I could send out a few more letters if you do."

Argus pushed her hand away when she tried to give him more broth, knowing that his stomach could deal with no more, that it needed a very gentle reintroduction to ample food of any kind. It was a weak gesture, his hand shaking, but she heeded it, setting the bowl aside. He prayed the weakness gripping him would fade soon.

"I was but newly back in England from a long journey on the continent when I was taken, so I fear I do not know the plans any of my family may have made for the summer. Best to just wait for a little longer." He tried and failed to keep his eyes open. "I am too weak to fight my enemy anyway. Are you certain that you are safe?"

"Oh, yes, quite safe."

There had been the slightest hesitation before she replied, but sleep dragged him into its smothering depths before he had the chance to question her any further.

Lorelei studied her patient. His bruises were livid swirls of color on his face and body, but the swelling on his eyes and mouth had gone down. She was now certain that all he needed was plenty of rest and food to heal. He could probably be moved to Sundunmoor soon. Lorelei was eager to get him as far away from his enemy as possible. Dunn Manor was too close to the prison from which they had just freed him.

She glanced at the blanket covering his lean hips. The white linen wrapped so tightly around his ribs was a stark contrast to his bronzed skin. It annoyed her that she had finally seen a naked man only to continuously be thwarted in seeing his manly parts. Curiosity was riding her hard and her fingers itched to lift that blanket up just enough to have a quick peek. The sound of the bedroom door opening brutally killed that urge.

"How is he?" asked Cyrus as he slipped into the room.

"Still weak, but I got quite a bit of hearty broth down his throat," she replied.

"Then I had best sit with him now, for he will soon be in need of a man's assistance."

"Ah, of course he will." Lorelei stood up, fighting a strong reluctance to leave Sir Argus's side.

"Send Peter to me with a nightshirt. Oh, and what we will need to clean him up and change the linen."

"You can do that?"

Cyrus made that strange expression, appearing to look all around the room in one fast sweep with his eyes, and Lorelei ignored that silent criticism of her intelligence. "How do you think we knew so much about the injuries he had? Who do you think cared for Papa when his horse threw him?"

"I rather thought that was your mother and his man Deeds."

"They were of little use. Mother has never had the stomach for tending to the ill or the injured, and Deeds could not cease fretting, quite loudly, about how he was certain Papa would never walk again. He did help a little, but we made certain that he spent as little time with Papa as needed until it was evident that Deeds's grim prediction was not coming true."

"Your father is fortunate to have you and Peter."

Cyrus grinned as he sprawled in the chair Lorelei had just vacated. "So we like to tell him. Go. Get some food in you and some rest."

Lorelei walked away, somewhat disturbed over her increasing reluctance to do so. Sir Argus Wherlocke was certainly a handsome devil and obviously had some fascinating skills, but she did not know him well enough to be as drawn to him as she was. She had met and flirted with handsome men before and not one of them had intrigued her as much as this man did. As she hunted down some food, she told herself it was just because he had been in danger and she had helped him, that he had been part of a true adventure in her otherwise mundane life. The little voice in her head that scoffed at such pathetic rationalizations was not easy to ignore, but she did her best.

Moonlight shone on her face when Lorelei opened her eyes. She softly cursed, for she had not meant to sleep for so long, leaving Cyrus and Peter to tend to Sir Argus. A quick look out the window at the position of the moon told her that most of the night had slipped away. She hurriedly washed up, dressed, and made her way to the room they had hidden Sir Argus in.

The sound of three men snoring assailed her ears as she entered the room and she nearly laughed. Cyrus was sprawled in the chair with his head flung back, and his mouth wide open. Peter was stretched out across the foot of the bed, looking as if he had been sitting there and simply fallen over. Sir Argus was still asleep, his snoring much softer than that of her cousins'. Lorelei was surprised that the noises the two younger men were making had not woken Sir Argus up. As quietly as she could, she woke her cousins and sent them off to find their beds.

Lorelei sat down and opened the book she had brought with her but found it impossible to read. Her

gaze kept drifting to the man on the bed. Her cousins
had dressed Sir Argus in one of their father's night-
shirts and the crisp white of the garment enhanced
the swarthiness of his skin as much as his bindings
had. She had seen enough of him to know that the
color was not from the sun, either. She also admitted to herself that she liked it, far more than she did
the pale or ruddy color of the men she knew. It was
possible that it was that very difference that made her
fingers itch to touch his skin, but she feared the urge
was born of something far more complicated than
simple curiosity.

Forcing her attention back to her book, she managed to read a few pages before her gaze was again
drawn to Sir Argus. The soft snore he had been making
had ceased. When she stood up to look at him more
closely, afraid that he had stopped breathing alto-
gether, he opened his eyes and stared at her. Lorelei
found herself captivated by his eyes. It was like staring
into a starless night sky. As the haze of lingering sleep
cleared from his eyes, the intensity of his stare began
to make her nervous, yet she was unable to pull away.

Argus stared at the woman standing by his bed. It
took him a moment to recall exactly who she was and
why she was there. Recognition was rapidly followed
by lust. Her dark red hair was loose, draping her slim
shoulders as it tumbled to her small waist. She was
very modestly dressed, but the way she leaned over
him gave him a tantalizing glimpse of the top swell of
her lush breasts. He wanted to press his face against
them, lick the delicate skin there, and breathe deeply
of her light, tantalizing scent. He reached out and
grasped a hank of her thick, silken hair, and tugged.

"Sir?" Lorelei tensed even as she bent into the pull on her hair.

"Beautiful," he murmured, his gaze fixed upon her full lips, lips he was compelled to taste.

"Thank you most kindly, but . . ."

His lips stopped her words. Shock held her in place while her mind raced. His lips were warm and soft. Also skilled. Lorelei had not been kissed very often in her three and twenty years, but enough so that she recognized that Sir Argus was well trained in the art. A soft nip to her bottom lip had her opening her mouth to the invasion of his tongue, an intimacy she had only experienced once, very briefly and with none of the pleasure she was experiencing now. This kiss drew her closer to him, lit a raging fire in her veins.

Just as Lorelei was about to climb into his arms, he tensed. She had to bite her tongue to stop her protest as he pulled away from her. The heat of embarrassment warmed her cheeks when she saw that she was clinging to his nightshirt. Finger by finger, she slowly loosed her grip. Recalling his injuries, she feared she might have caused him pain.

Argus struggled to beat down the fierce need to pull her into his bed and get her beneath him. And not just because his aching ribs would probably loudly protest such an action. This was the unwed daughter of a duke, he told himself. This was the woman who had saved him from Charles. This was not a woman he should be trying to seduce, no matter how loudly his battered body was demanding that he do so. The flush of desire on her cheeks and the damp of their shared kiss still glistening on her lips made it very difficult to fight that demand.

"My apologies, Lady Lorelei," he said, not surprised to hear the husky note of desire in his voice. "I should not have abused your kindness in such a manner."

The look that briefly crossed her face told Argus that he had just stepped wrong, but he was not sure how. His history with women was long and a little sordid, at least up until the last few years. He had never, however, had much to do with the ladies of the aristocracy. Tavern maids, shop girls, and courtesans were his chosen companions. Rarely had he mixed with the women of the gentry, for he believed such dalliances led only to trouble, or a very quick trip to the altar. Argus decided he was strong enough to use his gift to convince her that he had not kissed her, and then he could work very hard not to do so again despite how great a temptation she was proving to be.

"Apologies?" Lorelei muttered, surprised at how angry, even hurt, his polite words made her.

"It is of no importance," he said, holding her gaze with his own and infusing his voice with command. "You shall forget it happened. We just talked when you came to my chambers. There was no more than that."

Lorelei frowned. There was something a little odd about the rich, deep tone of voice he used, even the measured cadence of his voice. His eyes were much darker and his stare so intense it made her skin itch, the hairs on her arms standing up.

"Of course we did not just talk," she snapped. "Do you take me for a complete idiot? Talking does not involve a man sticking his tongue down a woman's throat, and why are you staring at me like that? Ha! Have I shocked you by not bowing to your manly will?"

"You could say that. Allow me to try that again." He did and she just looked angrier. "How very odd."

"What is odd is you trying to tell me we just talked when that is not what just happened."

Argus knew his gift had been fully engaged, yet she was obviously untouched. "Do you see things clearly?"

"What do you mean?"

"I mean, are you one of those women who needs spectacles but refuses to wear them?"

"Of course not. I see perfectly."

"And you have no trouble with your hearing?"

"None at all. Why?" Lorelei began to understand that there was more to this than some man thinking she was so lacking in wits she could be convinced that they had not kissed.

Argus idly scratched his chin as he tried to think of the best way to explain himself, and then winced when his fingers caused a bruise to start throbbing. "I believe I told you that I was taken captive because Charles Cornick wanted to steal my gift."

Lorelei slowly sat down in the chair, never taking her gaze from him. "Yes, and my father filled my ears to overflowing with tales of all the gifts the Wherlockes and Vaughns are believed to have. If I had not seen how you could send your spirit out in search of aid, I may have scoffed at it all. I rather thought that that was your gift."

"Ah, no. 'Tis but something I have been working on, a skill I have been fighting to perfect. No, my, er, gift is that I can use my voice and my eyes to make people tell me the truth, to make them even do as I wish, or to firmly believe in what I say even if all evidence shows what I said to be a lie."

"But it did not work on me." Lorelei suspected his attempt to play with her mind, to impose his will on her, would infuriate her later, but, for the moment, she was utterly fascinated, and not quite sure she completely believed him. "That is the skill Charles Cornick wanted you to give to him?"

"Yes. He believed I could simply hand it to him or, mayhap, train him to do the same."

"I imagine he felt it would be a most useful skill to have. Just think of all he could accomplish."

"I have, and very little of what I considered was good."

"Of course it would not be," Lorelei murmured. "A man willing to do all he did to you would not be one to use such a skill for good or innocent purposes. In truth, it is chilling to think on all the evil he could do with such a skill."

"He and whoever his allies are. Charles spoke of a *we* several times. What is also troubling is how much he knew about my family."

Lorelei could hear a touch of hoarseness in his voice and quickly moved to get him a tankard of cider, adding a little honey to soothe his throat and a few herbs to help him sleep. "My father knows quite a lot as well. It does appear that your family is of great interest to those who study such matters."

"That is not welcome news. When someone takes an interest in us it usually ends with us running for our lives. Lost many an ancestor to such interest."

"Such deadly persecution ended many years ago, although I know the fear of such gifts does linger. One can still see people make the sign to ward off the devil and some women are still whispered about, called witches, and shunned. We are a more enlightened people these days, however, and most of us have cast aside such foolishness." She returned to the side of the bed and held out the tankard. "Do you think you can drink this on your own, or will you need my help?"

Argus stared at the drink as he slowly eased himself up into a seated position, ignoring the painful protest of his body. "You have put something in it."

"Just something to strengthen your blood and help you sleep." She held up her hand to halt the objection he started to make. "Rest is the best healer. The pain you are in makes getting that much-needed rest difficult without such aid."

There was no arguing the truth and Argus reluctantly took the tankard from her. He used both hands to hold it as he drank, not wishing to embarrass himself by tipping the brew all over himself and the bed. It was not an unpleasant potion despite the hint of bitterness.

"That is the last time," he said as he handed her back the empty tankard.

"Once more. When we move you to Sundunmoor. It will make the journey easier."

Knowing the herbs would soon do their work, he started to lower himself down onto his back. Argus could not fully smother a hiss of pain that brought Lorelei closer. Her small hands gripped him with a surprising strength as she helped him lie down. He breathed deeply of her delicate scent, a touch of roses and clean skin.

She was just tucking him in, in a way that made him want to smile, when the door opened. Lorelei was startled, stumbling a little, and Argus wrapped his arm around her small waist to steady her. He fought the urge to cover the hand she had placed on his chest to stop herself from falling on top of him with his own and hold it there. Not that he would mind such a tumble into his arms if he were not such a mass of pain and bruises.

"My lady!" A plump maid rushed toward the bed, her attire marking her as an upper servant. "What is he doing to you?!"

"Nothing, Vale," said Lorelei as she straightened, the abrupt loss of Argus's touch causing her a pang that greatly troubled her. The man was wreaking havoc on her senses. "I was but aiding him in lying down and stumbled. What are you doing here?"

"You should not be in here, all alone, with a strange man."

"He may be strange, but he is also badly injured, and needs constant watching, Vale. At least for another night or two. I am in no danger."

"Your fine reputation would be utterly destroyed if this was discovered. You must get one of the maids to tend to him."

It was astonishing how many things would utterly destroy her fine reputation, Lorelei thought. "We are attempting to keep his presence here as secret as possible, Vale. If I drag a maid into this, it will not be long before most everyone for miles around will know there is a wounded man here at Dunn Manor."

"Vale, look at me."

Lorelei frowned at the tone of command in Argus's deep voice. She was not surprised when Vale immediately obeyed, but was disconcerted by how she also felt a fleeting urge to heed that order. The way Vale was rooted to the spot, her wide gaze locked with Sir Argus's, made Lorelei uneasy, however. She knew she was about to see the proof of the strange gift the man claimed to have, and a part of her wanted to put a stop to it. It did not seem right to play with Vale's mind and will in such a way. Yet, she also knew it was important to keep Sir Argus's presence at the manor a secret and Vale's concern over her mistress's reputation threatened that secrecy.

"You know I would do nothing to bring harm to your lady," Argus said.

"I know," said Vale, still unmoving, her voice oddly flat and lifeless.

"You will not concern yourself with her presence in this room. There is no harm in it."

"No harm."

"Precisely. No harm will come from her care for me. You will no longer fret over the safety of her good name."

"I will not."

"Good. You may leave now."

Lorelei nearly gaped as Vale left the room without saying a word, gently closing the door behind her. After staring blindly at the door for a moment, Lorelei looked at Sir Argus, only to find him watching her warily. And so he should, she thought. What he had just done was very disturbing, and a little frightening.

"Ah, and now you fear me." Argus wondered why that stung so badly, as he was well accustomed to such fear.

"A little," Lorelei admitted. "That is a very powerful gift you have. Vale was trapped by your gaze, your voice. I even experienced its touch although it was not directed at me."

"And does not work on you, either."

"So, it does not work on everyone. Vale is susceptible?"

"Most servants are, if only because they are well trained in obedience."

"I have never been very competent in the art of obedience," she murmured.

Argus smiled a little. "That does not surprise me, but it is more than that. 'Tis evident you felt something, but you shook it off with ease. Outside of those within my own family, I have yet to meet anyone who could. Fight it, yes. Know what I am doing, yes, especially if I want them to know. Break free of any command I give sooner than I would like, yes. Shake it off like dewdrops and tell me to stop, no."

"Perhaps if you had had more time . . ."

"No. When I first plied my skill, it did take time, but that was many years ago."

"And you have never used it to simply get what you wanted?" She wondered what was behind the hint of sadness she saw on his face, one not fully disguised by his rueful smile.

"I was young when my gift first revealed itself. Of course I used it to gain what I wanted, and I suffered from a youth's arrogance in knowing I had such a power. But, not for long. It was"—he paused to reach for the right word, the herbs in the drink already beginning to do their best to pull him into sleep— "uncomfortable and unsatisfying. Now, I only use it when there is good reason to do so."

"Such as protecting yourself from a maid's insistence that others learn you are here? Or, convincing a woman that you did not stick your tongue in her mouth?" She almost grinned over how irritated he looked.

"I did apologize for that and for the kiss." He stressed the last two words, not particularly liking the way she described their brief intimacy.

"No need to apologize. I am not without some experience in such matters."

"Really?" Argus wondered why he had the urge to demand names, find those men she had gained her experience with, and pummel them into the ground for daring to touch her. He decided the herbs were disordering his mind. "I am pleased that I did not shock your tender sensibilities." Despite his best efforts, he tried and failed to keep his eyes open.

Lorelei ignored the bite behind his words. She knew enough about men to suspect he was not pleased to think he had not given her anything special. He most certainly had, but she would keep that as her own little secret. A man's passion was a shallow thing unless it touched his heart. Lorelei was not sure what it was about Sir Argus Wherlocke that drew her, but she was sure that, if she gave in to her attraction for the man, she wanted far more than passion from him.

"Sleep, Sir Argus," she murmured and stood to settle the bedcovers more securely over his body. "'Tis the best cure for your injuries." Giving in to a sudden impulse, she kissed his forehead before she sat back down and picked up her book.

Argus nearly opened his eyes in shock when he felt her soft, warm lips brush over his forehead. It was a surprisingly tender gesture and touched him deeply. Lady Lorelei Sundun was a puzzle.

She was also a danger to his peace of mind, stirring a softness and longing he had thought dead a long time ago. It would be best to get away from her as quickly as possible, he decided as he let the thickening fog of sleep pull him under.

Chapter 4

Lorelei winced in sympathy as Cyrus and Peter helped Sir Argus out of her carriage. The journey from Dunn Manor had been taken as slowly and carefully as possible, but it had taken all day, and not every rough spot on the road could be avoided. Sir Argus was pale, lines of pain bracketing his tightly pressed lips. Sweat dampened his hair and glistened on his face despite the cool of the evening air. However, he still took the time and strength to convince the carriage driver that there had been no one else in the carriage save for her, and her cousins. It surprised her that her cousins were not disturbed by the way Jem, the driver, just smiled blandly, agreed that Sir Argus was not there, and drove away.

She hurried ahead of her cousins and Sir Argus, unlocking the door to the carriage house. One deep breath was enough to tell her that Max had done as she had asked and prepared the place for a guest. Sending Vale on ahead with the message had been a hurried decision and might not have been the wisest one. Max would undoubtedly question her later on all the secrecy she had insisted upon, but she could not worry about that now.

"Get him settled in the bed," she told her cousins. "I will go and see if Max left all I asked for in the kitchens."

Lorelei rushed into the kitchens only to come to a halt so quickly she stumbled and had to grab the back of a chair to steady herself. Max himself stood at the stove idly stirring a small pot of a rich-smelling broth and eyeing her in that way that always made her feel guilty, even when she had done nothing to feel guilty about. She stood up straight, brushed down her skirts, and attempted to act like the grown woman she was and not some child caught stealing biscuits.

Max was not like most butlers. He ruled the Sundun household far more than her father did. He and her father had been together since they had been small boys. Max had the common sense her father sometimes lacked. He had stood firmly at the duke's side through three marriages, three funerals of wives dead before their time, the burial of the late duke, her poor ill-fated Uncle Cecil the previous heir and his wife, and the arrival of every one of seventeen children, plus Cecil's two orphaned daughters and a vast assortment of young cousins. Lorelei knew her father loved them all, but, although the duke did his best, it was Max who was the guiding hand for all the children calling Sundunmoor home. She doubted Max would do more than quirk one dark brow in derision if she tried to play the haughty mistress with him now.

"Did you truly believe I would not wish to ascertain exactly who this mysterious visitor is?" asked Max. "Or why he must hide here in the utmost secrecy?"

"I had hoped such would be the way of it," she mumbled.

"It grieves me to dash your hopes." He ignored her snort of disbelief. "Who is he and why must he hide?" He set a cup of chocolate on the table and nudged her into a seat. "I expect you to leave no detail out of your undoubtedly convoluted explanation."

Lorelei took a sip of the rich chocolate as she hastily thought of what to tell Max. Once she was composed enough to speak calmly, certain that she could disguise any hint that she was being less than precise on the sequence of events, she told Max just how a wounded man had come to be hiding in the gatehouse. She avoided all mention of nakedness and kisses, but, when she was finished, Max was looking at her as if he knew she had omitted a few things. Lorelei hoped it was just a natural wariness he had gained from years of dealing with the large Sundun brood and not a true suspicion that she had not been completely truthful.

Max sat down across the table from her and sipped on his own cup of chocolate. "Wherlocke, Wherlocke," he mumbled, his brow creased with thought. "Ah, yes, I have heard of them. Head of the family is a young duke. A recluse named Modred Vaughn, Duke of Elderwood. I do not recall what number he is though, but it is an old title."

"Modred?" She shook her head. "I had not noticed that name when I sent word to him. I think his name was obscured, just the letter M and then a list of other more common names. Poor fellow. No wonder he just uses the initial when he can."

"Quite. I have heard whispers that the family has worked for the government from time to time."

It was not difficult for Lorelei to see how a man like Sir Argus could prove to be a great asset to king and country. With his gift he could unearth all manner of helpful secrets.

"I have also heard rumors that the men of the family are rogues," continued Max. "It is said that there is even a house in London where they place their many by-blows."

"Oh, dear. Well, at least they care for them. Too few do."

Max slowly nodded. "That is something in their favor. I believe I will take the broth to our guest. You will go up to the main house now."

"But . . ."

"No. You are a very clever woman, m'lady, but you are also quick to trust and have a very sympathetic nature. I must personally take the measure of this man before I can agree to keep this all secret, especially since I strongly suspect you have no intention of setting his care into the hands of the servants."

"The fewer people who know he is here, the safer he will be."

"True, but I wish to assure myself of the need for subterfuge."

Max allowed her to mix a few herbs into a tankard of cider and then ordered her home. She knew it was useless to argue with his command. Many of her class would find Max's ways intrusive, those of a man who was stepping far beyond the bounds of a servant, but the man was too intricately intertwined with her family for the Sunduns to be so rigid. As she made her way home, she prayed Max did not decide that she could not help Sir Argus. She knew she would fight that decision tooth and nail, and hated the thought of being on the wrong side of Max.

Argus looked at the tall, thin man setting a tray down on the bedside table. "Are you another cousin?"

"No." Max helped Sir Argus sit up straighter in the bed, cautious not to cause him much pain. "I am Max, butler to His Grace, the Duke of Sundunmoor."

"Max? Your surname is Max?" A stupid question, thought Argus, but he was too busy fighting the pain in his ribs to care.

"No. I do not choose to use my surname. It tempts people to make unseemly jests. My surname is Cocksbaine."

"Ah. Quite. Well, Max, I am Sir Argus Wherlocke."

"So I was told." Max sat on the edge of the bed and began to spoon-feed Argus a thick, rich beef broth. "I sent her ladyship home as I felt it was important that I make a judgment on all of this without her close at hand. Her sympathies are too easily roused. So, you are in real danger?"

"I did not do this to myself," Argus grumbled in between swallows.

Max looked him over. "You have evidently been hard done by, but an angry husband could easily be the cause. The tale that you have some strange gift that a man sought to steal from you is, as I am certain you know, a little difficult to believe."

"Let me show you what my enemy wished to steal," Argus said as he gently grasped the man's wrist, caught his gaze, and began to tell him that he should not interfere.

"It is my duty to interfere if I believe her ladyship is in danger."

Argus was so startled he released Max's wrist, got another spoonful of broth shoved in his mouth, and had to swallow before he could speak. "You felt nothing?"

"A brief inclination to heed your words, but it was easily shaken off once I realized it was not something I was inclined to do."

"Damn my eyes. First Lady Lorelei. Now you." He grimaced when he saw the way Max's dark eyes narrowed in suspicion.

"You tried that trick on her ladyship?"

"I was attempting to ensure that I remained well hidden and to protect myself." *From a highborn virgin's outrage or expectations,* he mused, but had no intention of telling this protective butler that. "And it is no trick. It also works quite well on most people. It was certainly easy enough to convince Vale that it would be best if the servants at Dunn Manor remained ignorant of my presence. As I told her ladyship, I usually only experience difficulty if I try to use it on members of my family."

"Or someone with a strong will?"

"Ah, yes, that, too. At times."

"I am also a distant relation to a Vaughn. Some great-great-someone. That, too, may be it. I did, as I said, feel a touch of compulsion to heed your command so I can accept that you have this gift. Just as I have to accept that you somehow managed to appear to her ladyship in her father's garden and asked for help. But, why would anyone think they could take such a gift away from you?"

"Madness? Greed strong enough to disorder good sense? Cornick and whoever is his ally thought I could just give it to them or teach it to them. Cornick even said he was bringing a witch soon to try to spell it out of me."

The soft noise Max made was so full of derision, Argus almost smiled. Instead, he dutifully ate the rest of the broth Max fed him. It was with great reluctance that he took the tankard of cider Max held out to him, however. He could smell the herbs in the drink and briefly considered holding Lady Lorelei to her word that the one he had drunk before the trip here was the last one. But, he could not deny that, after the long journey to Sundunmoor, he needed it if he was to get any sleep at all. The ache in his ribs alone was enough to keep him awake for hours. *Last time*, he promised himself, and began to drink the potion.

"How is it that you were able to tell her ladyship that you were in danger?"

"This may be difficult for you to believe." Argus decided that Max was very skilled at saying a lot with but one quirk of a dark brow and then proceeded to tell him of how he had arranged to reach his family, only to make a brief appearance in the gardens of Sundunmoor. "I am still not quite sure why I ended up in that garden instead of at my sister's or cousin's home although Lady Lorelei believes some old rune stones may have had something to do with it. It certainly was not where I had intended to be, and the few times I have done it before I went where I planned to."

"The stones may well be the answer to that puzzle. They are very old, set into the ground in a circle, and there are many old tales of such places holding a great deal of power. Or magic, if you prefer to call it such."

"So you believe me?" Argus was unable to hide his surprise.

"Let us just say that I am intrigued. Such things have long fascinated His Grace. Magic, odd skills that cannot be explained, spirits, and all that. He and I have spent many an evening discussing such matters. It also explains why her ladyship abruptly sent messages to three people she has never met. She also used everything necessary to make it clear that the missive came from a ducal household so that it would, perhaps, gain swifter notice."

"Do you recall who she notified of my need?"

"The Duke of Elderwood, the Baron of Uppington, and Lady Olympia Wherlocke, the Baroness of Stryke Hall. None have yet replied."

"Not surprising. At this time of year it can be difficult to catch anyone at home. Save Modred, but even he has begun to leave Elderwood from time to time. It has not even been a sennight yet." He studied Max for a moment. "You really are inclined to believe me, are you not?"

"I am, although I wish her ladyship had not involved herself in your troubles. Once she heard your request for help, however, there was no turning back for her. I am pleased that she has brought you here, for her own protection if not yours. Sundunmoor is well protected. And, yet, no place is truly impregnable, so I am hoping that your family comes to your aid soon."

"As soon as they get word, they will come." Argus had no doubt about that, was a little surprised that some of them were not already looking for him, as his family was always quickly aware of when one of their number was hurt or in danger. He just wished he could know which ones would appear so that he could better prepare his hosts. "I am grateful and rather surprised that Lady Lorelei found me so quickly. I had few clues to leave her with."

"Her ladyship has always had a true skill for finding things. Or people."

"A useful talent."

Argus carefully set the empty tankard on the bedside table. The herbs were already at work, dulling his senses and weighing down his limbs. He suspected the potion was working so quickly because the journey had stolen most of the strength he had regained at Dunn Manor. He did not like it, but accepted the need for it.

"I would suspect that yours is far more useful," murmured Max as he helped Argus into a prone position, gently arranging the pillows more comfortably behind his head.

"It is, but it carries a dangerous curse with it. One must ever fight the seduction of it." Argus wondered why he was being so honest with the man and decided he was just too weary, too concerned with the pain nearly every move he made brought him, to guard his words more carefully. "It is not a temptation one can walk away from, either. I carry it with me wherever I go."

"Rather like lust."

Argus stared at Max for a moment and then grinned. "Why, so it is."

"But a man learns to temper it."

"Max, if you are trying to be subtle about something, I pray you cease. My mind is too cursed hazy for such games."

"Lady Lorelei is a beautiful young lady."

"Ah, I thought that might be what you were ambling

toward. A warning to leave her be. Not to worry. I owe her my life and I am far from suitable for the daughter of a duke."

"You misunderstand me, sir. You are wellborn. I suspect you have a purse full enough to satisfy any father, too. I shall be blunt."

"Please do."

"Do not seduce the girl. She is too trusting and too soft of heart. An easy target for a rogue, despite her sharp wits. I but ask that you play no rogue's games with her. If something occurs between you and her ladyship, you *will* accept responsibility. I will not have her hurt or shamed."

"Agreed. Nor will I."

"Then I will leave you to get your rest," Max bowed, "for it is the best cure for the sort of injuries you have suffered."

"Why do you not just keep her away from me?" asked Argus.

Max paused in the doorway to look back at Argus. "You ask that concerning the young lady who crept about in the night dressed as a lad and dragged you out of your prison?"

"Point taken."

With a brief nod, Max left, and Argus stopped fighting to keep his eyes open.

Lorelei wondered if a heart could beat itself to death. Hers was pounding so hard she was surprised it had not echoed through the halls as she had crept through the house. Max was busy and her cousins were off fishing so she knew Argus was alone. No one else had been informed of his presence. She carried her sketchbook just in case she was caught and had to explain where she was going, but she hoped she was not forced to make excuses, for she knew she was a poor liar.

She had slept the night away and guilt was a heavy stone in her stomach. Lorelei knew it was foolish to feel so guilty, that Sir Argus was neither mortally wounded nor completely infirm and in desperate need of constant watching. He could tend to his basic needs without help once he had rested from the journey. Max had also assured her that he had left food, drink, and clean nightclothes for Sir Argus close at hand. There was no reason for her to suffer any guilt or worry, and yet she was gripped hard by a need to see him. She did not like to think of him all alone or in any pain.

The gatehouse was so quiet as she entered that she found it a little eerie. She was unaccustomed to being anywhere that was totally devoid of people, especially servants. She grimaced, afraid she had just allowed her imagination to run wild, filling her head with visions of Sir Argus calling out for help. Setting the pack that held her sketching materials down on the table in the hall, she pulled a book from the pack and started up the stairs. Lorelei hoped Sir Argus believed that she had simply thought to keep him company, perhaps read to him for a while. It would be unbearably humiliating if he guessed that she had been afraid for his health and safety. Sir Argus was a big, strong, worldly man. She was often described as delicate and knew she had led a very sheltered life. The man would probably laugh at the idea that she thought to protect him.

She reached for the handle of the door and then paused. Although she could not hear anything, she knew he could be awake, asleep, or even indecent. Lorelei rapped softly on the door, heard a muttered command to enter, and quickly did so.

The sight of Sir Argus stopped Lorelei after she had taken only two steps into the room. He was sitting up in the bed, his nightshirt open to his waist. She briefly noted that the bedcovers were pulled up to that trim waist, for it was his chest that captured her full interest. He did have a very fine chest, she thought. Broad, taut with muscle, and with only a small patch of hair. The bandage wrapped around him hid too much of him in her opinion. She had the strangest, strongest urge to hurl herself into his arms and rub her cheek against that smooth swarthy skin. She would enjoy it, but, considering his injuries, she doubted he would.

"Thought you were Max," Argus said and hastened to close his nightshirt. "You should not be here." He hoped he did not sound as prim to her as he did to his own ears.

Lorelei had to bite back a sigh of disappointment as his handsome chest disappeared beneath the crisp white linen of the nightshirt. "I have come to read to you, if you wish me to. You have been left alone for quite a while and I thought you might like a little company."

Argus glanced at the book she held. "A tale of an old battle between the Cavaliers and the Round-heads? Strange choice for a young lady."

"I have brothers, sir. They all enjoy this so I thought you might." She frowned. "Although, if you recognize it so quickly you must have read it already."

"Know of it. Have not yet read it."

"Shall I read it to you then?"

He wanted to say no, knew that was what he should

say, but he found he did not have the heart to dim the hopeful light in her beautiful eyes. Although he would never admit it aloud, he had been achingly bored, weary of having no company but his own thoughts. The short walk he had taken around the room had left him aching and so exhausted he had been unable to do more than lie there staring at the ceiling. It had been too soon to get up and move, but he knew he would keep doing so, for he had enemies and needed to get strong again as fast as possible. Argus decided listening to her read to him would be innocent enough. He was too weak to be any threat to her virtue anyway.

"It would be pleasant to be read to for a while," he said. "My own company was growing quite tiresome."

The smile she gave him was a lethal weapon aimed straight at ending a man's freedom, Argus decided. As she began to read, he realized her soft, lilting voice was not much safer. He had to wonder why she was not yet wed with a few children clinging to her skirts. She certainly looked old enough to have come out in society. Even here in the country there had to be men ready and willing to marry into a ducal family.

As he half listened to the rousing tale of an old battle, the author's tone surprisingly unprejudiced whenever the Puritans were mentioned, Argus attempted to understand why Lady Lorelei was still unwed. Her bare fingers implied that she was not even betrothed. She was beautiful, young but no longer childish, undoubtedly had a reasonable dowry, and was as highborn as any woman could be outside of the royal family. Her actions concerning his plight revealed a touch of wildness in her nature, perhaps even a touch of recklessness, but he could not really see that as a fault. Her butler saw her as sympathetic and too trusting, qualities most men would see as charming, might even be tempted to take advantage of. It took all his willpower not to interrupt her reading to ask her why she was still a maid.

It was not long before the soothing music of her voice aided the exhaustion brought on by exercise in making him sleepy. Argus tried to stay alert, not wishing to insult her in any way, for she was an excellent reader, but he finally found it impossible to keep his eyes open. He hoped the constant need for sleep would end soon as it made him feel like a weakling. That was something he had never liked, but he suspected the dislike was enhanced by the fact that he was acting weak before Lady Lorelei Sundun. That fact carried with it some dangerous implications.

Lorelei watched Sir Argus close his eyes but continued to read to him for a while longer. She could see that his color had improved since she had been at his side and decided that some sort of exercise had caused the paleness she had first noticed. She could readily sympathize with the need to heal and get strong as soon as possible. Sir Argus was undoubtedly spurred on by more than male pride, however. He had enemies, ones who were probably searching for him.

Certain that he was finally asleep, Lorelei rose and set the book on the bedside table for him to read later if he wished to. She lightly adjusted the bedcovers over his chest and touched a kiss to his brow. It was a shockingly forward thing to do, but she could not fully resist the urge to touch him. A startled squeak escaped her when his arms wrapped around her and tugged her down onto his chest.

Argus studied her blush-stained face, and ignored

the protest his ribs made about having any weight on his chest, even her light weight. "Why do you do that?"

"Do what, sir?" Lorelei was not surprised when he gave her a look of mild disgust, for her attempt to act innocent had been a pathetically weak one.

"Kiss me on the brow."

"'Tis but an innocent gesture, one of sympathy for someone in pain."

"Is that what you expect me to believe?"

"And why should you not believe me?"

"Because I think you are lying through your pretty white teeth."

Before Lorelei could protest that remark, even if it was the truth, he kissed her. This time she did not hesitate to give herself over to his kiss. Hesitantly, she threaded her fingers through his thick hair even as she parted her lips to welcome the seductive intrusion of his tongue. Lorelei could not believe how alive she felt in his arms, her every sense awakened by his embrace. The scent of him, all male with a hint of the soap he had washed up with, filled her head. The taste of him was as heady as the richest chocolate and she knew she could quickly come to crave it. The way his tongue played within her mouth, stirring up a passion she had begun to think herself incapable of, drove all clear thought from her mind. Even the heat of his body pressed close to hers seeped inside her, entering the very blood pounding through her veins. When he softly cursed and abruptly ended the kiss, gently but firmly setting her aside, she hastily swallowed a whimper of dismay.

"What the bloody hell am I doing?" Argus muttered, dragging the fingers of both hands through his hair.

"Kissing me again?" she replied sweetly, refusing to

flinch before the cross look he sent her. He was the one who had pulled her into his arms and kissed her.

"That must never happen again. You"—he pointed one long, graceful finger at her—"will cease to come here."

"Oh, no, I think not. Your presence is still a great secret and, if Max is busy as he so often is, I am the only one who can ensure that you have the food, drink, and clean linens you need." She shrugged. "You cannot choose who will aid you yet, sir."

"Fine. Then, when you must be here, you are to stay far away from me."

"As you wish. Rest well, Sir Argus."

Lorelei fled the room before he could say any more. He was a fool to think they could stay a proper distance apart at all times after sharing a kiss like that. She had the growing suspicion that she had finally found the man she had been looking for and she had every intention of staying very close until he agreed that they were a good match, or turned away from her so completely she could not mistake his rejection.

Argus glared at the door as it shut behind Lorelei. He knew she was not going to do as he asked and it was evident that he had very little control when she was near. Closing his eyes, he vowed to work harder to regain his strength so that he could run as far and as fast as he could. A little voice in his head whispered that he could run all he liked but he would never escape the memory of her kiss. He ruthlessly silenced it.

Chapter 5

"His Grace would like to speak with you, m'lady."

Nine little words should not make her heart leap with such alarm, Lorelei thought, yet they did. She had the chilling feeling that, somehow, her father had learned about Sir Argus. The man had been hiding in the gatehouse for a full week so it was certainly possible that even her sweet, distracted father could have noticed something suspicious.

As she set aside her needlework and rose to follow Max out of the parlor, Lorelei suddenly recalled the swift departure of Cyrus and Peter. They had barely paused in their escape from Sundunmoor to say a proper farewell. If she had not happened to enter the front hall just as they were going out the door, she doubted very much that they would have said a word to her about leaving. Her cousins must have told her father something, perhaps even everything.

"He knows about Sir Wherlocke," she said, looking hopefully at Max for a denial even though she doubted he would give her one.

"He does," replied Max. "I did not tell him, although I was not pleased that I had to keep such secrets from him. That is not my way, as you well know."

"I know. My cousins told him for some reason. That is why they fled. Do you happen to know just how much they did tell him?"

"No, but you should be aware that your father has taken to ambling about his estate, on foot, weather permitting. Every day, shortly after breaking his fast. It is quite possible he saw something that stirred his curiosity and pressed young Peter and Cyrus for some answers."

"And they crumbled like stale biscuits."

"Quite possibly."

"I wish they had had the courage to tell me precisely what they told him before they ran for their lives."

"It does not matter. It is time, I believe, to tell your father the truth."

Lorelei sighed, unable to argue with that no matter how desperately she would like to. Her father was often distracted, lost in his books and papers, but once his curiosity was roused, he could prove to be very persistent until he got the answers he sought. There was a very good chance that something had caught his eye as he had ambled over his property, perhaps passing right by the gatehouse. Whatever her cousins had told him in answer to the questions he had asked would only have sharpened that curiosity. All she could do now was hope that her father would understand the continued need for secrecy. Sir Argus was a great deal stronger than when he had arrived at Sundunmoor, but he was still not ready for a confrontation with Cornick and his men. If nothing else,

Max insisted that Argus should keep the wrapping about his ribs for at least another week.

Straightening her shoulders, she stepped into her father's library. He sat at his desk with his hands clasped in front of him. The fact that he had no book close at hand and had obviously been waiting for her did nothing to soothe her nerves. Lorelei glanced behind her, seeking some support from Max, only to find herself staring at the closed door. *The coward has fled*, she thought crossly, and turned to face her father again.

"You wished to see me, Papa?" she asked as she walked toward his desk.

Roland Sundun, His Grace, the eighth Duke of Sundunmoor, studied his daughter as she approached him. A small, sweet memory twisted his heart for despite having his eyes she looked so much like her mother, the only one of his three wives that he truly cared for. He could not let that softness sway him, however. She was keeping secrets from him and may well have involved herself in something dangerous. The babbled explanations of the Dunn boys had not been much help, but Roland was determined to get to the truth now. He suspected Max knew the truth but would not press his butler, and friend, to break a pact with his daughter by questioning him.

"Sit down, m'dear." He pointed to the chair set facing him across his wide desk. "I believe you have something to tell me."

"I do?" Lorelei clasped her hands in her lap, not wishing to reveal any unease or guilt.

"Lorelei, I know I am a negligent father. . . ."

"Oh, no, Papa. You are a wonderful father."

"You say so because we both know that, much of

the time, I have little idea of what is going on with my children."

"I suspect anyone with so many children would be unable to know everything that went on with them."

"Clever girl. Cease dancing about and tell me, who is the man you have hiding in my gatehouse?"

"Sir Argus Wherlocke. I would have thought my timid cousins would have revealed at least that much," she muttered, silently swearing retribution on her cowardly cousins.

"They babbled and ran. I gleaned enough from their nearly insensible rush of words to know that I am correct in thinking something is going on out at that gatehouse." He drummed his fingers on the top of his desk and frowned. "For a moment I had feared that I had forgotten that we had guests. Only, it does appear that this particular guest would prefer to be forgotten."

"Not forgotten, just well hidden."

"Young lady, you *will* tell me what you have managed to get yourself tangled up in. And, I suspect, poor Max, as well."

Lorelei sighed and told her father exactly what she had told Max. "So, you see, Papa, it is of the utmost importance that as few people as possible know where Sir Argus is. At least, until his family arrives to help him or he recovers completely from the brutal treatment of his captors."

Roland rubbed a hand over his chin, studying his daughter as he thought on all she had said. He knew he was indeed a somewhat negligent father, but he loved all of his children, as well as the ones who had been put into his care. He might spend much of his time lost in his books, but he was certain each child at Sundunmoor knew they could turn to him if they needed him, and many had from time to time. He was, therefore, not ignorant of all the ways his many offspring could manipulate the truth. His daughter had told him the truth, but not all of it. There was also a look in her eyes, a telltale shine, whenever she spoke Sir Argus's name. As far as he knew, no man had ever put that shine in his daughter's eyes before. This was definitely one of those times when he needed to keep his mind sharp and watch her closely.

"I believe I must meet this man," he said as he stood up.

"Now?" Lorelei asked as her father grasped her by the hand and tugged her to her feet.

"He has been here for a week, has he not? I think it is far past time I acted the proper host and welcomed him to Sundunmoor."

"Papa, it is truly very important that no one learns he is here."

He hooked her arm through his and patted her hand. "I am well aware of that. No need to keep reminding me. Although I think you gravely underestimate the servants if you believe none of them have guessed that you are hiding someone in the gatehouse." He watched as she grew a little pale and patted her hand again. "None of them will speak out of turn or spread gossip. Weeded that sort out a long time ago."

Lorelei reluctantly allowed her father to lead her away from the library toward the front door. He was not going to give her even the smallest chance of warning Argus that he was about to meet her father, the duke. This was a poor time for her father to become keen-witted and sharp-eyed, she thought crossly. She could only hope that he did not also decide to suddenly become obedient to all the rules of propriety, for she had no intention of staying away from Sir Argus Wherlocke.

Not that putting herself in his way was getting her very far, she mused. The man still kept kissing her and then pushing her away. If she had not sensed his desire for her, she would probably be hiding under her bed, crippled with humiliation. There was so much passion in his kisses she was both infuriated and impressed with the strength he revealed in reining it in before they indulged in more than kisses. She had none at all. The only good thing she could see in Argus's reluctance to seduce her was that it revealed that he honored her enough not to want to play any roguish games with her. That was all well and good. She was not playing any games, either.

The look on Sir Argus's handsome face when she entered the room arm in arm with her father almost made her grin. He was quite obviously stunned, but he quickly hid that shock behind an expression that bespoke courtesy with a touch of aloofness. Lorelei was rather envious of that skill.

"Your Grace," Argus said and quickly stood up to bow.

"Oh, sit. Sit," ordered her father. "You must be far healthier than when you arrived, but you still look like you lost a battle with a carriage."

Argus sat but slowly, making sure that the duke was intending to sit as well. Many outside of Sundunmoor would not take Lorelei's father for such a highborn lord, he thought as he studied the man, certainly not by ones who did not know him. Argus was not sure he would have guessed that he was facing a duke if the man had not come in with Lorelei and did not have eyes very similar to hers. His clothes were of fine quality but somewhat rumpled. His graying brown hair looked as if he had run his fingers through it many times and never bothered to check his appearance before leaving the privacy of his rooms. There was no air of arrogance about the man, no inbred sense of privilege.

There was, however, a look in the man's eyes that told Argus this man was no fool. Roland Sundun, His Grace, the eighth Duke of Sundunmoor, had a sharp intelligence. It made Argus a little uneasy to have that intelligence fixed upon him.

"You have apparently been my guest for a sennight and I decided it was best if I made your acquaintance," said the duke and smiled at Argus. "The lads who helped bring you here told me so, just before they decided there were some things they desperately needed to see to at home."

"Rotten little cowardly weasels," Lorelei muttered, but quickly smiled sweetly when her father glanced her way.

"Lorelei, m'dear, I think Sir Argus and I would like something to drink and, mayhap, a bite of something to eat," the duke said, smiling at his daughter with a sweetness to equal hers. "I am sure you can find something for us. In the kitchens."

Lorelei opened her mouth to dispute that gentle command and then quickly shut it. Her father had that look in his eyes, the one that said he was the father, and the duke, and she had better do as she was told. She curtsied and went to find some drink and food, intending to get back to the room as fast as she could.

Roland had to bite back a laugh. His daughter had spirit. Far more than any of her three sisters had shown. He looked back at the man he had come to judge, the man who put that shine in his daughter's eyes. Sir Argus Wherlocke was a fine figure of a man. The only thing that troubled Roland a little was the air of worldliness the man wore like a comfortable old coat. He was not sure his spirited but very sheltered daughter was a match for such a man, one who had done and seen a great deal in his life.

Yet, she was still unwed. He did not care if she chose to remain so, if she was happy to remain a spinster, but Roland did not think a life as dear Aunt Lolly the spinster was what would make Lorelei happy. He trusted his instincts and they told him that his Lolly wanted a marriage, a good marriage with a good man, and children.

"How is it that you fell into the hands of this man who foolishly believed he could steal a God-given skill?" he asked.

"He wished to meet to discuss some investments. I found nothing about him to suggest he was a threat and so I met with him." Argus frowned. "I do not believe I missed anything, yet, once his prisoner, there was much about him that made me think he was a man with blood on his hands."

"Which could have been gained in the stews and thus been kept very secret. Few care or know what happens to those wretches. I fear that simply gives evil a safe play to hone its skills."

"I suppose it does."

"Lorelei said that you believe this man has at least one ally."

"He said *we* several times."

"*We* could encompass a veritable mob of people," murmured Roland.

Argus nodded. "My fervent hope is that it is, at most, two or three. A small committee of fools who have gotten this idea that they can steal away Wherlocke or Vaughn skills or be taught them. Men trying to get something that will give them a power they have been unable to gain on their own."

"Or Cornick could be no more than a hired hunter."

"He seemed a little too interested, almost desperate, to gain hold of my skills. And, for a mere minion, he knew a little too much about my family." That was something that still chilled Argus's blood, for it was dangerous for people outside of their family to have such knowledge.

"Your family and the many rumors that have swirled around them for generations have always stirred an interest. I have a great deal of information on the Wherlockes and Vaughns, although most of it is speculative or a simple recitation of some rumor or gossip. Yet, I understand your unease. Too many people showing too much interest could prove a grave threat to your whole family.

"I also do not like the thought of such men working their evil so close to my family, the Dunns. Now they will be trying to follow you. However, Sundunmoor is far more secure than Dunn Manor. Yet, as long as you insist upon hiding here, it is a little difficult to offer you guards."

"Your Grace, if you feel I am a threat to your family, then I will most certainly leave," said Argus.

"And go where? No, stay here and wait for your family to come. They will help and they can be your guards. I will, of course, offer you any of my people you may need when the time comes. For now, it is wisest that you remain a secret, hidden away here like some mad aunt." He briefly grinned. "Even if this Cornick fellow sniffs you out here, he will be hard-pressed to get to you. My lands are well guarded. Part of being a duke and all, as there has never really been any threat to the family. Father had guards. So I have them. Tradition, I suppose, but it will be of a help now."

"I thank you for your help."

"I have done little. Lorelei is the one due thanks. And, now, let us speak on her, shall we?"

Argus silently cursed. He had hoped the man would not touch on the subject of his daughter. If the man found out how difficult Argus was finding it to keep his hands off his daughter, all offers of help would be rapidly withdrawn. And rightfully so. Worse, Argus did not really understand why he was finding the control of his lusts so difficult. He had learned such control a long time ago and easily resisted far more beautiful and experienced women.

"I had not intended to draw her into this mess. . . ." Argus began, only to hastily swallow his words when the duke waved a hand to silence him.

"I know that. You sought out your family. But, Lorelei is now involved. What I need to know is if you think this danger could pursue her as well."

"I cannot see why it would. She is not a Wherlocke or a Vaughn. These men seek the skills they have heard we possess. She is of no use to them."

"But she is the one who robbed them of their prisoner."

"They do not know that."

"True. Are you good with weaponry? Pistols? Swords?"

"All of those things, but mine were taken from me when I was taken prisoner."

"Then I shall see that you are well armed."

"Why not just order her to stay away from the gate-house?"

"Ah, no, that would not work. She is a good girl, but she has a mind of her own and a very strong will. Max has known of this from the beginning and he has seen no need to keep her away from here. I will follow his lead. And, I will trust you to be the gentle-man you seem to be."

Argus could almost feel the weight of that trust settle heavily on his shoulders. He wanted to tell the man that he should not trust him with Lorelei, but, again, it was not something one could say to a father. A man simply did not tell a father that he lusted after his daughter but was not in the market for a wife. He realized that, now that her father knew about him, he had hoped that a little parental control would be ex-erted upon the woman. It seemed that had been a vain hope. Lorelei's virtue rested solely upon his honor and ability to keep his lust chained. Argus was not sure anyone should count on either of those things at the moment.

Lorelei entered with a tray of bread, cheese, and tankards of ale. Argus turned his attention to the food, shaking off his worry about his growing inabil-ity to resist temptation. The duke sat with them at the small wooden table, eating the plain fare with evident enjoyment and questioning Argus on his ability and some of the ones he had heard others in his family possessed. Something about the man prompted Argus to speak with a frankness that surprised him.

It was late by the time the duke ended his visit.

Lorelei was down in the kitchens again when the man suddenly wished Argus a good night and walked out of the room, a look of almost joyous anticipation on his face. A rather young face for a man who had seventeen children, Argus mused, curious as to how old Lorelei's father was.

"Where is Papa?"

Argus stared at Lorelei as she brought in a tray with three cups of chocolate and set it down on the table. "He left. Why did you not know? Or go with him?"

Lorelei sat down in the chair her father had vacated and picked up one of the cups of chocolate. "He forgot me." She laughed softly and sipped at the rich drink. "You are to blame. His head is now bursting with new ideas and information."

"Perhaps too much," Argus murmured as he helped himself to some of the chocolate. "I was reckless, speaking with too much freedom about matters my family would prefer were kept very secret."

"Do not worry. Papa really is not interested in the who, simply the what. He does not care which members of your family can do what, only that there is such a gift, that it truly exists and there are people who have it. I did not notice you giving him any names, either. Simply my cousin, or one woman of my family, and other such useless terms. But, truly, he will not be speaking of all you told him, only studying it and comparing it to the information he already has. You can trust him to understand that your family needs protecting."

"I must do already or I would not have answered all those questions he had for me."

"It can be difficult to resist Papa when he is interested in getting answers. His interest in what was going on here is what brought him here to begin with." She hastily told him just why her father had learned about his presence in the gatehouse. "Once his curiosity is roused, there is no stopping Papa from getting what he needs to satisfy it. He saw something that stirred his curiosity and immediately sought answers."

Argus nodded and finished his drink. Seeing that she had done the same, he stood up and held out his hand. "And now you must leave."

Lorelei sighed but took his hand and let him tug her to her feet. "Papa will not come rushing back, if that is what you fear. You must have seen that somewhat glazed look in his eyes as he left. It means he is lost in his thoughts, his whole mind consumed by whatever interest has grabbed him or a theory he must now prove or disprove."

"It is not your father I am concerned about." He pulled her toward the door. "It is your reputation."

"Sir, my reputation cannot be destroyed because I come to visit you. You are not here as far as most of the world knows, and this is but another place upon my father's estate."

"You cannot be that naïve. The moment anyone learns that I am here, it will be recalled that you were flitting in and out of this house quite often, at all times of the day and night. The minute that is recalled the whispers will begin and your ruin will descend upon you like a summer cloudburst."

She stopped in the doorway and looked at him. "I never flit."

"Lorelei . . ."

"I am a grown woman, sir. Many would consider me a spinster. I am also a duke's daughter and, although such a position does not make me untouchable by scandal, it makes it a lot easier to escape one, no matter what is said about me. Why are you so reluctant to accept my company?"

He grasped her by her shoulders, intending to scold her about foolishly risking her good name. Touching her immediately proved to be a mistake. The warmth of her beneath his hands rapidly entered his blood. The way her sweet face was turned up toward his, her soft mouth but a breath away, proved that he was right to think he had lost all control over his lusts. The lecture he had planned fled his head as rapidly as a buck did a hunter's party. He lowered his mouth to hers, hungry to taste her again.

The moment his lips touched hers, Lorelei flung her arms around his neck and held on tight. His kisses were intoxicating. When she was near him, kissing him was about all she could think of. The memory of his kisses haunted her for most of the time she was not with him as well. He tasted good, smelled delicious, and the hunger his first kiss had stirred within her just kept growing stronger.

He pulled her hard up against his body and she nearly gasped. There was one particularly hard part of him that was pressing against her belly and it both enflamed and intrigued her. She shifted her body against him and a soft groan escaped him. His arms tightened around her and she reveled in the closeness of their bodies. When he slid his hands down her back to stroke her backside, she shuddered with surprised delight. She would never have thought such a caress could be such a dangerous pleasure.

A curse escaped her when he abruptly set her aside yet again. This was growing tiresome, she thought

crossly, as she scowled up at him. This time the fact
that he was nearly panting and there was a slash of
red color high on his cheekbones did not ease her
annoyance. Those signs of desire did not soothe her,
for his desire did not make him hold fast to her as she
wanted him to.

"I want you to leave now," he said even as he pushed
her out the door.

"You, sir, do not seem to know what you want,"
she snapped, a gnawing frustration firing up her
temper as quickly and hotly as his kiss had fired up
her desire. "One moment you cannot seem to stop
kissing me and the next you act as though I have
the pox."

"You think I do this because I do not know what I
want? Foolish woman. I know exactly what I want. I
want you naked and spread out beneath me in that
bed. I want to be buried deep inside you, feel your
skin against mine, and hear you cry out my name as
I pleasure you. That is where such kisses lead and I
will not behave the cad with you. Now go."

She went but not really because he had commanded her to. Lorelei was reeling from what he had
said. The words had been crude, but his deep, husky
voice had been pure seduction. The hot look in his
eyes had made her insides curl with heat and need.
She might be virginal, but she knew what that aching
she suffered meant. It was pure lust. Now Argus's
words had given her an image it would be difficult
to shake from her head and that was only going to
add to the hunger she had for him.

It struck her suddenly that she was running away
like a terrified child, just as he wanted her to. Lorelei

stopped and glared at the door he had shut. So, he thought he was the only one who wanted, did he? He thought it was he who was pulling the strings, perhaps even thought he was forcing his desires on a poor, deluded maiden. She might be innocent in body, sheltered from a great deal of the ugliness in life, for which she was heartily grateful, but she was far from ignorant. Perhaps it was past time that he knew that, that he knew she had her own wants and desires.

"Do you know what, Sir Argus Wherlocke?" she yelled, the unladylike skill well honed growing up with sixteen brothers and sisters as well as a growing clutch of cousins. "Do you, who are so bloody determined to play the gentleman, think your wants will send me into hiding? Maybe, just maybe, I am not the coward you are and will start reaching out for what I want. Ever consider that? Maybe, just maybe, I have a few wants of my own! Maybe, just maybe, it will be *I* who see *you* lying naked beneath *me*!"

The words were still echoing in the hall when Lorelei became fully cognizant of all she had just bellowed through the upper halls of the gatehouse. Her cheeks burned with the fierce blush that flooded her face, but she held her head up as she walked away. Inappropriate, even scandalous, as the words had been, they had been the utter truth and she would not run from them. Let Sir I Know What Is Best for You chew on them for a while. She intended to go home and, if luck was with her, sneak into her father's library. There was a book there that would show her what to do if she ever actually got Sir Argus naked and beneath her. She was not sure if he saw what she had said as a threat or a promise, but if he ever called her on it, she intended to be ready to act upon it.

* * *

Argus stared at the closed door and, realizing he was gaping, slowly shut his mouth. Her clear, pristine, and very loud voice had cut through the thick door without a problem. That was an astonishing skill for a wellborn lady of such high rank and more than enough to shock anyone. It was what she had said that left him reeling, however.

She wanted to get *him* naked and beneath her? He groaned and threw himself down on the bed, only idly noting how his still-healing ribs protested that action. Argus was certain she was a maid, as pure as new fallen snow, but she certainly had not spoken like one. She could also be right in calling him a coward, as it was not only a sense of honor that held him back. Instinct told him that, once he had her in his bed, he would be loath to let her leave it. That would require marriage and, even if he was not far beneath her in rank, such unions did not work well for his family.

Maybe, just maybe, I will get you naked and beneath me! If she had purposely plotted some revenge for the way he kept pushing her away, she could not have found a better one. Lorelei had not even had to bellow the words. Whispering them just loud enough for him to hear would have worked just as well. Honor demanded he not bed her unless he was going to marry her, and he had no intention of ever marrying. Honor, however, would not be enough to wipe his mind clean of the image she had just planted within it. Argus knew he was facing many a night of waking up hard, aching with need, and unsatisfied. The kisses they had shared had already caused him enough trouble.

Maybe, just maybe, I have a few wants of my own.

As his traitorous mind started to ponder on just what wants of hers he could try to sate, Argus cursed long and loud. He would be lucky if he ever slept peacefully again.

Chapter 6

"The Wherlockes are here."

"Uh?"

Lorelei opened one eye and glared at Max. She had not slept well. Finding out just what she could do with Sir Argus Wherlocke's fine body if she got him naked and beneath her had kept her from sleeping peacefully. She no longer saw it as lucky that she had been able to slip into her father's library and look at the books he thought were so well hidden. She had woken up so often through the night, aching and asweat with a need she had never felt before, that she now wondered why she had even stayed in bed.

Such dreams should have shocked and embarrassed her, but, instead, they had stirred her desire and her curiosity. Each time she had awakened she had cursed the fact that Sir Argus was not close at hand so that she could heartily satisfy both. That shocked her a little, but she decided it was all a result of knowing that Sir Argus was the man she wanted. And, now, here was Max, looming over her and telling her she had company when all she wanted to do was sleep. Then she frowned, for Max rarely entered her bedchamber to wake her, so something important had to be happening.

"What did you say?"

"I said the Wherlockes are here."

The words finally penetrated her exhaustion-clouded mind and she squeaked in alarm. "What time is it?"

"Eleven. In the morning."

"That is rather early for a call by people we have never been formally introduced to." Then Lorelei grimaced. "I sounded just like Old Miller, our last governess, right then. Foolishness. I wrote to the Wherlockes and asked them to come. They are here. I need to go and speak with them." She nodded as the recitation of those hard, cold facts pushed aside the last dregs of sleep.

"Send Vale here, if you will, and I will be down within the half hour." She frowned at Max. "Do you think that is too long a wait for them? Mayhap I should just throw on . . ."

"A half hour to respond to an unannounced visit is more than any would expect, even those whom you summoned. I will see to their comfort."

"Have you told Papa they are here?"

"Your father has taken some of the lads down to the pond to fish and, perhaps, learn a few things about whatever disgusting wildlife lurks in the mud there."

She silently cursed the fact that she could not look to her father for any help as Max left. Knowing the Wherlockes would be treated well as they waited for her, Lorelei leapt from her bed the moment the door closed behind Max. By the time Vale arrived, Lorelei had already washed up and was half dressed, much to her maid's obvious dismay. Despite Vale's protests, she had the woman put her hair up in a very simple style and then hurried down to the blue salon where all guests were placed, a little proud of the fact that she had done it all in only twenty minutes. Catching a glimpse of Max disappearing in the direction of the kitchens told her he had already served them some food and drink so she did not have to fret over that courtesy. Taking a deep breath to steady her nerves, she opened the door and stepped in to meet Sir Argus's family.

They are a disgustingly handsome lot was the first thought that went through her head as she looked at the four Wherlockes gathered in the salon. One woman and three men. The woman was stunningly beautiful, and the men had the dark, somewhat dangerous look about them that could make women sigh. And they were all so tall, she mused, as they all stood up to greet her. And then she realized she should have waited for Max to announce her, but hastily shrugged that concern aside. Too late now.

"Lady Lorelei Sundun?" When Lorelei nodded, the woman continued, "Allow me to perform the introductions," said the woman in a voice Lorelei suspected made most men think of cool linen sheets and soft candlelight. "I am Lady Olympia Wherlocke, Baroness of Stryke Hall." She gestured toward a tall, black-haired man. "That is the Lord Iago Vaughn, the Baron of Uppington." She patted the strong arm of the tall, dark-haired man with the jade green eyes who stood by her side. "This is Lord Sir Leopold Wherlocke, the Baron of Starkly. And next to him is Sir Bened Vaughn." She smiled at the large man with the odd silver eyes before fixing her gaze on Lorelei as one by one the men introduced stepped up to take Lorelei's hand in theirs and kiss the back of it. "We have come in response to your letters. You know where my brother is?"

"Sir Argus is your brother?" was all Lorelei could think to say, momentarily dazed by having three handsome men kiss her hand in greeting. "But, he is not titled, yet you are." *And was that not a foolish thing to worry about now?* a little voice in her head groaned in disgust.

"I gained my title from one that has been passed down through the female line ever since my great-grandmother's time. She gained it through doing a service for King Charles the Second."

Considering that king's sordid reputation with women, Lorelei managed to grasp the good sense not to ask what service had been done. As she attempted to collect her thoughts, she urged her guests to sit down and served them some of the tea and small cakes Maxwell had just set out for them. She tried very hard not to be intimidated by the beauty and poise of Argus's sister, but it was difficult. Lady Olympia Wherlocke, with her thick raven hair, sky blue eyes, and enviously curved figure made Lorelei feel small and thin, as well as young and awkward, despite the fact that Lorelei doubted Lady Olympia was all that much older than she was. It was bad enough that surprise, and nerves, had caused her to ask the woman something so irrelevant as why she was a baroness when Argus was only a knight. Now Lorelei felt witless as well as plain.

"You know what has happened to my brother?" asked Lady Olympia, a shadow of impatience in her voice that Lorelei easily understood, for news of Sir Argus was the whole purpose of this visit.

"Yes, first, please allow me to assure you that he is quite safe," Lorelei said and could actually see the tension bleed out of her guests, their postures becoming much more relaxed.

"We believed he had been badly injured."

"Oh, he was. It may be best if I begin from the moment he appeared to me in my father's rose garden."

"I beg your pardon? He *appeared* in your garden?"

It was obvious from the surprised looks upon the faces of his family that Argus had not told them about that particular skill. Lorelei hoped that was because he had not yet perfected it and was loath to do any boasting about it until he had. Whatever his reasons for keeping quiet about it, they did not matter now. His secret was out.

"Sir Argus told me that he has been, well, testing his ability to send his spirit out from his body. He had intended to send it to one of his family when he used it to try and get some help, but he ended up in our rose garden instead. I think the rune stones in the garden may have had something to do with that. There is a circle of them, which my father had made into the rose garden. Although, that must sound very foolish to you."

"Not at all. It could quite possibly have something to do with the stones," said Uppington. "There may be no true records of the power of such places, but there are certainly enough tales about them to make one wonder. So, you are saying that you saw an apparition in your garden and acted upon what it said?"

"Instead of running, screaming loudly, back into my house?" Lorelei smiled. "Yes. I did try to convince myself that I had been sitting in the sun for too long or that it was all a dream, but he took my shawl with him when he faded away." Lorelei inwardly grimaced at what she had just let slip and prayed no one would ask just why Sir Argus had had need of her shawl. "I could not explain that away so I sent word to his family as he had asked me to. Although, only two of you are ones I sent the letters to."

"Modred sent word to me," said Lord Leopold, "and Bened was with me at the time. The duke rarely travels, especially to places where he does not know the people."

"Ah, of course." Before they could pepper her with more questions, Lorelei gave them the full tale of what had happened from the time she had seen Argus in the garden until their arrival at Sundunmoor. As always she left out all mention of nakedness and kisses.

"What I do not understand is how this Cornick fool could even think that he could just take Argus's gift," said Lady Olympia.

"The man obviously believes it is something that can be given away, stolen, or taught," said Lorelei.

"Madness."

"Sir Argus rather thinks so. But that does not stop the man from being a danger to Sir Argus. Still, it might be best if you discuss all that with him."

Within moments, Lorelei found herself escorting Argus's family to the gatehouse. She had thought to introduce them to her father, but he and the youngest boys had not returned from their foray to the pond. A coldness was settling deep into her soul as she realized that these people could be here to take Sir Argus away. Every instinct she had told her that, if Argus left

Sundunmoor, she would never see him again. Lorelei was just not sure if there was any way she could prevent that. These four people were his family and this problem was a family one, while she was simply the woman who had pulled him out of his prison and nursed his wounds.

When they stepped into the bedchamber, they found Argus struggling to tug on his boots, wincing all the while. The way his relatives hurried to his side made Lorelei suddenly feel like the odd man out. She told herself it was foolish, but the longer they all talked amongst themselves, the more de trop she began to feel. Finally she decided it might be best if she just quietly slipped away and waited at home to hear what would happen next. She was just stepping out the door when a hand clasped her by the wrist and she looked to find Lady Olympia at her side.

"Where are you going?" asked Lady Olympia.

"I thought I should leave you alone so that you could make your plans," Lorelei replied, but she did not stop the woman from dragging her over to where the men were talking. "You know best what you are capable of and what resources you can bring to this battle."

"You and this place are an intricate part of all the planning that must be done. Is this place not close to where he was held prisoner?"

That remark implied that at least Lady Olympia thought Argus should stay where he was, but Lorelei smothered the sudden hope that rose within her. "About a half day's ride if one does not have to go very slowly."

"Then this is the area where his enemies will be. They are surely searching for him all around here and Dunn Manor. Well, if they realize that Dunn Manor is where he had to have been taken at least at the start. Once they figure that out, the connection to you, to the Sunduns can easily be made."

"It is possible, although we have had no word of anyone looking for him."

Lady Olympia stared at one of the windows, but a quick glance at her face was enough to tell Lorelei that the woman was not admiring the view. There was a faraway look in those lovely eyes she suspected men had written odes to. She wondered what gift Lady Olympia could lay claim to.

"You will," Lady Olympia said in a voice very close to a whisper. "Soon." She frowned and then nodded as if confirming her own words.

"How could that be?" Lorelei asked. "There can be no connection between me and Sir Argus. Our families have never even met. So this Cornick thinks Sir Argus was taken to Dunn Manor. It matters not for no one but me, my maid, and my cousins knew he was there and we moved him as quickly as possible."

"You were seen," Lady Olympia said, giving Lorelei a look that dared her to deny it.

"What?" Argus turned away from his cousins to stare at Olympia and Lorelei, revealing that he had been listening closely to what she and his sister had been talking about. "You did not tell me about that, Lady Lorelei. When were you seen? By whom?"

It was not something she had ever intended to tell him, and Lorelei cast Lady Olympia a cross look only to earn a sweet smile from the woman. "It was when we were getting you away from that place. When the men rode up just as we reached the top of the hill, I think one of them caught a very brief glimpse of me.

May have even seen me in the moonlight for the space of a heartbeat. But, we were not chased, were we? There was no outcry. I quickly hid in the shadows and I was in disguise. I do not see how the man could ever guess it was me and come here because of that."

"No, but he might get to your cousins."

"He did not see them. They had already gotten you to the horses that were tethered deep in the shadows of the trees. Also, it has been a week and there has been no word from the Dunns that there has been any search for you or any trouble for them."

Sir Argus said no more, but he did not look convinced by her assurances. In fact, he looked sorely tempted to do a great deal more arguing, perhaps even give her a few orders. Lorelei decided to be the coward and slip away for a little while until he could be well distracted.

"I will just go and see what Max may have left in the kitchens. Perhaps you would like to go down to the front parlor? There will be more comfortable seating there," she said even as she hurried out of the room.

Down in the kitchens Lorelei found a very impressive array of cakes, bread, and cheese, and a few bottles of fine wine. She busied herself making up a tray for Sir Argus and his family, and listening to them all come down the stairs. His obvious concern over the chance that she had been seen touched her, but she forced herself not to read too much into it. As a gentleman she had given aid and succor to, it was only natural that he would believe he needed to keep her safe. All she could hope for was that he did not speak of the possibility to her father or Max, or she could find herself burdened with a constant guard.

That would certainly put an end to her plots to make Sir Argus see that they were perfect for each other, she thought with a sigh. It was going to be a monumental task as it was. She did not need a constant shadow interrupting what little time alone she might steal with the man. That was, she mused, if he even stayed at Sundunmoor now. Somehow, when she joined them all in the parlor, she would have to have some good reason for them to agree to keep Sir Argus here. She had to have her chance to make him see that they were perfect for each other.

"Interesting situation you have tangled yourself up in, dearest brother," said Olympia as she sat next to Argus on the plush dark blue settee.

"I keep thinking over how I ended up trapped by that fool and can see nowhere I actually went wrong," said Argus. "I gathered information on him before I met with him and there was no hint that he would do something like this. Perhaps it was just the lure of a possible profitable investment that made me careless."

"Nonsense. Not only is it difficult to find out everything about a person, especially if they are careful to keep their sins well hidden, but we have had no hint of any trouble headed our way. No attempts have been made to take any of our family before this."

"Are you certain?"

"As certain as I can be. Our seers gave no warning and no one has reported any attempts to drag them off the streets."

"It is troubling that there appears to be one or more people so interested in us and what we do, however," said Leo. "We shall all have to be careful until we know exactly who is behind this."

"Aye," agreed Iago. "A warning should be sent out."

"We shall do so as soon as we know where we will be settled as we sort Argus's trouble out." Leo looked at his cousin. "You believe the man will try to hunt you down?"

"Yes," replied Argus. "He will have to if only to protect himself. I know who he is and what he did is a hanging offense. The *we* he spoke of may also insist that he silence me."

"Unless they have already silenced him."

"A possibility, but I cannot feel that this will all be settled so easily."

"You were very fortunate to be rescued."

"I know. After a fortnight in the man's hands, I feared that I would die there because there was no way to reach any of you. Lady Lorelei and her cousins, mere boys, came right after I had suffered the worst beating yet and I knew I would not survive much more of such treatment. He also kept me half starved and gave me little water. Nor did he treat the wounds I suffered." He smiled when his sister grasped his hand and held it tightly for a moment, the only sign that she had been upset by his tale of the abuse he had endured.

"What I do not understand is how he discovered what you can do," said Olympia.

"I have given that some thought myself," said Argus. "It may be that someone in the government, one who somehow learned of what I have done for them, decided he needed my skills for something the government would not approve of."

"I can have that looked into," said Leo.

"It might be best."

Lorelei entered with a large tray weighted down with food and bottles of wine. Before Argus could move, Leopold was at her side to help her. He discovered that he did not like to see her and his cousin exchanging smiles. That had the sour taste of jealousy, which astonished him. It had been a very long time since he had cared whom a woman smiled at.

It was silent for a moment aside from murmurs of thanks and requests for a choice of the offerings as Lorelei, with Olympia's help, served the food and wine. Argus suddenly realized that this woman, this daughter of a duke, had gone into the kitchens and set up a tray for her guests, with her own hands. Then he recalled that her own father had commanded her to do the same last evening. The Sunduns were evidently not very high in the instep.

He quickly shook aside his pleasure at that thought. It had him thinking foolish things, such as a woman like her would not look down on a mere knight. Argus decided it might be time for him to take a few hours and vividly recall all the shattered marriages littering his family tree. That would be certain to cure him of this strange need he had to see her as a woman he could have for his own. It was a thought that had sneaked up on him when he was not looking, and he intended to send it crawling back into the dark hole it had come out of.

Out of the corner of his eye he caught his sister studying him and Lorelei and felt a chill go down his spine. Olympia had long insisted that he needed to marry despite the fact that she was six and twenty and still unwed. He suspected she thought a wife would stop him from doing things for the government, things that put him deep in danger and secrets. When he got the chance he would have to have a long talk with his sister. He would not have her trying her hand at matchmaking.

"Have you come up with a plan?" asked Lorelei as she sat on a little chair angled so that she could see all of them.

"If it is acceptable, I think we should stay here," said Olympia.

"Although her father has already offered that, if in an indirect way, I am not sure that is a good idea," said Argus.

Lorelei refused to be hurt by his reluctance to stay near her. She preferred to think that he was simply acting like all bachelors and trying to stay free of the marital net he could feel slipping over him. A little voice in her head whispered that she was indulging in wishful thinking, but she shushed it. She had never had a man look at her as Argus did, or kiss her as he did. It had to mean something.

"Heed me, Argus," Olympia said. "You are not yet healed enough to travel far. If we attempt to take you somewhere else it will sap what strength you have regained. Do not think I do not know that your ribs are bound up tight, for you still wince faintly when you move a certain way. There is also the fact that your enemy is probably in the area searching for you to consider."

"And so we should lead him away from the Sunduns."

"An admirable sentiment, but impractical."

"I fear she is right, Argus," said Lord Sir Leopold. "This is where it happened, or near here. It is not a place someone brings a prisoner unless there is some important connection. London certainly has many a hiding place no one would ever find. And in London it is very easy to move a person from one place to another and never be seen. Yet, despite all those advantages, your captor brought you here. Here is where we must at least begin our investigation."

"There is plenty of room here in the gatehouse," said Lorelei. "Max can have the other rooms aired and readied in no time. And Father will readily allow you to make use of some of our men if the need arises."

"So he said," said Argus, knowing that Leo's words had sealed his fate. He wondered why a part of him was so relieved that he was not leaving Sundunmoor just yet.

"Then we shall speak to the duke as soon as possible," said Olympia. "He does know all about this, does he not?"

"He does. Only recently, but it was a hard secret to keep for long." He frowned. "In truth, the duke also knows a great deal about our family. It seems there are many who have recorded every tale and rumor about us, and he has studied them. The man is fascinated by what we can do."

Lorelei saw how all Argus's family glanced her way and she smiled. "Truly, the knowledge is safe with him. When you meet him, you will see that. As I explained to Sir Argus, what fascinates my father is the gift itself, not the one who has it. And, he fully understands the need to protect one's family."

"I trust him with the knowledge," said Argus, and hoped none of his too-perceptive relatives could tell how his heart actually skipped when Lorelei smiled at him.

Argus was almost embarrassed to admit, even to

himself, that his heart had skipped. Or that he had
been strongly tempted to smile right back at her.
Worse, he had the terrifying feeling that there would
have been a touch of besottedness in that smile. Lady
Lorelei Sundun was having a very strange effect upon
him. He was going to have to work harder at pushing
her away, especially as it appeared that he would not
be leaving Sundunmoor any time soon. He also had
the feeling that trying to use his family as a wall to put
her behind was not going to work.

Lord Leopold helped himself to some more wine.
"I fear our life of secrecy may slowly be coming to
an end."

"Why?" asked Lady Olympia. "This is but one,
mayhap a small group, but no real threat."

"There are those of us, Olympia, who have gifts
many would covet. If this man, or men, share their
belief that somehow those gifts may be taken or not,
then none of us are safe. This has to be ended here
and now before the poison spreads."

"I agree," said Lord Iago. "Think, Olympia. Think
of what some of us can do. It is not hard to see how
greedy men or men in search of a way to grasp power
could think to use those gifts for their own gain."

Lady Olympia sighed and there was a fleeting look
on her face, one of such profound sadness, it made
Lorelei want to pat her hand. She restrained herself
from doing so and from feeding her curiosity by
asking exactly what gifts they were all thinking of.
What Sir Argus could do was fascinating. She could
only guess at some of the gifts the others in his family
might have. It was possible that some of the things
her father had talked about were not simply the imag-
inings of people who paid too much heed to rumors.

Then again, in the not too distant past, it needed only a rumor to have one decried as a witch, tortured, and executed in a variety of cruel ways.

"How will you find these men?" she finally asked. "The one who imprisoned Sir Argus is known by name, but none of his allies are. And I suspect the man who held Sir Argus prisoner is deep in hiding."

"The first thing we will do is go to the place where they held Argus," said Lady Olympia.

"I can show you to the place in the morning," said Argus.

"No, you cannot. You still have some healing to do."

Any argument Argus was inclined to make was halted by a sudden noise in the front hall. It sounded as if someone had just burst into the house. The noise of rapidly approaching footsteps brought everyone to their feet. The men stepped in front of her and Olympia before Lorelei could move to see what was happening.

The door to the parlor burst open and her two cousins, Cyrus and Peter, ran in only to stumble to an abrupt halt. They were in sad shape, covered with dust and looking very sweaty. A heartbeat later they also looked terrified, every drop of color in their overheated faces disappearing. Lorelei was a little afraid they were about to swoon. She peered around Argus to see what had her cousins looking so terrified. All four men had pistols aimed straight at her cousins' hearts.

Chapter 7

"Damn my eyes, I think my heart stopped." Cyrus blushed and looked at Lady Olympia. "Pardon, m'lady."

Lorelei idly wondered why she did not deserve a pardon as well. Her cousins still looked a little pale, but Peter had already recovered enough to help himself to some food and drink. She told herself to try to watch how much of the wine he drank, for he had very little tolerance for it.

"Why are you back here so soon after you fled like little cowards?" she asked, smiling at the glares her cousins gave her. "Papa is not that scary."

"He is when he is trying to dig the truth out of you," muttered Peter. "And acting like the duke."

"He is the duke."

"You know what I mean, Lolly."

"Yes, I suppose I do. So, why have you raced back here?"

"Have some bad news," Cyrus said after hastily swallowing the biscuit he had filled his mouth with.

Lorelei exchanged a worried glance with Argus before asking, "What bad news?"

"I think those men who took Sir Argus may know who got him out of that prison." He flushed when everyone stared at him. "Someone beat poor old Chambers near to death. He managed to tell us they were asking about a Sir Argus Wherlocke."

"Is Chambers going to recover?" Lorelei allowed her very real concern for the aging gamekeeper to hold back the fear for Argus that was already churning in her stomach.

"Mrs. Ratchet thinks so, but he will be abed for a long time. The only other thing he said was that the beating got real fierce because he thought they finally believed him when he said he did not know what they were talking about. Either they got very mad or they meant to kill him. Papa has all our people on guard now."

"And we shall put ours on guard as well."

Even though she recognized her father's voice, Lorelei was startled to see him standing in the doorway. Argus and his family looked far more than startled. She wondered if it was because they believed at least one of them should have realized her father was there. As their shock eased, however, Argus's three cousins looked as if they were about to pull out their pistols again.

"Papa!" Lorelei hastily cried, making it clear that this man was no threat. "I thought you were with the boys at the pond."

"We were on our way back when I saw these two lads"—he nodded at Cyrus and Peter—"riding for here as if the devil himself was snarling at their heels. Sent the boys on to the house with their tutor. Gave Pendleton our bucket of fish to take to the cook."

It was difficult to swallow the laugh tickling her

throat, but Lorelei managed. Later she would savor the image of the prim, meticulous Pendleton handed a bucket of smelly fish. *The man will probably demand a bath and all his clothing aired*, she thought, and then had to bite back a grin.

"So, Sir Argus, I see your family has finally arrived," her father said, smiling at everyone, who now scrambled to their feet as he approached them.

Lorelei had to wonder what Argus's family thought of her father. He looked less like a duke than he usually did with mud caked on his boots and splattered on his breeches. His hair was windblown into an untidy mess. His valet had given up years ago, contenting himself with simply making sure the duke was decently attired when he left his bedchamber, and saved his moments of sartorial elegance for the rare times her father went to some important event. She saw no lack of respect in the faces of Argus's family, however, as the introductions were made.

"Sit," the duke said. "All of you, please sit. I am getting a pain in my neck from looking up at you all and I had never thought of myself as short." Without waiting to see if they obeyed, he sat down on the arm of Lorelei's chair and looked at Cyrus and Peter. "So there was some trouble at Dunn Manor, was there? Your father is well though, I hope."

Cyrus nodded and explained why they had come back. "'Tis why we raced here. Thought it was something Sir Argus should know as soon as possible and Papa agreed. After he burned our ears for keeping secrets," he added in a sullen voice.

"And so he should have. Be grateful a little ear-burning is all he did. But, good work, lads, for this is indeed something Sir Argus should know."

The duke turned his head to look at Argus, and Lorelei knew exactly when her father spotted the food set out upon the small table centered amongst the settees and chairs. His face lit up like a child's. Her father loved so many foods she was astonished that he was not as round as a ball.

"Ah, bless me, lemon tarts." He grabbed one and hummed lightly with pleasure as he ate it. "Excellent. Now, Sir Argus, have you and your family made any plans yet? It does appear that your enemy is close at hand and determined to get you back. Or silence you." He listened intently as the Wherlockes and Vaughns told him what they had been discussing. "Why do you wish to see where he was kept?" he asked Lady Olympia. "Not a thing a young woman ought to be seeing, is it?"

After studying the duke, Cyrus, and Peter carefully, Lady Olympia replied, "I may gain some information needed to put an end to this threat. We believe the threat could be aimed at all of us, not just Argus. He was merely the first one they tried to get hold of."

"Quite right. He is not the only gifted one in your family. Do you think this Cornick fellow left a clue behind at that house?"

"Yes, but not as you think. I am able to see, well, the memory a person or event leaves behind. If I can go to that house, walk around it, I may be able to gain some important information from the memories of what happened there. When the event is born of violence, as this would be, the memories are often very clear."

"Such a wonder," he murmured. "Of course you must go."

"I thought I could take them there in the morning," said Sir Argus.

"No, that will not do at all. Bouncing around on the back of a horse will set back all the healing in your ribs. If it was but a short ride, one that could be done in a day at an easy pace to and fro, mayhap you could do it. That is not the case here. No, these lads will show your family the way. I cannot see that you would have seen much of the way to get there anyway, not in the sad condition you must have been in then. I have a fine stable of horses to choose from and will tell Gregor One that you will be needing some strong mounts come the morning."

Argus really wanted to argue that plan, but could not. The duke was right. He had seen nothing of the ride from his prison to Dunn Manor and just a little when they traveled to Sundunmoor. Pain had consumed him. He could easily get them all lost. This was his fight, however, and he wanted to be in on it. The fact that his injuries still prevented him from joining in the hunt for his enemies was beyond irritating.

"You shall have your turn soon," said the duke, and Argus feared his frustration was far too clear to read on his face.

"Max believes it will be but a few more days," said Lorelei.

"Let us hope Max is right," said Argus. "I need to stop this fool."

"Max is usually right." The duke smiled and stood up, quickly snatching up another lemon tart. "Now, lads," he said to Peter and Cyrus, "go on up to the house and clean up. This parlor begins to smell of sweaty horses."

Peter and Cyrus quickly departed. Lorelei wondered why her cousins were always so intimidated by her gentle father. She suspected their mother, who was awed by the fact that her family was now related to a duke, had something to do with that. Her father spoke and drew her attention back from thoughts of trying to get their mother to stop seeing her father as something close to a king.

"I shall send some servants to aid you during your stay here," said her father.

"Very kind, Your Grace," said Lady Olympia, "but we would prefer that the servants do not move in here with us. You know about us, but we would rather the servants did not learn too much. If you would permit, I could set up a schedule that would give us any help we need yet allow us the privacy we find so necessary. I will send for a few servants of our own, if I may, and then they can relieve your people of the care of us."

"You have servants you trust so completely? Ones who do not fear what you can do?"

"There are two families that have given us faithful servants for generations. There are a few others who are not from those families, but choosing the right servants for ones like us takes a lot of time and must be done with extreme care."

"Of course. Well, I will send some to air out the rest of the rooms here and bring you some supplies. They should arrive within the hour. We dine at seven and would greatly appreciate your company. Just a warning that most of the family joins me at the evening meal."

The duke nodded at the Wherlockes and Vaughns and then left. Lorelei could see by the thoughtful looks on the faces of Argus's family that they were trying to decide exactly what sort of man her father was. Most people did and most of them failed, if only because they became too set upon the fact that he was a duke.

"You need not worry about the crowd at the evening meal," she said. "It will not be as large as it sometimes is. My three eldest brothers are in Greece with two of my cousins who live here. My brother Winslow is staying with a friend of his in Surrey." She frowned as she tried to think of any others who were away from home at the moment. "The two youngest are not allowed to dine with us yet and the twins Axel and Wolfgang still have a few days of punishment remaining for demonstrating the waltz on the table just as dessert was being served about a fortnight ago." She smiled when the men laughed and Lady Olympia just shook her head and grinned. "We do still have five cousins staying with us, plus five of my brothers who have not done anything to be banished from the dinner table. Yet."

"Your father takes in a lot of your cousins, does he?" asked Argus.

"We have room and the tutors needed to ready the boys for school. With seventeen children, Papa has more than enough skilled people at work in the house to add a few more now and then. He is also godfather to a vast army of children, takes in any of the family who are orphaned, or those whose parents have fallen on very hard times. The entire Prudhome family live in a part of the east wing, mother, father, grandmother, and three children, but you will probably not see them either as they are battling a severe bout of the ague right now."

"Your father likes a full house, does he?"

"Papa does not care if the place is bursting at the seams with people as long as they stay out of his library. He spends a great deal of his time there. The number of family within the main house is one reason this place is kept empty. Some people do not like the way Papa allows the children to be seen and heard."

After a few moments of idle conversation about her family, Lorelei left. She knew they needed time to talk amongst themselves. Argus's family did not know her, except that she was the one who had rescued and sheltered Argus, so they did not yet feel comfortable speaking with complete freedom while she was there. It was understandable, but she hoped it would soon change for, with every kiss he stole, and despite the way he then pushed her away, Lorelei knew Sir Argus was the man she wanted. She had plans to join that family.

"So that was the Duke of Sundunmoor," said Leopold and then grinned. "A pleasant fellow, if a bit odd. The talk of who stays there and whom he supports does make me wonder if he is being poorly used by his family, however."

"I think he is too intelligent to be used for long, but, even if he does not see when it is done, Max does," said Argus. "The butler is the common sense the easily distracted duke sometimes lacks. And, the duke heeds the man's words." He turned his attention to his sister. "You are determined to go to that house, I suppose."

"Argus, you know full well that I have a good chance of finding some useful information," said Olympia.

Even as he tried to think of a way to tell her why he would rather she did not enter his prison, the servants from the main house arrived. Leo's men, Wynn and Todd, followed on their heels with the luggage. Argus promised himself that he would find time to speak with Olympia before she left in the morning. Knowing what she might read in the charged air left behind by his ordeal, he could not let her walk in there blind.

He and his family retired to the surprisingly spacious garden while the servants worked to make the gatehouse ready for so much company. They worked with an efficiency that astonished him and every single one of them was clean and genial, and had a glow of health about them that too few servants did. Argus had to approve of the way the duke treated his servants.

They were able to get back into the house in plenty of time to prepare for dinner with the duke and his family. Argus had barely led his family through the door into the dining room, Olympia on his arm, when he nearly stumbled in surprise. If not for the wide range of ages of the people moving to stand by their seats, it could have been an elegant dinner party at any of the homes of the highest echelons of society. Everyone was dressed in his or her best clothes and the table was set as if the king himself was expected to attend.

To his dismay he found himself seated next to Lorelei. She looked beautiful in her dark green gown that complemented her fine eyes. The delicate lace fichu tucked into the low neckline to make it appear more modest did its work well, yet then tempted a man to keep trying to see the shadow of the cleft between her fine breasts through the lacy web. Her thick dark red hair was elegantly done, a rope of fine pearls woven through it and several fat curls dangling down to brush teasingly against the smooth skin of her shoulder. She smelled so good he had to grit his teeth to stop himself from burying his nose in the curve where her long slim neck met her shoulder.

He forced his attention to the others at the table, noticing that Leopold had been set at the duke's right side and the two men were deep in conversation. Argus suspected that, despite the way he often lost himself in his books and papers, or even because of all that reading, the duke knew a great deal about the world around him. Olympia was seated between the two Dunn lads, who appeared to be cursed with a tendency to blush. Iago was seated next to a young girl who could barely have stepped out of the schoolroom and who appeared to be awestruck by her dinner companion. A quick head count revealed that there were eight and thirty people at the table, and he could recall the names of only a few despite having been formally introduced to them all. Then he saw that there was another table set far in the corner where a man, a woman, and six young children sat.

"What is that over there?" he asked Lorelei.

"Ah, it is the night when the ones who will soon join us at this table are allowed to be in the room as they are taught their table manners," she replied.

"You will soon need a bigger table."

"Oh, we have one in the formal dining room."

He blinked, glanced around the huge room, and decided not to ask where that was and just how huge that table was. Then the old woman on his other side started to talk to him. He savored the delicious food served and tried to be polite to the woman, who rambled on at his side, not much of what she said making any sense to him. Then suddenly the old woman leaned around him and said to Lorelei, "A dark blue, eh, gel?"

"Oh, yes, Aunt Gretchen. That would be lovely," replied Lorelei.

Aunt Gretchen looked Argus up and down as if he were a horse she meant to purchase and then muttered, "Long." She scowled at the other men in the family. "Huh. All long. A nice gray, two shades of green." She studied Olympia. "And a fine bright blue." She then turned and began to speak to the youth seated at her side whose name Argus could not quite recall.

"What was that all about?" he asked Lorelei.

"Oh, you will all be going home with a scarf," she replied. "Aunt Gretchen knits all the day long. Once Papa teased her that she would set him into the poor house with the cost of the yarn she uses. She immediately learned how to spin her own and even how to dye it the color she wished it to be. Does very fine work, too. Sells some to the shops in town. Shares the profit with Papa since she uses his sheep and all. But she makes so many things that no one who comes to visit ever leaves without a scarf, or shawl, or something for a babe if they have one. Loves to tat as well, so your sister may well get a nice shawl or something instead of a warm scarf."

The Sunduns were eccentric, he decided. He had thought it was only the duke but now realized it ran in the blood. In a less obvious way, even Lorelei was a bit eccentric. That could be why he and his family were treated so calmly and welcomed by the duke. That was why she had not run screaming when she had seen him appear in her garden but had, instead, come looking for him. Argus was just about to ask Lorelei if she actually had an exact counting of how many relatives lived in the house when he felt something brush over his feet. He started to look beneath the table when Lorelei grabbed him by the arm.

"Ignore it, please," she whispered. "It is just Cornelius. Papa will deal with it."

A glance over at the children's table revealed the man and woman seated there looking around. There were only five children at the table now. Argus was just deciding Lorelei was wrong to think the duke was aware of what was happening when the man calmly spoke between bites of his tender braised beef.

"Cornelius, why are you beneath the table again?" the duke asked. "Do you think yourself a dog and have come to look for scraps?"

A boy of about seven poked his head out from beneath the tablecloth. "No, Papa. I had to talk to you."

"You did not need to sneak about to ask for a meeting with me. What do you wish to talk about? We can meet in my library after the meal."

"I want to talk about what Mr. Pendleton and Mistress Baker were doing in the linen closet."

The duke's hand hesitated only briefly before he put another piece of meat in his mouth and slowly chewed. "I suspect they were discussing their wedding plans."

"Oh."

Argus noticed that, although blushing fiercely, the woman seated with the children looked delighted. Assuming the man at the table was Pendleton, he looked as if he were about to be ill. Not a match made in heaven, he mused, but then the fool should have stayed out of the linen closet in a house that obviously swarmed with young eyes and ears.

"Were you hoping I would toss them out?" asked the duke.

Cornelius crawled out from beneath the table and stood by his father's chair. "I thought you might."

"I would just hire another tutor and governess, Cornelius. You cannot get out of your lessons this way."

"May we still have a talk?"

"About what?"

"I think I may need the manly talk now."

"I will consider it. You will meet me in the library one hour after dinner is over. We will also talk about such things as telling the secrets of others simply to get what you want. Now, back to your seat. Unless, of course, you need to untie a few shoe ribbons beneath the table."

Argus choked on a laugh when the boy sighed and scrambled back under the table for a moment. The duke probably needed the quiet and peace of his library with such a large and mischievous brood. It reminded him a little of the Wherlocke warren in London.

His belly nicely full of a very fine repast and his palate soothed by a glass of port with the duke, Argus strolled back to the gatehouse arm in arm with Olympia. He struggled to ignore the glint of disappointment in Lorelei's fine eyes when he left, giving her only the most courteous of farewells. At the moment he could not concern himself with Lorelei's feelings, despite his errant mind's determination to do so and the pinch in his heart when he had seen that look in her eyes.

Slowly falling back until he was certain he could

speak with Olympia without his cousins overhearing every word, he said, "We need to talk before you leave tomorrow and this appears to be the only time we will have."

"It can wait until we can sit in the parlor," she said.

"No, for I can see that you are more than ready to seek your bed. Olympia, I know you will see a lot tomorrow. As you have said, the more violent the emotion or event, the more memories it leaves behind. I was there for a fortnight and when I was not being beaten, I was healing from the beating. I was also always cold for they left me with no clothes, no more than a rat-chewed blanket, hungry, and thirsty. They left me no food and water, or only the barest minimum to keep me alive. The wounds from the beatings were never treated so I lived in constant fear of infection. I was also chained to a nasty little bed in a room with no light unless you count the faint moonlight that reached into the tiny window or the lantern Cornick brought with him each time he visited."

"I knew it was bad, knew from the moment you disappeared," she said as she stopped and hugged him. "I had not realized it was quite that bad."

"I was treated worse than some men treat their dogs," he whispered, the pain and humiliation of it rising up in his memory. "Just before Lorelei rescued me, I had grown resigned in some ways. I could not fight off the big-fisted lads he brought with him and they protected themselves from my gift. They wore tinted spectacles and had strips of linen stuffed into their ears to dull the effect of both my eyes and my voice. Another such beating would kill me, of that I was absolutely sure. I was helpless, Olympia, and it is a feeling that can still leave me nauseous."

"And in your tiny man's mind you believe that somehow you should have been able to be less helpless? How, with a sheet to cover your nakedness? A salve to spread on your wounds? You were chained, naked, and regularly beaten. For a fortnight! Many men would have tried desperately to give their captors what they wanted, but you did not."

"Perhaps. I certainly misstepped in my judgment of the bastard. But I tell you all this because it could be a very ugly lot of memories you see when you go there."

She stepped back, slipped her arm through his, and resumed walking toward the gatehouse. "I understand, but I will still go. Somewhere in that house may be a small scrap of memory that will tell us how to find this bastard and kill him."

"Ah, well, we should probably keep him alive long enough to tell us who his allies are," he said, a little amused by his sister's fierce words.

"Fair enough. And then we will kill him *and* his allies."

"Making ourselves judge, jury, and executioner?"

"It has to be done. If only Cornick dies, what is to stop his allies from finding more men to come hunting us? There are too many of us to keep a close guard on and most of them will never accept hiding away until this threat is ended in a slow, completely legal way. I would certainly have trouble doing that." She sighed. "I know it is wrong to think such things, but this is the safety of our whole family we are concerned with. At least that is what I fear."

"I fear it as well, but we must still tread warily. We do not know who his allies are. If they are powerful people we could simply be putting an even larger target on our backs. And, of what good is it to kill but one of our enemies and then lose several of us to the hangman or exile?"

Olympia grimaced. "Had not considered that. Then we take it slow for now. I believe, however, that the man will die. From the moment I knew you were in trouble, I knew the man who hurt you would die. But you are right to say it is best to try and find out who is his ally." She glanced back at the main house and then gave Argus a sly smile. "A very nice family and a very beautiful rescuer."

Argus shook his head as they entered the gatehouse. "Get that matchmaking glint out of your eyes, Olympia. You know how I feel about marriage. Wherlockes, and Vaughns, are doomed to only suffer when they wed."

"Oh? What of the marriages we have seen in recent years? Chloe's, Penelope's, and Alethea's? Do any of them seem to be suffering?"

"No, but then the abilities to see ghosts and have visions do not stir up as much fear and superstition as many of our others do. I also think they were very lucky. I am not a man to trust in luck when it comes to my own life." Once inside the hall, he kissed her on the cheek. "Go to bed, Olympia. You will face a long, difficult day on the morrow and should be well rested."

When she sighed and went up the stairs, Argus stepped into the parlor, where he knew some fine brandy had been put out, only to find his cousins already enjoying some. "Do not become too accustomed to such riches," he drawled as he poured himself a drink and sat down on the settee facing them.

"Why? Because you plan to have this problem all solved within a few days?" asked Leopold, who slowly grinned. "Or because you mean to run as fast as you can as soon as you can to get out of reach of a pretty green-eyed lady?"

Argus considered punching his cousin right in his bright straight teeth. It would be useless to argue the truth of those words, however. Worse, in the course of the argument he might expose the cowardice concerning Lorelei that was riding him hard at the moment. Instead, he just gave Leopold a cold smile and silently toasted him with his brandy.

"Both."

Chapter 8

"'Ware, Olympia."

Olympia paused a foot from the door of the deserted house where her brother had been held prisoner, and looked at Iago. "You sense that something is wrong?"

"There is a very angry spirit here," Iago said.

"'Tis a sad-looking place. I am not surprised there is some disgruntled spirit wandering about here."

"Not disgruntled. Angry. Furiously angry."

"Dangerous?"

"I do not think she has the skill to be so, no. And she died recently. A little over a week ago, just about the time Argus was being liberated."

"Damn." Olympia dug around in the small bag of supplies she had brought with her, pulling out long strips of linen and a bottle of heavy scent. "Glad I thought to bring these."

"What is wrong?" asked Cyrus as he and Peter stepped up beside Olympia.

Olympia looked at the two youths and sighed. "I think it might be best if you two stay right here. There is a body inside the house." She nodded when they paled and stared wide-eyed at the door. "It has been in there only a little over a sennight, so it will not be looking or smelling very pretty."

"How do you know that? That there is someone dead in there?"

"Lord Vaughn sees spirits. And, as for knowing it will be a foul mess in there, I fear I have seen a few bodies in my time." She could see no fear of that news in their eyes and relaxed. "Argus did say that you knew about us, but I was not sure."

"Oh, yes, we know," said Peter and he nodded. "We do because Sir Argus had to make Vale do as he wanted or she would have told the world and its mother that he was there. And the carriage driver who took all of us to Sundunmoor." He looked at Iago. "You truly can see that someone died in there, m'lord?"

"Yes," replied Iago. "An old woman, and she is not happy about it. It was not age that killed her, either."

"Should we go and tell our father? He is the magistrate here."

"That would be helpful, but we do not need a lot of people here too quickly."

"We will just bring Papa back here," Peter said even as he and Cyrus hurried back to their horses.

Leopold watched the two youths as they rode away. "Such easy acceptance," he murmured.

"I think we can thank the duke for that," said Olympia. "From what little I learned at that dinner last night, His Grace's door is open to all his relatives and many of the young roam free there. I think the Duke of Sundunmoor is a very good man and a man of reason, if just a little odd." She shared a grin with her cousins but quickly grew serious again as she handed each man a heavily scented strip of cloth. "It appears he has passed that reason and calm on to a great many of his relatives. Now, let us be done with this."

The stench of death hit them the moment they opened the door. Olympia left the door wide open and breathed through her nose until nearly all she could smell was the strong perfume on the cloth she wore tied around her nose and mouth. It did not take long to find the body and it took only a cursory examination to know exactly how the old woman died. Olympia left Iago to gather what information he could from the enraged ghost and, with Leopold and Bened at her heels, she made her way to the place where her brother had been held captive and beaten.

Olympia entered the damp, dark prison where Argus had been kept captive and nearly fell to her knees. It was not just the sight of the chain that had locked him in place, the pitiful dirty bed he had been forced to stay on, or the single chair where his captor had sat as Argus was beaten that stabbed her to the heart. The memories of his abuse were so clear that she feared she would be ill. When Leopold wrapped his arm around her shoulders, she leaned against him and struggled to regain the strength to seek out the information they needed.

"They kept him here, chained, naked, nearly starving, always thirsty, and alone in the dark," she whispered. "How could we not know how he suffered?"

"We knew he was in trouble, Olympia. I believe the warnings started not long after he was dragged in here. We just could not find him." Leopold looked around. "Argus is a very strong man, but, I think, he is damned lucky that girl found him when she did."

When Olympia pulled away from him and straightened up, he asked, "Did you say he was naked?"

"That is what he told me when we talked last night, and I suspect I will soon read it in the dark memories that are crowding this room."

"So that is what happened to Lady Lorelei's shawl."

"What are you talking about?"

"Do you not recall what she told us when we arrived? She said she thought Argus was naught but a dream or some vision brought on by spending too much time in the sun, but he had taken her shawl away with him when he faded from sight. She no longer had it. It is why she believed in what she had seen and heard enough to send for us and search for him."

For just a moment the vicious memories of Argus's imprisonment faded back into the shadows. Olympia stared at Leopold, who just grinned. Bened did the same. She shook her head and laughed softly.

"So, the duke's daughter not only saw Argus in all his manly glory in her father's rose garden, she then went out and hunted him down. If that became known, those two would be standing before an altar faster than one could say the word naked."

"Yes, and get that idea right out of your head," ordered Leopold. "Argus is a man who must walk to that altar willingly. I think it would be best for Lady Lorelei if he did so as well. For her own peace of mind, if naught else. I also believe it will happen without any help from you."

"Aye," agreed Bened. "So do I."

"Have you seen something?" asked Olympia.

"No vision or dream if that is what you are asking," replied Leopold. "I just know it."

"They are a perfect match," said Bened. "She knows it. He is still fighting it."

"But Argus has always said that he would never marry," said Olympia. "Until recently, every marriage he ever saw was an utter failure that made everyone concerned miserable. Our own parents included. I will admit that when I first saw Lady Lorelei, I thought she would be perfect for Argus, but I still believe that some sort of nudge will be needed to make him open his eyes and see it, too."

"Nudging is fine," said Leopold. "Easily done. We just make certain that they are alone together as often as possible. That will plant the seeds and grow the bond." He frowned. "Argus will still fight, but something will make him surrender. I do not know what, however. I only know that he will face a crisis of the heart and it will end his battle against what he wants but thinks he cannot have. Now, let us get this miserable chore done with."

Olympia nodded and began to study the memories of all her brother had suffered at Cornick's hands. The room was filled with the energies from those confrontations. By the time she was done all she wanted to do was find some place very private, curl up, and weep. She accepted Leopold's assistance up the stairs and out of that dark place where her brother had suffered so much. The moment they stepped out of the kitchens and headed to the room where they had left Iago, Olympia doubted she would find that time alone any time soon. Young Cyrus and Peter, both looking as if they were holding the contents of their stomachs in by sheer will alone, stood outside the parlor door. Someone inside the room was speaking quietly with Iago. The magistrate had arrived.

After introductions were made, Squire Dunn looked down at the body again. "That is Old Belle. Thought herself a witch. Did a lot of wandering about. She was knowledgeable about her herbs, though did not always deal in the ones meant for healing. Nearly got herself hanged two years back when a man died. She had sold the angry wife a potion. Wife confessed in the end. Said the old woman's potion had not worked and so she had made her own. Old Belle was crafty enough to talk her way out of being hanged for trying to help a wife kill her husband."

"The man who did this did not give her the chance," said Iago.

Olympia watched Iago and Squire Dunn talk and realized that the squire was not troubled in the least by the fact that Iago claimed to be talking to a ghost. It truly was as if the easy nature of the duke ran in the blood of his whole family.

"Who owns this house?" asked Iago.

"It belongs to a Mr. Wendall. Fellow lives in London." The wry tone of the squire's voice revealed his contempt of that arrangement. "Takes the profits from the land's bounty but does not care to live here or spend a groat on the old place. Rumor has it that he is looking to sell it."

"He may find some trouble doing so. This ghost has a mean spirit to it and it is very angry."

"Sounds like Old Belle. She could make trouble, could she?"

"Oh, yes, once she gains the strength and knowledge. Yet, I am puzzled as to why she is still here. From what you have just told me, she is not one who sounds as if she is headed to a better, more beautiful place. And . . ." Iago blinked and stared at the floor. "Well, that solved that problem."

"Gone, is she? By the way you are looking at the floor, I must assume she did not fly up to heaven. You can actually see that, can you?"

"Not always. And some ghosts who should have been dragged right down to hell have lingered longer than anyone would have liked. It is rare, though."

"Huh. Devil is not a patient man." He shared a grin with Iago.

Olympia shook her head. "You have no trouble with the fact that he can see ghosts, do you?"

"No, m'lady," replied the squire. "Do not see why I should. Church says we all have a soul. Makes sense they might not rush off to heaven when their time comes and also makes sense that some people can see them. Cousin Roland, the duke, says one must always have an open mind and be ready to accept things we might not understand. Grew up with him, so some of his opinions stayed with me."

"Of course." Olympia could not help but think how this was the perfect family for her brother to marry into. "Is there anyone around here who might know more about the man who owns this house?"

"I can give you the solicitor's name and direction, but he is in London, too. As you can see, no one pays heed to what is happening to the house and the steward only comes down now and then to collect the rents and profits."

"Then I suppose we may as well make our way back to Sundunmoor," she said. "I thank you for your assistance, sir."

* * *

Argus silently cursed and rubbed his hands over his face. He sat in the duke's library along with the duke and Lorelei, going through books, letters, and papers trying to find something out about a family named Cornick. It was not a terribly common name, yet they had already followed several trails and gotten nowhere.

He knew some of his frustration came from the fact that he was sitting in a room sorting through piles of the written word while the others were out actually following the trail of his kidnapper. Argus knew the tedious work he was involved in could actually lead them somewhere, but he hated it. The fact that his sister was at the house where he had been imprisoned, reading all the violent, sordid memories of that time, did not soothe his rising temper either.

"It is as if the man does not exist," he grumbled. "I think you have the family lines of nearly every man, woman, and child in England here, Your Grace, yet we cannot find one idiot named Charles Cornick."

"Is it possible that the man is not really named Charles Cornick?" asked the duke. "He was, after all, involved in a criminal venture. It would not be beyond the realm of possibilities that he would use a false name or alter his real name in some way."

"Then this would make all this work useless."

"Not really. It but worked to send one in a different direction."

"You have far more patience than I, Your Grace."

"Research requires it, and an acceptance that, at times, you might follow the wrong path." He frowned when someone rapped on the door. "Come in. Ah, Max, what is it?"

"You have company, Your Grace," Max announced. "The widow Benton and her daughter."

The duke looked horrified. "Tell them I am not here."

"Your Grace, they have come because last week you had me tell them you were not here, but that you would be here now and they were to come back today."

The duke's shoulders slumped and he nodded. "Do remind me never to do that again, Max." He stood up. "Well, I had best go and play the host for a while. How long?" he asked Max. "Ten minutes?"

"A half hour, at least."

"Purgatory," he grumbled and started out the door.

"Do you intend to greet your guests looking like that?"

The duke looked at his ink-stained vest, shrugged, and combed his fingers through his hair. "She is the one who keeps coming to my home. She can take me as I am."

The moment the door shut behind her father and Max, Lorelei laughed. "Poor Papa. The widow makes no secret of the fact that she would very much like to be his fourth wife."

"Would you mind?"

"If she caught him in her net? Yes, but only because she would make him utterly miserable and he has already suffered a miserable marriage twice. He married when he was only fourteen, his bride the same age as he. She saw the marriage as her path to all the delights in London, Paris, and anywhere else she could spend buckets of his money. He just wanted to stay here. She gave him three sons and three daughters and died. His second wife, my mother, loved the country and he was, for a short time, very content, according to Max, but Mama died bearing twins. His third wife entrapped him, easily getting poor Papa into a compromising position that honor demanded he marry her. She, too, wanted to play the duchess all about London."

"What happened to her?"

"She died in a carriage accident shortly after giving Papa his thirteenth son. She was running away with an artist."

The first thought that went through Argus's mind was that one obviously did not have to be a Wherlocke or a Vaughn to end up in a miserable marriage or be left behind. He and Olympia had suffered badly during their parents' miserable marriage, but Lorelei and her siblings had been blessed with one constant in their lives—the duke. Argus's constant was Olympia and, with that thought, he was back to being frustrated and angry at being left behind.

Lorelei watched as Argus got up and strode to the large windows that overlooked the garden. Something in the tense way he held himself told her he was troubled. She could think of many reasons why he would be, but wished he would simply tell her what troubled him. Biting back a sigh, she got up and walked over to stand beside him.

"They should be back before dark," she said, gambling that he was worried about his family.

"I should be with them," he said, his anger at being left behind roughening his voice.

"You could not and that must be accepted. You still have your ribs tightly wrapped and bouncing about on the back of a horse could end with you being more a burden than a help to them. They can hunt him down as well as you can." She was a little startled when he whirled around to face her, his expression tight with anger as he grasped her by the shoulders.

"*I* need to be the one to find him," Argus said, giving the core of his anger and frustration voice. "*I* need to be the one to catch him, to face him as a whole man instead of the shivering, beaten, half-starved creature he made me."

Lorelei reached up to stroke his cheek. "And so you will once you have healed more. You would not be able to accomplish what you want if there was a fight and your injuries caused you a loss of strength and agility at the wrong moment, would you? If you want him to see you strong, to see you as a real threat to his life, then finish healing."

Argus placed his hand over hers. She spoke to him much as Olympia did, not really tempering the truth with pretty words. He liked that, liked it far more than he should. He also liked the way she was looking at him, a warmth in her gaze that drew his mouth down to hers, despite the warning bells clamoring in his head.

The moment his lips touched hers, Lorelei locked her arms around his neck. This time she knew there would be an abrupt end to their kiss for they were standing in her father's library, but she saw no reason not to take what little he could give her. She savored the taste of him, shivered with the strength of the desire he stirred within her as he stroked the inside of her mouth with his tongue. Daringly, she returned that caress with her own tongue and he groaned softly, a faint tremor rippling through his body. His hold tightened briefly, and then he began to caress her.

Lorelei was no longer shocked by the touch of his hands on her backside; she just pressed closer to that hard ridge pushing out the front of his breeches. She murmured in disappointment when he moved his mouth off hers, but then sighed with pleasure as he began to kiss her neck. It was not until he dragged his hands up her body and caressed her breasts that she stepped out of the sensual fog he put her into, but only for a moment. Her surprise at such an intimate caress was washed away by the pleasure that rushed through her body, a pleasure that increased tenfold when his warm lips touched the swell of her breasts above the neckline of her gown.

He turned and pressed her up against the wall as he continued to stroke and kiss her breasts. When he tugged the neckline of her gown down to free one, then licked the hard tip, she almost screeched from the pleasure of it. She thrust her fingers through his hair and held on as he suckled her, each pull of his mouth tightening the knot of desire low in her stomach.

And it all came to an abrupt end. She was released, her gown hastily put right, and Argus already several feet away before she cleared her head enough to know that she had been pushed away—again. Anger bubbled up inside her, but before she could say anything, she heard her father's voice and had to grit her teeth tightly to fight down the blush that threatened to flood her cheeks.

"That was a very childish thing to do, Your Grace," said Max as he opened the door to the library and let the duke walk in.

"I suspect it was," replied the duke. "And no surprise about that as I learned it from Cornelius."

"Papa, what did you do?" asked Lorelei, pleased with how calm her voice sounded.

"He kept coughing each time she tried to speak to him," replied Max. "The woman did not stay long, for I suspect she thought he had the ague or the like and feared catching it."

Lorelei did not like the way both her father's and Max's gazes narrowed briefly as they looked at her and then glanced at Argus. She had the distinct feeling that they guessed that she and Argus had not spent the time alone just talking or looking for names in the reams of paper her father had. Neither of them said a word, however, so she began to relax, and smiled over her father's trick to be rid of the woman.

"She will be back," she said.

"I fear so, but not too soon, I hope," said her father.

They worked for a little longer, searching for names, but Lorelei finally slipped away. She was not surprised to look out the window once she reached her bedchamber to see Argus striding toward the gatehouse. She supposed she ought to be grateful that he had retained enough sense to hear the approach of her father and Max, but she was only slightly so. She was getting very tired of being all stirred up and then tossed aside.

Roland stared at the door for a moment after it closed behind Sir Argus Wherlocke. "Tell me, Max, did my daughter look as if she had done more than talk while I was gone?"

"She did, Your Grace, as did Sir Argus, although an admirable attempt was made to hide the fact," replied Max.

"Should I interfere?"

"Not yet, Your Grace. Wherlocke men have good reason for being hesitant about marriage. From what I read in your papers after he arrived at the gatehouse, Wherlocke and Vaughn marriages usually end up as a complete and miserable disaster. I suspect he has a deeply bred fear of that honorable institution. It will sort itself out, for he is besotted with our girl. He just needs to accept that."

"Fair enough. I thought he was, too, but a father worries. I have no doubt she wants him and I did not wish to see her hurt."

"Even fathers cannot always stop that, but, this time, if I judge that man right, she will end up quite happy."

Argus was still cursing himself for an idiot as he walked into the gatehouse. He had been pressing a duke's daughter against a wall as if she was some common trollop and nearly got caught doing so by that duke. Insanity had obviously taken root in his mind. Or his groin, he thought with a touch of self-disgust.

He stepped into the parlor and quickly pushed aside all thoughts of Lorelei and how sweet her skin tasted, as well as how close he had come to finding himself dragged before a vicar. His family had returned, and, by the look on their faces, they had either failed to find anything or there was some bad news. He poured himself a brandy and sat down next to a slightly pale Olympia.

"Not successful?" he asked.

"Aye and nay," she replied and sipped at her own brandy. "I know what the fool looks like as well as his trained dogs. I also know that he has something to do with that house but is not the owner. His contempt for the place was there, but no sense of ownership. It was what else we found when we got there. There was a body there."

"One of his men?"

"Sadly, no," replied Iago. "An old woman. According to Squire Dunn she was a wandering herb woman who was not above making potions that had nothing to do with healing." He briefly related all the squire had told them of Old Belle. "She was a very angry ghost, but, fortunately for whomever ends up living there, she could not stay. She was shot between the eyes and just left there, so the one who shot her must have felt there was little chance of her being found."

"She must have been the witch Charles claimed he was going to bring," Argus said. "He was going to try and get the woman to spell my gift out of me and put it in him, or some such nonsense."

"She was fool enough to demand the money he owed her, telling him it was not her fault he had lost his prisoner, and then he shot her between the eyes. I would have thought belief in witches and spells had died a quiet death."

"I do not think Charles believed in it all, but someone wished to try it."

"We also discovered that the house is owned by a

man Mr. Wendall and he lives in London, as does his solicitor. Dunn did not know who the steward was or even if there was one, for the only purpose the property is put to is to bleed away all profit from the lands and rents."

"I will have my people look for him," said Leopold. "The squire said he thought the man's Christian name was Henry, so I will add that with a caveat about it being just a guess."

"And once I have time to think over all I learned, I may uncover something else I did not see clearly, not right away at least," said Olympia.

For over an hour they discussed what little had been learned until Olympia suddenly excused herself. Argus hurried out of the room after her, catching her part the way up the stairs. "Are you unwell?"

Olympia looked at him and smiled sadly. "Nay, just weary. I find the cruelty one man can inflict upon another very hard to bear at times. It also made me think on the past, on the tales of those unlucky ancestors who were taken up as witches. I cannot help but wonder if attitudes have really changed all that much and it makes me sad. My fury at Cornick also tired me. If he had been within my reach I think I would have tried to kill him with my bare hands." She kissed his cheek and started back up the stairs. "I will recover. Do not worry o'er me."

Argus shook his head and began to return to the parlor, to his cousins and the brandy. He did worry about Olympia, for a woman should never have to see such things, but she was too strong a woman to hide behind the protection of the men in her family. He also worried about himself. He was losing all control when it came to Lorelei, he could not find his enemy, and his enemy could well be a threat to his whole family. Stepping into the parlor, he went right to the stock of brandy. It was, perhaps, time to drown a few of his troubles.

Chapter 9

Argus breathed a sigh of relief as Max removed the binding from around his ribs. "It is good to have that off."

"Do not celebrate yet. I may have to wrap it back around you," said Max. "It is only because you whined so that I agreed to take the wrapping off today. Nor can you now leap on a horse and gallop round the countryside."

As Max pressed the area around his ribs, the bruising there now a sickly fading yellow color, Argus prepared himself to hide any pain he might feel. To his surprise he felt very little. He followed all Max's orders, turning, bending, coughing, and taking deep breaths, but suffered little or no pain as he did so.

"It appears that you are a fast healer or your ribs were not as badly damaged as we had thought they were. Rest, drink, and a lot of food did not hurt, either," added Max as he assisted Argus back into his shirt.

"I am healed then."

"You are better. No more than that. You should not

do anything too tiring or exert yourself too vigorously for at least another week. I cannot see inside you so I cannot say with a certainty that you are completely healed. If your ribs were badly cracked you should not be feeling as good as you appear to be. I will say that much. Yet, the bones could also have merely healed just enough to end the pain and give you a greater ease of movement, so take care. The fact that the ribs were injured at all means that the bones there will be weaker for a time yet. The healing needs to go a lot deeper than it has had time to."

Argus nodded. Being cautious was a great deal better than being unable to do anything. Now he could more fully aid his sister and cousins in finding Cornick. Now he might not be so confined that he found it almost impossible to avoid the temptation Lorelei constantly provided by her mere presence. Now, a little voice in his head whispered, he could give in to cowardice and run.

It was humiliating, but he had to admit that that little voice was right. Having Lorelei so close all the time had brought his control to the breaking point, something he did not like at all, for he prided himself on his control in all matters. With Lorelei, all he wanted to do each time he saw her was pull her into his arms. He could now put some real distance between them.

"Thank you, Max." He grinned at the man. "You have proved to be very skilled at doctoring people."

"With so many young boys to watch over, that should come as no great surprise."

"Why does the duke take in so many when he already has seventeen of his own?"

"His Grace cannot abide to see a child in need. Nor

can he abide the thought that, for lack of funds, a child of his family might go without a full education. I consider it a good thing for another reason. It ensures that the younger Sunduns and all their young kin are not little more than strangers. They are family."

"Yes, that is a good thing. Olympia said that Squire Dunn grew up with His Grace and his boys run free here. Family, not simply relations."

Max nodded as he pulled a fine silver watch from his pocket. "I must leave now, for His Grace has a meeting with his steward and I need to make certain he recalls it."

As soon as Max left, Argus tried another series of movements just to see at what point his ribs protested what he was doing. There were not many twinges of pain, but he made careful note of each one. He was not sure how long it would take to end the threat Cornick presented, and he had no intention of doing anything that would destroy what healing had occurred. He then finished dressing and went to see where his family had wandered away to.

He found Olympia sitting in the parlor, sipping tea, and staring out the windows. For just a moment, she looked sad. Argus moved toward her and that look abruptly disappeared as she turned to greet him.

"So, are you now unwrapped?" she asked.

"Yes, but Max has warned me that I should be cautious in what I do. I may not have been as damaged as was first thought, but he is right when he says that, once injured, the bones will remain weak for a while." He sat down beside her and asked, "Are you well? When I first entered you looked very pensive, or sad."

"Pensive, of course," she said so quickly that Argus

knew she was lying, but he decided not to press her on the matter. "This is a very troublesome business."

"Very. It does not help that we can find no information on Cornick. I have to think that what information I found before was set out for me to find."

"It still makes no sense that we can find nothing. The duke appears to have information on everyone."

"True. Leopold was fascinated." He exchanged a quick grin with her. "Where are the others?"

"They went into the village. They claimed they needed a few things, but I suspect they have gone to listen to the talk in town, gather some gossip, and ask some questions. Before they left, Leo sent word to his people about Wendall, the man who owns the house where you were held prisoner." She shivered.

"That is over, Olympia. Firmly in the past," he said quietly. "I am healed now and Cornick will pay for what he did."

She briefly clutched at his hand. "I know. Him and whoever that *we* is. I pray, for the sake of the youngest members of our family, that Cornick and his ally, or allies, are but a very small group of idiots. And, what happened to you proves just how far they are willing to go to get what they want. That terrifies me."

"I, too, hope that we are dealing with a very small, very secretive group. I am also hoping that someone in the government is behind it, for their knowledge of the various gifts within our family is limited to those of us who have worked for them."

"Ah, there you are," said Leopold as he strode into the room, Iago and Bened right behind him.

Argus watched as the men helped themselves to some wine. "Anything happen in the village?"

"In other words, did your spying gain you any information?" said Olympia.

Leopold sprawled in a chair facing Argus and Olympia and grinned at her. "The duke is loved by all, but a few quietly admitted that they speak first to Max if there is a problem they need tended to," he replied as Iago and Bened sat down. "A few also complained that a certain widow is making a complete fool of herself over the man, for he has had three wives and does not want another. Nor does he need one for he has thirteen sons. There were even a few who thought that, while it was true that he did not need or want a wife, he should perhaps get one anyway for he is only six and forty."

Argus choked on his wine and grimaced when Olympia slapped him on the back. "Well, I suppose that could be true for Lorelei told me that the man was married when he was fourteen and a father by fifteen."

"Obscene if you ask me," said Iago. "He was naught but a child himself at the time."

"True," agreed Leopold. "And even, what? Two and thirty years ago having someone so young get married would have been considered unseemly. However, until the current duke, the Sunduns had great difficulty producing sons. There was great rejoicing when a second son was born to the old duke, but the heir died and left behind only two daughters. The duke raised them."

"Fascinating," drawled Olympia, "but just what does all that have to do with our troubles?"

"It has something to do with us, in a small but important way. Every man, woman, and child on Sundun lands knows they must alert the ducal household to any stranger who is doing more than simply riding through on the way to somewhere else. That there is someone out there whom the duke sees as a threat."

"And you believe they will do that?"

"I do. The duke's people are loyal to the bone. I found no lies when they spoke of him, not even a hint that someone was merely saying what they thought I wished to hear, all the while quietly seething with anger. The duke settles all problems quickly, keeps his people housed comfortably, fed well, and working so that there is a coin or two for spending. He also tends his lands well and keeps his rents reasonable. And, even better, when he does make an appearance, he speaks to all he meets and knows all their names, their children's names, and so on."

"Astonishing. One has to marvel at his prodigious memory."

"Quite. It also seems that he has a lot of men working here who are named Gregor. Seven of them I believe. Their grandfathers settled here about sixty years ago. All Scots. The accents are still very thick."

"Stap me, the Sunduns were sheltering Mac-Gregors while they were still a proscribed clan. That could have caused them a great deal of trouble, what with all that Jacobite business." Argus shook his head. "But no word of any strangers yet."

"Nay," replied Leopold. "And no word from my people yet, either."

"These people have covered their trail very well."

"It would seem so, but my people are very good." Leopold sighed. "Unfortunately, good or not, such things take time. The fact that there is a chance someone in the government is behind this means it might take even longer. Caution must be taken so as not to alert the ones behind this. It would help if we could get information on that fool Cornick," Leopold muttered. "I do not know how you could have found anything about him to prove he was either good or bad. Whatever was shown you is long gone. And, yes, I had my men go through the papers you told me about, but they found nothing. They must have been taken and whoever did so was very good at his job."

"This just keeps getting worse," said Olympia. "All that you are saying points to someone with a very long reach and power. Government." Leopold nodded and she frowned. "And the part of the government where falsified papers and ones who can steal things from people without even disturbing the dust on the desk are easy to come by, causing no hard questions or raised eyebrows." She looked at Leopold. "The part of the government all of you work with."

"I know. And that is why it will be difficult to quickly get the answers we need, but we will get them. My superior is enraged that there is even the hint of one of his people being behind this. He understands all too well that, if our family is put in danger, especially by his own people, he will rapidly lose the Wherlockes and Vaughns as tools he has found very useful in the past."

They talked over what other things they could do to try and get Cornick until Argus's head began to pound from the strength of his frustration. He needed some air, he decided, and left the house, stepping out into the back garden. A stone bench was placed beneath an old tree and he sat down there, resting his head back against the gnarled bark on the thick trunk.

There had to be something he was missing, something that would help them catch Cornick and whoever was behind his acts. Argus knew Charles had talked a great deal during the violent visits he had paid him, but, unfortunately, the sound of fists pounding on his flesh made most of what the man had said indecipherable and hard to recall. He did not want to think about his time in that cold, damp prison, but it was time to do so. Argus was determined to pull all memories of his captivity out of hiding.

"Are you certain there is a spirit out here?" asked a sweet, lilting voice that yanked Argus out of his dark thoughts.

He looked through the dappled shade of the tree he sat under to see Iago, Lorelei, and her little cousin standing near a thick brick wall at the back of the small garden. They all stared at a small doorway set into the wall. All except for Lorelei's young cousin, who seemed incapable of looking anywhere but at Iago. Argus was not sure how his cousin endured it.

"Aye," replied Iago. "I can see her even now, sitting right in front of this wall, facing us." He pointed to a place a foot or so to the right of the small door.

"Is she clear to see? Her gown and all? Her face?" asked the young girl, surreptitiously stepping closer to Iago as she stared at the place he had pointed to.

"She is a bit misty, Miss Lilliane," Iago replied. "I think she has been here for a very long time."

"Why does she not go to heaven?"

"I have found that a spirit lingers because the person it belonged to felt there was something that needed to be done yet, something that needed to be finished. When that is done, most of them fade away."

"I was hoping we might see something, even if it was but a shadow."

"I think, Lilliane, I would rather not see too many ghosts," said Lorelei as she subtly hooked her arm through her cousin's and pulled the girl close to her, away from Iago. "I also think it is about time for your dancing lesson. You had best get back to the house."

For a brief moment the girl hesitated, and Argus almost laughed at the sight of her being torn between two desires. Then she made a hasty curtsy and fled to the house without a backward glance. Argus decided he could stop hiding away now and stood up.

"I am sorry, m'lord," she said to Iago. "Lilliane . . ."

"Is a sweet child experiencing her first love, infatuation, fascination, call it what you will. It will fade." He grinned at her. "As mine did and the woman, and her husband, were very happy about that."

Lorelei laughed and then saw Argus stepping out from the shade of the huge old oak, the one that several of her ancestors had actually fought a battle over to save it from becoming a mast for a ship. The sight of him made her smile even more. That was dangerous, and she knew it, but there was no halting the welcome she knew she gave him in her eyes and her smile. He took her by the arm to lead her back into the house and began to discuss Iago's ghost.

"It is sad," she said as she sat down in the parlor and he served her some wine after Iago politely took his leave. "I think I will try to find out if there are any old tales of some lost or murdered girl in the family histories. I do not like the thought of some poor spirit being stuck here so long, wanting to get something done, but none of us able to see and help her."

Argus only briefly wondered where his family had all disappeared to, for no one had mentioned any plans, and then he turned his full attention on Lorelei as he sat down beside her on the plush settee. He was dangerously close to the very woman he should be running away from, but, for the moment, he did not care. After watching her with her young besotted cousin and Iago, seeing how carefully she dealt with the girl and how she showed no doubt that Iago was telling the truth, he needed to be near her.

He needed her clean scent, her purity and sweetness to wash away the dark memories he had been wallowing in before she and Iago had interrupted. She was his savior, his torment, and his pleasure. She was everything he could ever want, he suddenly thought. She was clever, kind, had the sort of open mind that allowed her to accept his family and its gifts, and she made his blood burn with just a smile. And, she was the daughter of a duke, so he would certainly be marrying up, whispered a cynical voice in his head.

"You are frowning so fiercely," she murmured. "Do you think I should just ignore the ghost?"

"Nay, if you wish to try and discover who the poor woman is, do so. I have always thought it a good thing to bring peace to a restless spirit." He stroked her hair, a few thick strands having been pulled free of her pinned-up hair by the breeze in the small garden. "You have very beautiful hair," he whispered, enjoying the thick silk of it beneath his fingers.

To her dismay, Lorelei felt herself blush. "It is just red."

He kissed the hollow at the base of her ear, and she shivered, delighting him. "You do not take compliments well. It is the deep, rich red of an excellent burgundy. Warm, thick, soft as the finest silk."

Placing his hands on either side of her face, he slid them up her cheeks until his fingers were buried deeply in her hair. There was a slight flush on her cheeks and her lips were slightly parted as she stared into his eyes. Argus had the fleeting thought that he could look at that face forever and then kissed her.

For one brief moment, Lorelei considered pushing him away for a change, but then he pulled her close to him as he thrust his tongue into her mouth, and she surrendered. Such fire and need were too tempting to turn away from. Before she lost all ability to think clearly, she told herself that one could not make sweet memories by resisting that temptation. There was a ferocity to Argus's passion that stirred her blood and she wanted to savor it, wallow in it.

Argus soon had Lorelei beneath him on the settee. The feel of her there, her soft body embracing his so perfectly, put him into a fever of need. A little voice reminded him that she was a maid, but he shrugged it aside. She shared his passion, of that he had no doubt, and it was that heady sharing that he badly needed right now.

A faint touch of cool air followed by the heat of Argus's mouth against her skin was Lorelei's first warning that he was undressing her. The thought that she ought to protest such a thing since they were in the parlor, in the middle of the day, entered her mind and was swiftly silenced when he kissed her breasts. The way he teased the tips of her breasts with his tongue soon had them hard and aching for more.

A soft cry of pleasure escaped her, and she arched up against him, when he gave her more, his mouth closing around the crown of her breast. Each slow draw of his mouth pulled at her desire until her whole body ached with need for him.

He was tormenting her other breast with his clever, skilled mouth while sliding his hand up beneath her skirts when a sound slashed through the passionate daze Lorelei had fallen into. She clutched at his shoulders and tried to ignore it, but it pressed upon her mind until she began to tense as she listened more closely. When she realized she was hearing the voices of young boys drawing closer to the house, their young laughter coming in through the open window, she nearly cried out in horror. Instead, she pushed at Argus's shoulders, hard enough to shake him free of passion's tight grip.

"My brothers are coming here," she said, trying to wriggle out from beneath him.

A heartbeat later he was on his feet, tugging her off the settee, and straightening her disordered clothing with skilled speed. She touched her hair but decided it was no more disordered than it usually was at that time of day. Lorelei resisted the urge to look into the mirror when Argus stepped away from her. She knew she would see kiss-swollen lips and other faint signs of what they had just been doing. She could only hope that her brothers were too young to notice such things.

In silent accord they sat facing each other on the matching settees, each holding a glass of wine Argus had hastily poured them. She could not help but marvel at how quickly he had banished all sign of their lovemaking. He was so skilled that she had to wonder how he had come to be so, but hastily banished the thought. At least this time she was the one to push him away, she mused as she sipped her wine. She then wished that Argus would kiss her in some place where such interruptions could not occur.

It also astonished her that they could sit there sipping wine as if the passionate moments they had just shared had never happened. If not for the fading flush on Argus's cheeks, and the way he had to struggle to even out his breathing, she might think that Argus's desire was easily doused. Her body still burned with need. It was comforting to think that his did as well.

The twins, Axel and Wolfgang, strode into the parlor a moment later and Lorelei had to smile. They looked a great deal like her father, even to their untidy clothing. Despite the fact that they were very prone to getting into trouble, they displayed excellent manners as they greeted Sir Argus and gave her the message they had been sent to deliver. Apparently Mr. Pendleton and Miss Baker had had a rousing argument and now Miss Baker was weeping. In her father's eyes, a weeping woman was a catastrophe of biblical proportions, and Lorelei was not surprised he had immediately sent for her.

"Ah, well, then, I had best go and see what I can do," she said as she set her wineglass down and stood up.

Argus stood up as well and a plainly awed Axel stared up at him. "Damn, he is tall."

"Axel, watch your language," said Lorelei, although she had to agree and idly wondered how it was that their bodies fit so well together.

"Pardon, sir. Pardon, Lolly. My stars, he is tall!"

Axel sounded so much like their Aunt Gretchen, Lorelei had to bite the inside of her cheek to keep from laughing. She nodded to Argus, who was obviously fighting to hide a grin. "I am certain I will see you again soon, Sir Argus." She smiled sweetly at him. "Such a shame that this time it is I who must run."

Before Argus could respond, Lorelei hurried the twins out of the gatehouse. As she rushed home to try and settle Miss Baker before her father hid himself away behind the locked door of the library and did not come out for days, she hoped Argus was suffering as she was. Constantly having her desires stirred to a fever pitch only to have everything end before it had fully begun was not a comfortable situation. It was only fair that the one who caused it share in the discomfort.

Argus stared out the window watching Lorelei hurry up to the main house with the twins. He wanted to run after her, throw her over his shoulder, and bring her back so that they could finish what they had begun. That was madness. Taking the maidenhead of a duke's daughter was the quickest path to standing in front of a vicar or a bullet. He was not sure which he would prefer at the moment.

Shaking his head, he went back to his seat, sprawled on the settee, and slowly finished his wine. His body ached with unfulfilled desire, but he tried to think of it as a just punishment for his actions. Even if he ignored the fact that he had been close to relieving a duke's daughter of her virginity in a parlor in the middle of the day, he could not ignore the complete lack of finesse he had shown as he had attempted it. He had pushed her down onto the settee, bared her breasts, and begun to shove his hand up her skirts all in an embarrassingly short period of time. He had not been making love to a tender virgin but ravishing her, his hunger controlling him. It would be comforting to blame the long time he had been without a woman for his actions, but it was a lie he could not tell himself. It was Lorelei and Lorelei alone who made him mad with lust.

Her parting statement had made it clear that she was tired of being pulled close and then pushed away. He was tired of it, too, but he suspected her solution did not match his. He would keep her at a distance. Argus believed her plan was to pull him closer, yet he could not make himself think that it was because she wanted to try and trap him into marriage. Lorelei would never be so underhanded.

That did not mean she would not want or expect marriage, however. She was a very highborn virgin. Such women did not take lovers, at least not until they were married, had provided the heir, or were widowed. He shook his head. Lorelei would never join the ranks of those women. Her passion was leading her now, and he, as the more experienced, needed to show some control. She was a woman you wooed and wed, a woman you planned a life and children with.

It was a pleasant dream, one that caused him a pang of longing. Despite the recent happy marriages he had witnessed, Argus did not believe marriage could work for a Wherlocke, or a Vaughn. Nor could he marry a woman just to gain a few children. He already had two and he really did not need a legitimate heir, for he had nothing much to leave one. Money, but no estate. Most of his family had endured wretched marriages, ones that left husband or wife bitter and, often, heartbroken, and children with scars that never really healed.

He admitted to himself that a marriage, a home and family, with Lorelei made for a nice dream. Argus knew it could easily turn into his worse nightmare, however. If she turned on him as so many other wives and husbands of his relatives had turned on them, and then left, he would be destroyed. He did not wish to think about what that said concerning his feelings for her, he just accepted it as hard, cold fact. And after what happened with his two sons, he had no wish to see yet another child tossed aside by his mother simply because he was a little different.

As he moved to pour himself some more wine, he paused. The drink might dull the pain and fog the confusion he suffered, but it did not solve anything. It was time he made a decision about her and stayed with it. It was not fair to her to keep pulling her close and then pushing her away. Argus was amazed that she still spoke to him.

He needed to look at the matter with eyes clear of need, of the passion he had for her. He had to look at whether he wished to gamble that he might find, as his recently married cousins had, that some Wherlockes could marry. It just required finding the right partner, the one who could live with what he and the rest of his family were and with what any child she might give him would be.

"Damn," he muttered. "It appears that what I really need to think about is whether or not I actually want to get married."

Chapter 10

"Someone was here."

Argus looked at the signs of a campfire that Iago pointed to and nodded. For three days they had carefully ridden over Sundunmoor lands, regularly inspecting the more remote places where strangers might be able to hide themselves. This was the first sign they had seen that someone was sneaking around the duke's lands.

"Could be just a poacher," he said.

"Let me have a little wander around," Olympia said. "Out here it may well be difficult to gather any memories left behind, but it cannot hurt to try."

"Do not go far," Argus said as she began to walk away.

"Nay. There is no use in doing so."

Iago grinned at Argus. "In other words, she is obeying you because she was not going to do that anyway." He began to carefully look around the ashes of the fire. "If whoever stayed here were poachers then they had a very poor night. There is no sign of a kill here." He wandered a little farther away from the fire, his gaze fixed upon the ground. "They also had horses, three of them. I have not got Bened's skill, but, by the boot prints I can see, I would think there were also three men."

"The number is right," Argus said. "Cornick always had two men with him." A ghostly reminder of the pain Cornick's two men had inflicted rippled over Argus, but he shook it away. "Men hired in London judging by the accents they had. Dockside, I would guess. So there is a connection to London there."

"Then Leopold's men will find it." Iago returned to Argus's side, looked around again, and nodded. "Three men. Three horses. One fire. No sign of a fresh kill. Not poachers."

Argus looked toward the wooded area Olympia had disappeared into. "Might as well leave then. Did you see what direction they rode in when they left here? The ashes of the fire are cold and have been dampened down so it is almost impossible to know exactly when they left this place, but it might help to know where they rode off to."

"Into the wood." Iago's eyes suddenly widened. "The wood Olympia went wandering into."

Iago had barely finished speaking when Argus drew his pistol and went after his sister, Iago but a step behind him.

Olympia frowned and looked around her. She had gone farther than she had intended to and would be hearing a lecture from Argus for it. There was no sense in continuing to look around, either. All she had found were faint echoes of what and who had passed this way. One very angry man and two men filled with a love of violence. There was enough to tell her that Argus's enemies were in the area, however. The echoes of the men themselves closely matched the much stronger ones she had seen in the prison Argus had been kept in. One of the men had also spurred his horse too hard, the pain and fear of the animal leaving enough of a memory to tell her that the horses being ridden were not ones a poacher or poor traveler would own. It was not much, but it would have to be enough.

She turned to go back to where Argus and Iago waited for her when, suddenly, all the hairs on the back of her neck stood up on end. Olympia spun around to look behind her just in time to see a large, ugly man on a horse. She had been so lost in her own thoughts that she had never heard his approach. Even as she turned to run back to her brother, the man spurred his mount forward, leaned down, and grabbed her around the waist with one thickly muscled arm, pulling her up to his side.

"Not the one he wanted," said the man, "but might be good enough."

"Bastard!"

She squirmed, kicked, and pounded the man with her fists to stop him from dragging her up on his horse. Olympia knew that if he did, she would be lost. He cursed her with the rough speech of a London dockside laborer. His grip loosened when her fist connected with the side of his head, but before she could take advantage of that, he punched her. Only the fact that she flinched away as he swung at her saved her from a direct blow to the face. His rough knuckles connected in a hard, sliding blow on her left cheek. The pain and the force of the blow made her head swim and allowed him to tighten his grip on her again.

Just as Olympia feared that she was going to be taken away, Argus and Iago burst into view. She slumped in her captor's hold, going completely limp. Argus fired his pistol and she heard a grunt of pain before she was picked up and hurled toward her rescuers. She hit the ground hard, Argus and Iago unable to reach her in time to catch her. As she sprawled on the ground fighting to remain conscious, she heard her attacker ride away.

Leaving an armed Iago to stand watch, Argus knelt by Olympia's side. "Ollie?"

"Do not call me that silly name," she snapped and then groaned when the simple act of speaking sent shards of searing pain slicing through her cheek. "The bastard punched me in the face." She gasped when Argus began to slide his hands over her body. "Stop that."

"I am trying to find out if you have broken anything," he said.

"I have not, so you may cease to maul me. Help me up."

Argus cautiously moved her until she was sitting up and became alarmed when she just slumped against him. "Olympia?"

"I just grew a bit light-headed for a moment. I am fine now."

She began to stand up and Argus quickly moved to help her, keeping an arm around her waist to steady her when she swayed. "Still light-headed?"

"Nay. Now my head feels as if some monstrous weight has been set upon my shoulders and someone is pounding on it with a very large hammer. Oh, and a great many parts of me are beginning to complain about the hard ground they just met."

"I will take you up on my horse with me."

"That might be best. I do not suppose there is any chance that the wound you gave that man will prove to be a mortal one."

"Nay."

"Such a shame."

It broke Argus's heart to hear her soft sounds of pain as, with Iago's help, he got her up before him on his horse. He knew she was trying not to make a sound, but he easily recognized the strangled moans deep in her throat. He had made a lot of them himself not so long ago. She had hit the ground hard and, although he was as certain as he could be that nothing was broken, she had to be hurting in a lot of places. Argus wanted to travel slowly to try and keep her from suffering even more pain, but he also wanted to race back to the gatehouse so that her injuries could be immediately tended to. In the end, he compromised, holding her as steady as he could to lessen her pain.

Half the way home they met up with Leopold, Bened, Wynn, and Todd. Argus told them what had happened and soon found himself with only Wynn to accompany him. Wynn had been left as a guard for him and Olympia. The others had raced back to where she had nearly been taken from them, all hoping that it would be easy to trail a bleeding man. Argus wanted them to be right, but instinct told him it would not be that easy, not even with Bened's keen hunting skill at their disposal.

Briefly he wondered if he was making Cornick into a greater foe than he actually was, one more clever and elusive, just because the man had bested him once. Then Argus inwardly shook his head. Cornick's elusiveness could be no more than a keen sense of survival. Even men as thick as two bricks could prove to be very cunning when their lives were on the line. The inability to get any information on the man could be due more to the cleverness of his allies, especially if Leopold was right and this was a trouble caused by someone in the government. All he was certain of was that Charles Cornick would continue to hunt him, to either capture or kill him. Argus was the only one who had seen the man's face.

The sight of Lorelei walking up to the front of the gatehouse, even as he reined in before it, was a very welcome one, and not just for the usual reasons. She could help with Olympia. He recognized the girl with her as the one who had sat next to Iago at the dinner they had attended in the duke's palatial dining room. As he dismounted, and then lifted Olympia into his arms, Lorelei rushed to his side.

"What has happened? Was she thrown from her horse?" Lorelei asked as she followed him into the gatehouse.

"No, she met up with one of the men we have been so assiduously hunting for," Argus replied as he started up the stairs. "He tried to take her with him."

Lorelei ordered her cousin to go and get Max. To see the strong, beautiful Olympia bruised and being carried to her room like a child alarmed her. She hurried into Olympia's bedchamber just ahead of Argus and pulled the covers back so he could lay her down.

"I am not sure Olympia will want Max looking her over," said Argus as he helped Lorelei take off his sister's boots.

"Her modesty will not be infringed, if that is what worries you. Max will have me tend to anything that might do that. But he is very good at tending wounds. We could call for the doctor if you wish."

"Max," said Olympia. "Stop speaking as if I am not here."

"I had thought you had swooned," said Argus as he brushed Olympia's tangled hair from her face, careful not to touch her injured cheek. "Did he say why he was trying to take you?"

"Just said that I was not the one he wanted but I might do." She groaned as Lorelei began to tug off her coat.

"Are you certain nothing is broken?" asked Argus.

"Nothing is broken, but I believe everything is well bruised, scraped, and cracked. Damn but I wish your shot had hit the bastard's heart."

"As do I."

With Lorelei's help, he got Olympia stripped to her shift by the time Max arrived. Argus could tell by the faint sheen of sweat on the man's brow that he had run down from the main house, but neither his clothes nor his hair look ruffled by the exercise. He quickly stepped aside when Max moved to examine Olympia. Argus watched carefully and felt his heart twist with sympathy at every wince and gasp of pain that escaped his sister. When Lorelei stepped to his side to clasp his hand, he returned the grip, welcoming the support. It was harder than he could say to watch his sister suffer.

"Well, Lady Olympia, there is nothing broken," said Max.

"Said that myself," she grumbled, but her voice was weak and a little hoarse, revealing the pain she was in.

Max ignored her ill-tempered remark. "You will have to rest a lot and I will send a salve for all those bruises and scrapes. Ice for your cheek as well to hold down the swelling. I ordered some maids to prepare a bath for you in the adjoining bedchamber. It should be ready by now. Lady Lorelei can assist you in bathing now if you wish."

"I wish."

Argus helped Olympia get out of the bed. Lorelei quickly moved to his sister's side, and put an arm around her waist to support her. The way Olympia shuffled out of the room, vainly trying not to lean on the smaller Lorelei too heavily, had him clenching his fists as he fought the urge to help. He turned to Max, hoping that talking about Olympia's injuries and what needed to be done to help her heal would take his thoughts off the urge to rush to her aid.

"She hit the ground hard when he threw her down," he said.

"That can easily be seen in the bruises that are already appearing," replied Max, "but she is a strong woman."

After unthinkingly glancing toward the door to make sure Olympia was not there to hear that, Argus had to smile. "It is a good thing she has already left, for you would not want her to hear you call her that."

"Ah, yes, women can often misunderstand. I merely point out that she is not some frail, easily broken miss. Nothing is broken, but she will ache for a few days, everywhere. The bruises may not cover her from head to toe, but the mere fact that her body was thrown to the ground will cause all of it to ache."

"And she just has to endure?"

"Yes, unless you wish something to stop her pain?"

"Nay, she would not take it anyway. Some of those herbs Lorelei kept pouring down my throat should be acceptable to Olympia."

"I will check the supply before I leave, and Lady Lorelei can show you how to mix them."

There had been a faint stress put on the word *lady* and Argus hid his wince. He had called her simply by her Christian name. Even in his mode of address he was failing to push her away, he thought with a flash of irritation.

"Do not let Lady Olympia do anything too strenuous for a few days," continued Max. "As I told you, since one cannot look inside the body, it is difficult to judge what abuse the bones have suffered. A break is easy enough to find, but lesser damage requires far more skills than I, or most doctors, have and nothing much can be done to fix them anyway. They have to heal on their own."

"I will do my best to see that she rests."

"Good. Stay here so that you can hear if Lady Lorelei calls for help, although I do not feel she will need it. Between Lady Olympia's stubborn refusal to let unconsciousness intrude and Lady Lorelei's determination, they should be fine, and your sister will feel better for having had a hot bath. The heat of the water will ease a few of her pains."

Argus started to show Max out, but the man waved him off. Walking to the door of the room where Olympia was bathing, Argus leaned against the wall and waited. After the struggle to help Olympia take her bath, Lorelei might welcome some assistance in getting his sister back to bed.

* * *

Lorelei decided that Lady Olympia had a very impressive vocabulary. She washed the woman's back as gently as she could but did not need all the muttered curses to tell her that the bath was causing some pain. Looking at the mass of bruises blooming brilliantly on the woman's back, Lorelei was not surprised.

"You fought him hard," she murmured, almost able to read the story of the struggle in the bruises and scrapes that peppered the rest of Olympia's body.

"As hard as I could," said Olympia, accepting Lorelei's help in leaning back against the side of the tub so that Lorelei could wash her hair. "I knew that if he took me away from that place, it would be hard for me to get back. Not only would I be a prisoner, if they did not kill me first, but I would then become a weapon that could be used against Argus."

"As a threat, perhaps a trade."

"Exactly. And do not forget, I am now all too aware of how they treat the ones caught in their grasp."

Lorelei shuddered and concentrated on washing Olympia's hair. It was not spoken aloud, but they both knew that it would not only have been their fists those men used to hurt Olympia. What they had done to Argus was appalling enough. Lorelei did not even want to try to imagine what they would have done to Olympia.

By the time she helped Olympia out of the bath, after gently rubbing and brushing the woman's hair until it was more dry than wet while she soaked in the healing warmth of the water, the woman was as pale as the fine linen cloth Lorelei used to help her dry off. She then grabbed the soft nightdress and thick robe the maids had set out. Getting her dressed obviously took the last of Olympia's impressive strength and Lorelei feared she would collapse completely before they reached the bedchamber only feet away.

"Argus," she called and ignored the way Olympia half opened one eye to stare at her over the familiarity of using Argus's Christian name. It was not a look of insult, however, but one of calculation, and that made Lorelei a little nervous.

It did not surprise Lorelei when Argus immediately appeared. She had suspected that he would lurk close by. His concern for his sister was heartwrenchingly real and ran deep. He ignored Olympia's muttered complaints and picked her up, carrying her back to her bed. Within moments of being tucked in and forced to drink the herb-strengthened cider Lorelei hastily mixed for her, Olympia was asleep.

"She will be in pain for a few days, but at least she was not taken away," Lorelei said as she studied the dark look on Argus's face.

"These are my enemies and my fight," he said in a voice that was little more than a growl, filled with such anger that Lorelei suspected he could kill those men with his bare hands if they were in reach. "She should not have been injured by this, should not have become involved."

Lorelei lightly stroked his arm, the tightness of his muscles telling her that he was eager to bring the men to justice, to make them pay for what they were doing to his family. "She had to be involved. She is your sister. You would not let her fight alone. You would not sit at home if she disappeared without word for a fortnight."

"Nor would you, if it was one of your siblings. Right?"

"Precisely right. I love them. How could I not do all that was in my meager power to help them?"

"Exactly what Olympia would say, although she would probably not mention the love so easily as she likes all to think her a hard, fierce woman."

He took a deep breath and let it out slowly, trying to force the worst of his fury out of his heart and mind, and then he looked at Lorelei. Her gaze held both understanding and sympathy. He needed both at the moment or he would run out of the gatehouse in some vain attempt to hunt the men down, not stopping until he was dead by their hand or from exhaustion. His anger would make him reckless and that would be dangerous. His work for the government had taught him that being slow, precise, and cautious was often the best way to defeat an enemy, and survive the encounter.

"And it is really not just my battle anymore," he said as he gave into temptation and pulled her into his arms, letting her softness ease his spirit. "I was but the first they went after."

She hugged him, rather enjoying the warm but not passionate embrace. "And you are all certain that they will go after others if this is not stopped now."

"Very certain. In their eyes, mine was but the gift they thought they could best use of and so they wanted me first. I may not have given them what they wanted, but I doubt it has made them believe that they cannot take such gifts from us so they will try again. My biggest fear is that they may decide to try their vicious games with the weaker ones of our clan, the women and children."

"You will stop them."

"Such confidence in me."

He smiled at her and kissed her but made it a soft and gentle one. Argus knew he would like nothing better than to lose himself in her kisses, in her body, for a while. It was not only all the other reasons why he should not touch her that kept him in control but the fact that this was a poor place and time to give into his needs. Not that he had been all that careful about time and place before, he thought wryly.

"Max said you can show me how to mix that herbal potion you were so fond of giving me," he said as he stepped back.

Recognizing the end to the moment of comforting and sympathy, Lorelei nodded. She led him down to the kitchens and carefully instructed him on how to mix the herbs into the cider. As soon as she was sure he knew what he was doing, she took her leave. He was consumed by concern for his sister and she had already done all she could to help him with that. Now he needed time to wrestle his fury and grief under control, and that was something he had to do by himself.

Argus was sitting at Olympia's bedside watching her sleep when he heard the others return. He stood up, brushed a kiss over her forehead, and went downstairs to meet them. When he reached the bottom of the stairs he suddenly recalled how Lorelei had always kissed his forehead when she thought him asleep. Did that show that she cared for him, that she had done so from the beginning? And why did that possibility thrill him so very much when he was determined to keep her at a distance? He shook away the thoughts, promising himself he would consider it all later, and went to meet with his cousins.

"The bastard got away," he said as he took one look

at his cousins, saw the disappointment on their weary faces. He went to get a drink of the brandy they were all savoring.

"He did," replied Bened. "Even I lost the trail, which, as you well know, rarely happens. Have to wonder if the bastard has a little gift of his own that he just does not know about. He is certainly cunning. He took the chance of being seen by crossing roads so the horses of others might hide his trail, somehow managed to stop the bleeding so that trail ended quickly, and even used the river to hide his trail. I cannot even say if I have an idea of the area they are in, for he could have easily turned round and come back this way."

"Not good news except that it offers us some explanation as to why we are having so much difficulty in finding them," said Argus.

"How is Olympia?" asked Leopold.

Argus gave them a full report on her condition and saw the relief in their faces. "The worst of it is that she is not injured so badly that she will be abed for days. Do not get me wrong, I would not wish a serious injury upon my sister, but one might keep her from getting into any more trouble while we hunt these bastards down." The muttering of agreement from the men pleased him.

"Idiot. I ought to let you bleed to death," snapped Charles as he bandaged Tucker's arm, ignoring the man's soft curses as he inflicted as much pain as he could. He had done the same while digging out the bullet.

"I just happened on them," Tucker said. "Thought

that you getting one of them would ease the way with your boss."

"You know nothing about my boss. He wants Sir Argus."

Charles walked over to the battered table that held his brandy. The place where they cowered was little more than a hovel, but he had made sure he had the important things with him as he waited to get Sir Argus back. It had only taken one exchange of letters for him to understand he had few choices. Either he got Sir Argus back or he ran, as far and as fast as he could. Since he did not have the money to make a reasonably comfortable exile, Charles had decided that he would get Sir Argus back.

"You said you were sure she was family?" he asked Tucker.

"Had the look."

"Obviously the others have begun to gather 'round him."

"Then why not grab one of them, one that ain't so damned hard to hold on to or break. Bet we coulda broken that fine woman easy enough."

"What did she look like?"

"Like him a mite. Big woman. Tall and strong with all that black hair."

"So speaks a man whose thoughts do not rise above his waist. It sounds as if it was his sister so she may have been useful as a way to bring him into our hands."

"Maybe one of the other ones. I be betting that the woman will not be coming near enough to grab now."

"No, they will keep her close. You saw the other ones?"

"Aye, damn fools trailed me for hours. One big

fellow seemed to be able to find my trail no matter what I did." He described the men who had chased him for hours.

"One of them sounds like Lord Sir Leopold Wherlocke." Charles spit out a string of curses. "This mire we have fallen into just gets deeper and deeper."

"'Course we could grab us the little lady what keeps trotting over to where the bastard is hiding."

"You know where they are hiding? Did you not think I would like to know?"

"Thought you did and that's why we was here."

"We followed what little trail we could find. All that told us was that someone had come here from Dunn Manor. That was the only place I was certain of, although that old man was no help. But you have actually seen where they are?"

Tucker nodded and scratched his stomach. "Know that place you called a demmed palace? That duke's place?"

"Please, do not tell me he is in the duke's home."

"Not exactly. He is in a house down the end of that long road leading to the duke's palace. I took me a wrong turn and found meself riding too close to that place, but afore I was in full retreat, saw me a pretty little thing with fine red hair meeting our boy at the door. Thinking they are close."

"Red hair, did you say? Did she have a very fine arse?"

"Very fine. Ah, you thinking she is the one you saw?"

"The duke and Squire Dunn are related. And close. We followed Sir Argus from there to here. There is only one daughter left at home. Of course, it could have been a maid."

"Not in them clothes."

"I must think about this. Do you think we could get

close enough so that I might see this gatehouse? See Wherlocke for myself?"

"They have a lot of guards, lot of servants, and workers, but I think I can get you close. Have to be watchful for the men hunting us though."

"I just need to see that he is there, mayhap see the woman if I am lucky, and then we can return to hiding here while I plan a way to entrap him."

"It be a risky thing, but think I can get you there long enough for that."

Charles felt the first stirring of hope since he had found Sir Argus gone. The path that led them here had been one mapped with rumor, suspicion, and very little fact, but the trouble they had had since then confirmed his opinion that Sir Argus was here. It was risky to snatch a duke's daughter, but, even if she and Sir Argus were not close, the man would do anything Charles wanted to get her safely back to her father. There was a chance, a very small chance, that he might yet come out of this mess with his life and a full purse.

Chapter 11

After a brief visit with Olympia, who was already on her feet after only one night, Lorelei collected her sketching supplies. She intended to spend time at her favorite spot in the apple orchard. It was one of the few places where she could find some peace, as the children rarely went there. Even Gregor Three would have finished his daily inspection of his precious trees. For just a little while she wanted to be completely alone with her thoughts at a time of the day when her mind was at its sharpest, and sketching often helped her to think.

She settled herself comfortably beneath a tree at the farthest end of the orchard, where there was a cluster of trees that shielded her from view unless one walked too close to them. Gregor Three constantly bemoaned the wild growth of the trees, but he did nothing to change them. The trees were no longer producing a great quantity of fruit, but Lorelei was of the opinion that the apples from these trees were the sweetest.

As she began to sketch she was not surprised to see

Argus's face begin to appear on the paper. She thought of him all the time. At night in her bed she could feel the heat of his hands on her body, taste his kiss on her lips. Despite how he kept pushing her away, she knew they were getting closer to becoming lovers. Each time he kissed her, touched her, the passion between them flared hotter and it took him longer to come to his senses, to recall that he needed to push her away. It was a maddening dance he had pulled her into.

Lorelei knew she had to decide whether or not she would become his lover. She needed to make that decision when her blood was not running hot and her mind was not clouded from the power of his kiss. Taking a lover was not something that should be done lightly or in the blind heat of passion, not when one was the maiden daughter of a duke. Most men insisted on their wives being untouched when they first took them into the marital bed.

She would be gambling her future on the hope that Argus's desire for her could become love, that it already ran deeper than a man's normal need for a woman, any woman. The question was, could she trust her own judgment? It was not something she had any great experience in. Once her maidenhead was gone, there was no retrieving it just because the man she chose did not want to get married, or could not love her as she loved him.

And she did love him. He was firmly entrenched in her heart, mind, and soul. Sir Argus Wherlocke was the man she wanted at her side for all the days she had left in her life. She wanted to have his children. If he left her, returned to his old life once his enemies were defeated, she knew her heart would always ache for him. She would probably turn into Dear Aunt Lolly the Spinster within a very short time.

She studied the picture she had drawn and sighed, a new tendency that was beginning to annoy her. Argus's face stared back at her with that heated look of desire she so loved to see in his eyes. A man like that was worth any gamble, she thought. So was his love and that was the prize she sought. If nothing else, she mused, if I become his lover and he still leaves me, I will still have some very fine memories to cling to as I do my tatting.

Argus strode through the orchard and tried not to feel guilty for leaving Olympia alone. He had returned early from the daily search of the duke's lands to see how his sister was faring and to keep her company. She very pithily, and somewhat profanely, told him she ached all over and to go away. Olympia was not a good patient. He grinned. She was, in truth, bad-tempered and foul-mouthed. He suspected he had had the ill luck to arrive just after she had tried to do something that had made every bruise scream in pain and he knew her poor bruised face was part of that. After what he had been through he found it easy enough to sympathize.

It felt good to take a brisk walk in the sun. Too much sitting and riding were not good and had caused some of his healing injuries to ache enough to remind him that they were not fully healed yet. Argus had always believed that a walk was also the perfect way to sort out one's thoughts. That or talking the problem out with someone he trusted. Unfortunately, aside from catching Cornick, the matter that preyed most on his mind was what to do with Lorelei. He was not inclined to discuss that with anyone.

He ached for her, dreamed about making love to her, and could not keep his hands off her. She smiled and his heart skipped like some untried, infatuated boy's. If he was not careful he would begin sighing like some lovelorn maiden. Or making sheep's eyes at her like her young cousin made at Iago. The mere thought of that fate made him shudder.

Last evening he had considered going into the village to relieve the lust twisting up his insides. The girl serving ale at the tavern there had made it very clear that she was more than willing to serve him in a more intimate way, and he was sure she had the experience to sate a man's desires. Of course, she had blessed Iago, Leopold, Wynn, and Todd with the same come-hither look. It was not that which had made him shake away the thought, however. He had not only been reluctant to go, but had experienced a sense of guilt as if he would be betraying Lorelei if he even considered touching another woman. That had scared the lust right out of him.

"Dangerous," he muttered.

He had exchanged no promises with Lorelei. The kisses they had shared might linger sweetly on his mouth, keeping him constantly randy, but they meant nothing. They certainly never had before with any other woman. Yet, he knew his mind and heart had balked at the mere idea of touching another woman because both were lashed to her like a man tied to the ship's mast in a storm. That made his rational self want to get as far away from Lorelei as he could, as fast as he could, but he was discovering that he was not his usual rational self when it came to Lorelei.

"Most assuredly dangerous."

"What is most assuredly dangerous?"

It was only the sound of a voice so close at hand when he had thought himself alone that startled Argus, for that musical voice emerging from the trees was already achingly familiar to him. He looked around and finally caught sight of a small foot shod in a red slipper sticking out from under a tree. Stepping into the thick cluster of apple trees, he found Lorelei sitting on the ground, her sketchbook resting on her lap.

"It is dangerous for any of us to be out alone," he said and, despite the warning from his rational side, he sat down beside her as she quickly closed her sketchbook. "Poor Olympia is clear proof that my enemies are close at hand."

"Poor Olympia," she said. "She is truly quite miserable, but Max assured me that her pain will ease quickly, for he found no serious injuries. Her face suffered the most from that brute's fist. I fear her cheek will be very colorful for quite a while, but Max does not believe there will be any scarring."

"As long as the pain eases, that will not trouble her overmuch. I hope Max is right for an Olympia in pain is not pleasant company."

"Fled the house, did you?"

"As fast as I could. Have you escaped as well?"

"Well, not from Olympia, for she was pleasant enough when I was there. But I have fled in a way. I come here for the quiet, to have a little time to myself. That can be so difficult at home and one grows very weary of locking oneself in one's bedchamber. Not that that stops anyone from pounding on the door. So, I told a miserably sulking Mr. Pendleton that he might consider the possibility that he is not the only tutor in the world, grabbed my sketchbook, and fled the chaos."

"And your father will keep him and Miss Baker on even after they are married?"

"Yes. Papa says it is foolish to demand that one's servants remain unwed or achieve a higher state of morality than most of their employees." She grinned when he laughed. "All he wants is that they do the work they are paid to do, show proper respect, be loyal, and commit no crimes."

"Very reasonable. So, what have you been drawing?" He reached for the book only to have her slap both hands down on top of it. "No need to be shy. I expect you are very good at drawing."

"No, really," she protested as he tugged at the book. "There is nothing of interest in there. My skills are but passable."

The fact that she was trying so hard to prevent him from looking only made Argus more determined to do so. He kissed her and, when her grip loosened, he snatched the book out from under her hands. Her work was excellent, he thought as he turned the pages, admiring her drawings of places on the Sundun lands and ignoring the glare she was giving him. Then he froze. He was staring at a drawing of himself. He slowly turned the page to find another, and another. When he reached the picture she had been working on when he arrived, his eyes widened. She still made him look far more handsome than he was, or ever could be, but she had caught that look of hunger in his eyes perfectly.

"You are too modest," he said. "You are very skilled indeed. Your only fault may be that you make me look far more handsome than I am." He glanced at her drawing. "You have, however, caught that particular look in my eyes perfectly."

He was probably about to make a big mistake, Argus thought as he set the sketchbook aside. He knew he was going to do it anyway, and he would worry about the consequences later. Looking at the drawings she had made of him, of the hard proof of her admiration of him, had brought his hunger for her roaring to life. She wanted him. It was there to see in her drawings. This would be no seduction but the sating of a mutual hunger, a sharing. Argus found he did not have the strength to turn away from that.

When he looked at her, he found her blushes and unease adorable but was wise enough not to say so. He pulled her into his arms and kissed her, letting her feel the hunger she stirred within him. As he had suspected, had indeed hoped, she was quick to respond, making him fully aware that she felt the same sensual greed. Lady Lorelei might be innocent, but she was not hesitant, and he planned to revel in her daring.

Lorelei made no protest as Argus pushed her down onto the ground. There was a look in his eyes that told her he would not be running away this time, would not stir her passion to a feverish height and then push her aside. This time she would get what her body had been clamoring for since the day she had seen him in her garden. The apple orchard on a bright sunny day was not where she had ever expected to have her first experience with the art of lovemaking, but she would not balk now.

She tilted her head back as he kissed her neck and ignored the unlacing of her gown. Lorelei hastily reminded herself that she had never seen any glaring fault in her body, so surely a man enflamed by passion would not do so either. Despite that she barely stopped herself from trying to cross her arms over her chest when he tugged her gown and shift down to her waist.

Argus sensed Lorelei's shyness and did his best to keep her desire hot enough to burn it away. He wanted to see all of her, touch every inch of her soft skin, and taste her, kissing her from her head to her toes and back again. When he kissed her breasts and then drew the hard tip of one breast deep into his mouth, she arched against him with a soft cry of need, and he knew how to keep her locked tight in passion's hold as he rid her of her clothing.

Lorelei thought she would go up in flames or die from the ache gripping her low in her belly. When Argus ceased tormenting her with his passionate assault on her breasts, she tried to pull him back into her arms. It was not until he sat back on his heels to remove his clothing with an admirable speed that she realized she was naked. She was lying on the ground beneath an apple tree, bathed in sunlight, without one stitch of clothing on.

"Nay," said Argus, quickly stopping her from trying to cover herself with her hands. "You are beautiful and I like to look at you. Let me look at you." He kissed the palm of each hand and pressed her arms down beside her body. "And very soon I plan to be as naked as you are." He slowly released her hands and, when she did not try to cover herself again, he rapidly removed the rest of his clothes.

She was indeed beautiful, full where a woman should be, yet lithe. Argus did not think he had ever seen a

woman as beautiful as Lorelei. She had smooth, soft
skin that shone golden in the sunlight. Her breasts
were full, high, and firm; her nipples a soft pink and
temptingly long. The curls at the juncture of her
slim, strong thighs were a brighter shade of red than
the hair on her head. A tidy little shield of curls he
had every intention of becoming intimately acquainted with.

He tossed aside the last of his clothing and looked
at her face. The admiration he saw in her expression
stroked his vanity as no words ever could and he had
to resist the urge to preen before her. Then her gaze
settled on his groin and her eyes widened. Argus suddenly realized that, although she had seen him
naked, that part of him had always been shielded
from her view. By the look on her face, it might have
been wise to continue to shield it from her eyes, at
least until she knew the pleasure he could give her.

Lorelei thought she could be quite content to
stare at a naked Argus for hours. He was all dark skin
and lean muscle from his broad chest to his long,
strong legs. For such a dark man he did not have an
abundance of body hair, and she decided she liked
that, liked that there was so much of his smooth
warm skin to touch. Then her gaze slipped to his
groin and she almost gasped. His man part was not as
large as the ones pictured in the books in her father's
library, but it was not small either. It stood up hard
and long from a nest of black curls. She was just starting to get a little nervous when Argus returned to her
arms, all that smooth warm skin she so admired
pressed firmly against her. All of her concern about
man parts fled as she took the opportunity to touch
that beautiful skin everywhere she could reach.

The way she caressed him with her small soft hands had Argus fighting for control. He needed, and wanted, to go slowly, to not frighten her with the ferocity of his passion. He kissed her, caressed her, and discovered that her passion was as fierce as his own. Determined to make certain that her first time with a man was not a painful disaster, Argus worked to make her so wild with passion that she would welcome the loss of her maidenhead just so that she could have him deep inside her, which was exactly where he wanted to be.

A moan of protest escaped Lorelei when Argus slowly moved out of her reach as he kissed his way down her body. The occasional little nip he gave her, and soothed away with his tongue, had her shivering with delight. A tickle of awareness crept through the haze of passion clouding her mind when she felt him kiss the inside of her thighs, his silken hair brushing against her womanhood. Before she could utter a protest or move away, he kissed her there. Lorelei went rigid with shock, but its tight grip was shattered with only a few strokes of his tongue. She could hear herself panting, knew she was brazenly opening herself to him, but what he was doing was making her so wild with need and pleasure she did not care. It was as if every drop of desire in her was rushing down to her groin to welcome his intimate kiss.

When the ache there became almost more pain than pleasure, she called out his name, but he ignored her. And, abruptly, the ache became a shower of wondrous joy rushing through her body, a sensation that had her crying out his name again. She was still reeling from it when he loomed over her, settled himself between her legs, and thrust himself inside of her.

A quick, sharp pain made her gasp, but she clung to him. He was in her, all around her, kissing her as if she was a well he was desperate to drink from. As he thrust in and out of her, she continued to cling to him, wrapping her legs around his waist, and there was no fear in her when the ache began to build again. He slid his hand down between their bodies and touched her in a way that brought back the exquisite explosion of tingling fire that rushed through her veins. Still caught up in the gasping intensity of it, she was only vaguely aware of when he thrust into her with a renewed ferocity and then shuddered as he called out her name. There was a brief rush of warmth deep inside where he rested within her, and Lorelei realized that was his seed and held him even closer to her.

Argus roused enough from his sated stupor to realize he had collapsed on top of Lorelei and hastily shifted to the side. He eased his body free of hers and then held her close. His heart pounded and he actually felt a little weak, but pleasure still thrummed through his veins, warming him. He nuzzled her neck at the point where it met her shoulder and knew he would never regret this moment. He had never shared such pleasure with a woman before. Argus wished he were man enough to claim her so that he never had to give that pleasure up, but there was no ignoring the hard cold facts. A knight did not marry a duke's daughter. And, since the thought of marriage still sent an icy chill through his body, he could not really offer her that anyway. Marrying a Wherlocke never ended well.

He raised himself up on one elbow to look at her. "Lorelei, I am . . ." He frowned when she clapped one small hand over his mouth.

Lorelei could tell by the tone of his voice that he was about to offer gentlemanly regrets, or, even worse, call what they had just shared a mistake. "Do not tell me this was wrong."

Argus pulled her hand away. "This was not wrong. This was perfection, utter bliss. I, however, am wrong. I am wrong for you. You deserve better than anything I have to offer."

"Argus, you do not do yourself justice. Are you not a knight of the realm? Are you not of good blood? Have you not gained honor serving king and country? How can you say you are less than I deserve?"

He pressed his forehead against hers. "Wherlockes make poor husbands. Trust me in this. Our history is that of ruined marriages and deserted children."

She sighed and idly stroked his back. A part of her wanted to poke and prod until he told her everything about that history, but she fought the urge. He at least felt he should be offering marriage, but, for reasons he did not feel inclined to tell her, believed he was a poor marriage prospect. Argus seemed to think some history of poor marriages was important, but he did not tell her why, and she could not understand why whatever happened in the past should matter to them now. That was something to deal with at another time. Right now she was in the arms of the man she had hungered for and she did not want to spoil it by talking about why he was wrong for her. If nothing else, she did not want such a beautiful interlude spoiled with talk of guilt and mistakes, and she was sure that such words would seep into a discussion if she allowed it.

The only solution she could think of was to relieve him of the problem. He thought he should have left her alone because he could not offer marriage. So, she had to make it clear that she had not and would not expect that of him. All she could do was hope he would believe her.

"We are lovers now," she said, and caressed his back, enjoying the texture of his sun-warmed skin.

"Aye, we are." He was not sure what she was trying to say, but he understood that she did not want any discussion of the right or wrong of what they had done.

"So, how do lovers who live amongst so many people meet, find some time alone?"

"Whenever and wherever they can."

"Do you have a trysting place in mind?"

"Well, there is that big old oak in the garden at the gatehouse. Its trunk is as wide and thick as any wall."

Lorelei laughed. "True."

"It is probably not wise to play that game, however. Cornick has already tried to catch one of us. Who knows what trick he might try next. One of us would be vulnerable for a while as we slipped back and forth during the night."

"Such practicality. I would think that one of us would find it easy enough to remain in the shadows, the night being a perfect shield."

He laughed and kissed her on the nose. "We will work something out, for now that I have had you in my arms, I do not think I will be able to go long without wanting you there again."

Lorelei decided that was as much of a declaration as she would get from him, and she kissed him. It was not long before they were making love again. She was astonished when the same joy rushed through her, not dimmed at all by her growing knowledge of what was happening between them.

Her shyness returned not long after the warmth of their lovemaking began to leave her body. Blushing so strongly that she suspected her face was as red as her hair she scrambled into her clothes. Even so, she managed to sneak many a look at him as he dressed. It was hard for her to believe that she had just been as intimate as a man and woman could be with such a beautiful man. She tucked the memory of his body away in her mind, assuring herself that now she could pull it out whenever she had need of it.

It was not until she was back home, slipping into her bedchamber intending to wash up, that Lorelei realized no plans had been made for another meeting. For a moment her heart clenched with sorrow, her mind declaring that she had already been cast aside. Lorelei took a deep breath to quell the panic rising inside of her. Argus had already chosen the spot where they could meet. She suspected it was his concern about his enemies that kept him from immediately choosing a time for her to meet him there. He simply wanted to plan the safest way for them to have a tryst.

It was not going to be easy to be his lover, she decided. The fact that they would have to be so secretive troubled her, as did the fact that he had spoken only words of desire, none of love or even the beginning of such an emotion. He had given her no hint that there was even a seed of love there that she could nurture. She would need a lot of patience if she were to hold fast to Sir Argus Wherlocke.

* * *

Argus stood in the little garden of the gatehouse and stared at the big old oak tree. It would be a perfect place to meet with Lorelei. The problem was, how to get together without putting her at any risk. Cornick and his men were somewhere in the area and had already attacked one of the family. He did not want his need for her to make him act foolishly.

As if he had not already, he thought and kicked at a stone in the path he stood on. He had bedded down with the virgin daughter of a duke, a man he liked and respected. A man who had opened his home to him and was ready to help him stay safe as he hunted down his enemies. If that was not the definition of an utter cad, he did not know what was.

Even disgusted with himself as he suddenly was, Argus found himself staring at the tree again. He could almost see him and Lorelei making love in the shelter of it, its huge trunk protecting them from prying eyes. Argus knew he would continue the affair he had begun tonight because the thought of never touching her again, never tasting her again, was more than he could endure.

"And mayhap you ought to give that fact some hard thought," he muttered.

"Talking to yourself?"

Argus turned to look at his cousin Iago. "Trying to work out a few problems."

"The first of which is a fair young maid with hair the color of a fine red wine?"

"I believe that might be my business," he said, but

the repressive tone he put into his voice only made Iago smile. His relatives were not easily intimidated.

"Since we are here on the sufferance of His Grace, her father, you might want to reconsider that opinion." Iago patted him on the arm and started back into the house. "Just came to tell you that food is on the table. Mayhap a full, contented stomach will help you sort out your twisted thoughts."

"My thoughts are not twisted," Argus protested as he followed Iago.

"Nay? Beautiful woman who saves your life, looks at you as if you hung the very moon in the sky, and, I think, shares a passion with you that could set the woods afire, and you stand about and frown as if you have some great weight upon your shoulders."

"I do. Its name is Cornick."

"True, but you just try to distract me now. Very well, I will let it go."

Argus sincerely doubted his cousin would let it go for long. What was it about family that made them think they had the right to stick their long noses into your business? he wondered, scowling at Iago's broad back. He had the sinking feeling that Iago was but the first one to try, however, and he had not heard the end of it, not by any means.

Chapter 12

"M'lady, there is someone here demanding to see Sir Argus Wherlocke."

Lorelei looked up from the book she had been trying and failing to read. Coming into the morning room to read had not succeeded in making her stop wanting to rush over to the gatehouse and see Argus. Although she now knew how wonderful lovemaking could be and she needed more, she would not keep hurling herself at him until she got it. She wanted to show him that she was a mature woman who could be a lover without pressing him for more than he had to give. Lorelei was rather hoping that Argus would come to her or at least attempt to arrange some romantic tryst. It was difficult to be patient, however, and she frowned at Max, hoping whatever he was talking about would occupy her mind as reading had not done.

"Demanding?" she asked.

"Quite vigorously."

"Surely Sir Argus's enemies would not come right

up to the door of Sundunmoor and demand we show them where he is," she muttered.

"Ah, no. These are not his enemies. They are two young lads."

"How young?"

"About twelve, maybe a little more, or a little less. Quite hard to judge at that age."

"No one else is with them? It is just the boys?"

"It appears so. Shall I bring them to you?"

"Yes, Max, I think you had best do so. We do not wish to send them straight to Sir Argus without knowing what they really want. It could be something he needs to be warned about. Perhaps some food and drink for them, too. I will attempt to discover what this is all about."

She frowned when Max left. It had sounded very much as if he had said, "Do not think you will like it." That made no sense. Why would she not like two young boys? Her home was filled with young boys and she was fond of them all. She also did not think there was anything two boys could do or say that would upset her. Talking to them before taking them to Sir Argus was merely taking a precaution, and, she ruefully admitted, satisfying her curiosity.

Lorelei had barely managed to set her book aside, stand up, and brush out her skirts when Max showed the two boys into the morning room. They looked as if they had endured a long, hard journey. A closer look made her certain the boys were related to the Wherlockes or Vaughns in some way. The family definitely had a distinctive appearance or, as her father liked to say, they bred true.

"What have you done with our father?" demanded the taller of the two boys.

"Here now," said Max in his sternest tone of voice. "Gentlemen do not speak so to a lady. This is the Lady Lorelei, daughter of the Duke of Sundunmoor, and you will show her the proper respect. Now, bow and introduce yourselves."

For a moment Lorelei feared the boys were going to make the mistake of arguing with Max. Her entire family could line up and attest to the fact that that was a waste of time. Max was the undisputed master of the stare that intimidated and the final word that made any further argument make one sound like an idiot. They glared at him, but then the taller boy elbowed the other in the side, and they both looked at her. Neither boy was looking particularly friendly, but they performed their bows with grace and no hint of insult.

"I am Darius Wherlocke," said the taller boy, "and this is my brother Olwen. We are Sir Argus's sons and we want to know where he is."

Shock held Lorelei silent for what seemed like hours, but she knew it could only have been a minute or two, for Max had not cleared his throat. Max had said exactly what she had thought he had as he had left the room to fetch the boys and, as always, he had been right. She did not like this. Various emotions were clawing at her heart and none of them were good ones.

We are Sir Argus's sons.

It was often said that words could hurt, but Lorelei had never fully believed that, thinking unkind remarks could easily be shrugged aside as the ignorance of the person saying them. She believed it now. Argus had two sons and had never told her. Was there a wife he had also neglected to mention? She groped for the training her governess had pounded into her, pulling the cloak of good manners around herself and letting it smother her confusion and pain.

"Come in and sit down, please," she said, waving the boys toward seats at the small table set before the wide doors leading into the garden. "Max will bring us some refreshment and we will talk." She heard Max leave as she sat down at the table, the boys revealing enough good manners to wait until she was seated before they, too, sat down. "Before I answer your demands"—she was pleased to see both boys had the grace to blush faintly—"I want you to tell me how you got here, and where is the adult who should be with you?"

"We came here by wagon," replied Darius. "And coach. We stay at Radmoor with our cousin Penelope and her husband Ashton Pendellen Radmoor, the Viscount of Radmoor."

"'Tis a huge place, like this," said Olwen, "but as soon as our father finishes our home in London we will stay with him now and then."

"Only now and then?"

"Well, we do not want to leave the others."

"What of your mother?" she asked as Max returned to set out the food, including several thick slices of bread placed around a healthy supply of meat and cheese.

"Our mothers left us with Penelope. All the others were left by their mothers, too."

Max straightened up and looked at the boys. "So you came here alone. You ran off like cowards because you knew you would not be given permission to make this journey."

"We left a note for Pen," said Darius. "And we had

to come. We heard that something had happened to our father, but no one would tell us what, even when we asked. They said they would tell us when they knew for certain. Then we heard that he was here. Iago, Leopold, Bened, Wynn, Todd, and even Aunt Olympia were here, too. So we decided we needed to come here and see what was happening to him for ourselves."

"Max, we need some writing materials, please," said Lorelei.

"Immediately, m'lady," he said and left to get them.

"But we left a note," protested Olwen.

"Eat." As soon as they began, she continued, "You are how old? Twelve?" They both nodded. "And yet you traveled here all alone. I think you are clever enough to know that was wrong. And clever enough to know that simply leaving a note to say where you were going does not correct your misjudgment. The viscount and the viscountess are undoubtedly worried, if they have not already begun to hunt for you."

"They were not at Radmoor when we left."

"Oh, this just gets better and better," said Max as he set the writing materials down on the table.

"I would not try to stare Max down," Lorelei said, and both boys stopped glaring at Max to look at her. "He has had many years of practice in outstaring wrongheaded children. As soon as you are done eating you will write a letter to Radmoor. You will explain where you are and apologize, profusely, for worrying them." She took a piece of paper and dipped the quill into the pot of ink. "I will include a message of my own to assure them that you are safe here.

Then you will explain what you have done when you see your father."

"He *is* here!" declared Darius. "Where is he?" He glanced at a frowning Max and hastily added, "m'lady."

"I will escort you to him once you have written to the Radmoors. Then you can assure yourself that he is safe as you try to explain your idiocy to him." She glanced up from the message she was writing to find them both staring at her.

"You have brothers," said Darius.

"Thirteen of them. Three older, ten younger." She smiled to herself when Olwen choked slightly and Darius had to slap him on the back, especially when Max winced at the cloud of dust that rose from Olwen's coat.

Accompanied by the sounds of two young boys filling their obviously very empty stomachs under the stern gaze of Max, Lorelei wrote to the Radmoors. Concentrating on what to say was not enough to silence her thoughts, however, and it was a continuous struggle to maintain her composure. She feared she could easily make herself ill caging in such fierce emotions.

What she wanted to do was rush over to the gatehouse and demand some answers from Argus. Yet, a part of her did not wish to hear how Argus had come to have two sons so close in age by two different women. And why were his children living with the Radmoors? She quickly shook the thoughts from her head, for they threatened her tenuous control over her riotous emotions.

By the time she had finished her message, the boys were ready to write theirs. Lorelei sipped at the tea Max served her and watched him direct the boys in what needed to be said. When they were done, they watched Max carefully as he looked over their work and then slumped with relief when he nodded. It had always astonished her how children, especially the boys, all wanted to see that nod of approval from Max, including herself.

Max collected the letters. "I will see that these are sent out immediately, m'lady. I will also have Gregor Four ready to escort you to the gatehouse."

"Thank you, Max." She did not want a guard, but did not argue. After what had happened to Olympia, Lorelei doubted she could get two steps outside the door without a guard before Max dragged her back in.

"Why do you need someone to escort you to your own gatehouse?" asked Olwen.

"Your father will explain," she replied, "after which you will be very fortunate if he does not banish you to the attics with naught but bread and water for being such complete idiots."

"Do you talk to your brothers like that?"

"All the time. Come along then," she said as she stood up and they hastily did the same. "Let us get you to your father." Just saying the word *father* caused her pain and she sternly told herself not to be an idiot.

"This is a grand place," said Olwen as they walked along the path to the gatehouse.

"Yes, it has been in the Sundun family for many, many years," replied Lorelei.

"Is that house over there the one where our father, aunt, and cousins are staying?" asked Darius, pointing to the gatehouse that was just coming into view.

"It is. We keep it for guests, for some of the ones

who come to visit do not really appreciate the freedom the children here are given. Papa knows which ones they are and always offers them the gatehouse, allowing them to graciously accept so everyone is happy and no insults are made."

"Sneaky," said Darius, but he grinned.

"I prefer the word clever. Mayhap even diplomatic."

"Does sound nicer," said Olwen.

"You do know that you should not have traveled here all on your own, do you not?" she asked them and almost smiled when they both sighed heavily.

"Aye, but no one would tell us what had happened to our father and Olwen was worried," said Darius.

Lorelei shook her head. Olwen was obviously the one who got blamed for things, Darius being the stronger of the two. Glancing at Olwen, she suspected he had a sweeter nature. She realized, too, that the Wherlockes must have been raised in the country, for all the adults staying at the gatehouse occasionally said aye and nay. Her governess had made sure that she stopped even though they both knew she would never be spending much time amongst the London aristocracy.

When they reached the gatehouse door, Lorelei hesitated for a moment. She suddenly did not want to see Argus acknowledge the boys as his sons. It would all become so real then. Instead of thinking he had kept a very large secret from her, she would know it for a fact. Glancing at the boys, she shook free of the hold that uncertainty had on her. They were just boys worried about their father. She would not allow them to be caught up in some confrontation between her and Argus even if she did think a man should inform his new lover that he had children already.

Lorelei rapped on the door and waited. Iago answered and smiled at her. He glanced at the boys and that smile disappeared like dew beneath the morning sun. The next look he gave her was one of uncertainty with a touch of alarm. She had the answer to what small doubt she had still clung to. These boys were Argus's sons.

Before the man could say anything, Darius asked, "Where is our father?"

"Argus, best you get out here," called Iago over his shoulder.

"What is it?" Argus said as he strode up to the door a moment later.

"You have guests."

Argus looked at Lorelei and wondered why she was not smiling at him, and then a nudge from Iago had him look to her right. He tensed in shock as he stared into Olwen's face. A look to his left had him staring at his son Darius, who looked cross. This was not the way he would have wanted Lorelei to find out that he had two sons.

"How did you two get here?" he asked his sons.

"We came to find you," said Darius, not answering the question.

Argus looked at Lorelei. "Come in and we will straighten this out," he said, hoping she would understand that he meant more than just what his sons were doing so far from home.

"No, I think not," said Lorelei. "This is a family matter. The boys and I have already written to the Radmoors to let them know that they have arrived safely and are with their father. They will now tell you why they are here and how they got here. Best if you do that on your own, as a family." She looked at the two boys. "It was nice to meet you and I am sure I will see you again." She nodded to Argus. "Good day, Sir Argus."

Lorelei was proud of how calm and polite she had sounded as she walked away. What she had really wanted to do was find something very heavy and hit him over the head with it a few times. She never had such violent feelings and decided that was all Argus's fault, too. If he thought she would just ignore this, he was a fool. Sir Argus was going to have to explain himself, and then she would decide if she could forgive him.

Iago cleared his throat. "A little chilly," he murmured.

"A little?" Argus ushered his sons into the parlor. "Ice. Pure ice."

"She was angry with you," said Darius as he sat down on one of the settees.

"I believe I noticed that." Argus sat down across from his sons and crossed his arms over his chest. "Now you can tell me why you are here and not at Radmoor where you are supposed to be."

"Olwen had a vision," said Darius.

"Just a little one," murmured Olwen.

"We knew you were in trouble, but no one would tell us anything so when we found out where you were, we decided we needed to come and find out if you were all right. Olwen was not sure."

"If you are quite done trying to put all the blame on Olwen for this idiocy, I would like you to answer the question as to how you got here."

As they told him of the journey they had taken from Radmoor to Sundunmoor, Argus felt his blood chill. It was pure luck that they had managed to get to him unharmed. He glanced at Iago, who looked as horrified as he felt. Just as he opened his mouth to begin a long, ear-burning lecture, someone knocked on the door. Iago jumped up to go and see who was there and Argus wondered if the man had sensed the lecture about to commence.

The voice he heard speaking to Iago was familiar enough to halt Argus's lecture before it had even begun. He was not surprised when Iago brought Stefan into the room. The way Stefan glared at Darius and Olwen told Argus exactly why the youth was there.

"Is there anyone left at Radmoor, or is poor Pen going to come home to find that all her little birds have flown?" he drawled.

Stefan winced as he sat down. "I saw their note to Pen and thought I could catch them before they got too far."

"How is it that you came here and did not go up to the main house?"

"I stopped to ask this man driving sheep over the road if he had seen two boys. He asked my name and I told him. He stared at me for a moment, nodded, and said, 'Aye, you be one of them,' and sent me here."

"One of the Gregors, I imagine," said Iago. "I think one of them is the sheepherder. They all have a keen eye and Stefan does have the look of us."

"Yes, well, Stefan, you are in time to share in the lecture I am about to give my sons," said Argus and almost smiled at the youth's look of dismay.

All three boys sat stoically as Argus informed them

of their idiocy, of every danger they avoided by sheer
luck, and how they had better grovel for forgiveness
to Penelope, who will worry about them. He also told
them about Cornick and stressed how they had just
blindly walked into danger since the man was lurking
around Sundunmoor. Argus did not think he had to
point out how easily they could have been taken and
used against him, but he did anyway. He then got
quill and paper and had Stefan write to Pen, adding
a few words of his own. It was not a good time for the
three boys to be at Sundunmoor, but it would be even
more treacherous to try to send them home.

"Lady Lorelei said we would be fortunate if you did
not banish us to the attics with only bread and water,"
said Olwen, who still looked as if he wanted to cry.

"Actually you are very fortunate that I am not a
man who believes in the adage of spare the rod, spoil
the child," said Argus.

"Good God," said Olympia as she hobbled into the
room. "Are we to expect the rest of Radmoor to arrive
soon?" She hesitated for a moment before allowing
Iago to help her to a seat.

"Aunt, what has happened to you?" said Olwen in
alarm as he and Darius rushed to her side. "Did you
fall off your horse?"

"Olwen did not see that, hmmm?" Argus had to
bite back a grin at the guilty look that skipped across
Darius's face.

"I fear I met up with a very bad man," said Olympia,
ruffling each boy's hair and smiling when they
grumbled.

"The bad men you three did not know about while
you were blindly riding through the very area where

he is lurking," Argus said and smiled when all three boys cast him a wary glance.

"I can help," said Stefan as he stepped up to Olympia.

"If you are but newly arrived from a long journey, will you not be too tired? It can wait until you have rested," Olympia said.

"Nay, you are in a lot of pain and the injuries are not so severe."

Argus watched as Stefan did his magic. The healers in the family always amazed, even awed him. He was not sure how such a gift worked, but it was miraculous to watch Olympia's bruises fade and see her sit up straighter, the pinched look of pain leaving her face. Stefan only looked slightly paler when he was done, accepting the kiss of gratitude from Olympia and blushing, before he returned to his seat.

"Where did they all come from?" asked Olympia as Iago returned from the kitchens he had rushed to with a large tankard of cider and some sweet honey cakes for Stefan.

Argus quickly repeated all he had been told, and nodded when Olympia looked at all three boys in horror. "Aye, they have been very lucky."

Olympia looked at Argus after studying each boy for a moment as if to reassure herself that they were hale. "Lorelei brought them to you?"

"Darius and Olwen went to the manor first," replied Argus and nodded at her look of chagrin.

"She was unhappy, I think," said Darius. "When I first saw her I thought she had a very pretty and bright aura, but after we told her who we were, there was a darkness there, like a big bruise."

Argus winced. "She was just surprised as she did not know that I had any children." He tried not to fidget beneath the looks all three boys gave him as he could read their skepticism in their eyes. "She is the woman who saved me," he said and gave them a brief summation of how Lorelei had taken him out of his prison.

"I wager Max did not like that," said Darius.

"Ah, so you have met the butler."

"We did. She told us that it was useless to try and outstare the man, and I could see that it was. He has an aura like some soldiers I have seen and acts like he commands an army."

"Since you will be staying here for a while, I suspect you will meet Lady Lorelei's family and will see that, in many ways, that is exactly what Max does."

"So she really does have thirteen brothers?" asked Olwen, revealing his awe over that possibility.

"And three sisters and a vast array of cousins who live there or are visiting. And at least one aunt." He glanced at three scarves that had arrived at the door earlier and then looked at Olympia's exquisite tatted shawl. "I suspect you will all soon have new scarves," he murmured. "Now, I believe you need to clean up and may want a rest after your long, foolish journey."

Stefan and the younger boys all stood and headed toward the door. As they walked out of the room, Olwen paused. "Me and Darius did not bring any clothes"— he looked at his cousin's sack—"like Stefan did."

Argus sighed, but before he could say anything there was a knock at the door. Iago moved to answer it, the boys all watching him closely. When he returned he stood before them with a large package.

"Max has sent you some things to wear," Iago told

the boys as he handed them the package, "for, as he put it in his message, you probably need to be deloused."

It was difficult, but Argus held back his laughter until all three boys were gone, Stefan assuring them that he would see that the younger ones scrubbed themselves vigorously. "I begin to think it is a good thing that the Sunduns do not mix with all that much of society, for someone would surely have stolen that butler away by now."

"They would have tried," said Olympia as she stood up, "but Max will live and die here with his duke."

Argus did not have to consider the truth of her words for long. "Aye, he will. You are looking much better. I cannot help but wonder if fate had a hand in letting Stefan be the one to find out what the boys were doing."

"If so, I send Dame Fate my warmest thanks. Now, I will see if Stefan needs any help and then I am going for a walk."

"Olympia, you were barely shuffling your feet only a short time ago. Do you think it wise to go for a walk?"

"Very wise. I have things I must think about," she murmured and left the room, pausing at the door just long enough to add, "I will take Todd with me."

"She is going to try and find Lorelei," said Iago as he sat down and smiled at Argus.

Argus groaned. "Interfering woman."

"Very much so, but I think she decided it when Darius spoke of the bruise in Lorelei's aura. Perhaps you should have mentioned your sons."

"The fact that I have two illegitimate sons is not something one tells a well-bred woman."

"But it is something one might mention to a lover."

"I never said we were lovers."

Iago shrugged. "Did not have to. You have the look of a man who finally eased a fierce knot of frustration. And it was bound to happen, as the two of you stank of want from almost the first day, I suspect. Have never seen two people with that much, well, fire in them."

Argus growled softly and stood up. "There are times when I could wish many of my family to perdition," he snapped and walked off to the sound of Iago's soft laughter.

The sound of Argus's footsteps had barely faded when Iago heard the softer sound of a lady's slippers on the floor. "Olympia," he called and smiled when she peered into the room. "Going to have a talk with Lady Lorelei, are you?"

"Clever cousins can be the bane of a person's existence."

"I live to serve. You might try the orchard as Argus was brushing away apple-tree leaves yesterday when he returned home from his walk. I would also suggest you do whatever you can to not have to see what someone has done there."

"Oh. You think she would actually go to the place where she and Argus made love when she is so angry with him? Hurt, too, I think."

"I may be wrong, but I believe that is exactly where she has gone. Just what do you intend to say to her?"

"A little of this and a little of that." She sighed when Iago just stared at her. "I want to know exactly how she feels about the boys and I intend to tell her a few things about why my brother is so cursed reluctant to even say the word marriage." She turned and walked away.

"Good luck!"

Chapter 13

She would not go up to the gatehouse again. She would not even look in the direction of the gate-house. She would just forget that the gatehouse was even sitting there with a lying, rutting cur inside.

Lorelei repeated that litany as she marched toward her favorite spot in the orchard. It was probably the wrong place to hide away and lick her wounds, but there were few others that allowed her the privacy she needed. She was certainly not going to hide in her bedchamber like some lovelorn maiden. And, per-haps, sitting in the same place where a rutting, lying cur had robbed her of her virginity would keep her anger to the fore, smothering the pain she knew was just waiting to bring her to her knees.

When she reached her private spot in the orchard, she sat down, crossed her arms over her chest, and glared out at the world through the leaves. For a while all she did was silently call Sir Argus Wherlocke every bad name she could think of. Then she began to make up new ones. She almost wished he could be there so she could express her opinion of him to his lying, rutting face. It took some time, but finally her anger was spent and she slumped back against the tree trunk.

Argus had two sons born on the wrong side of the blanket. Considering how close in age Darius and Olwen were, Argus must have had himself a very busy time thirteen or so years ago. She was not sure of Argus's age, only estimating that he was near thirty, so he could have been little more than a boy himself.

She frowned and thought that over several times. Argus would have been sixteen or seventeen, maybe even younger. Her eyes widened. And he had had two mistresses? Just as she had begun to see it all as a youthful folly, the facts painted him as a hardened rogue at a very young age.

What Lorelei really felt like doing was having a glorious tantrum, one full of heel drumming, cursing, and the pulling of her own hair. She had gambled her future and her heart on the man. Lorelei hated to think that she had risked so much for the sake of a fine chest and a skill at kissing a woman senseless.

"Sulking?"

Lorelei jumped in surprise, put her hand over her pounding heart, and glared at Olympia as the woman sat down beside her. Glancing out through the leaves she saw a large man idly pacing around just far enough away to guarantee them privacy. Then she abruptly recalled what Olympia's gift was, of how the woman probably knew exactly what had happened here, and she had to fight the urge to blush and then run away. Instead she studied the woman. For a woman who had been so bruised and battered a short time ago, Olympia moved with an agile grace. The horrific bruise on her face was almost gone as well.

"You are looking a great deal better than you did even just yesterday," she finally said.

"Shortly after you left, our cousin Stefan arrived. He had found the note those idiot boys had left and came after them. Another letter has been dispatched to Penelope. Stefan is more man than boy, but he is still only sixteen and her brother so she would worry. He is also a healer and worked his magic on me." She gave Lorelei a little smile. "And, yes, yet another bastard, but Argus still has only the two. Penelope has cared for all of them since she was little more than a child herself."

"All? How many are there?"

"With Penelope? Eleven. The men in our family do not always take the care they should. Of course, Argus was not very old when he became a father. Twice. He has since learned to temper himself and take care."

"They, the children, were just given up?"

Olympia nodded. "Despite being given a healthy annuity, each mother threw away her child. Penelope's two brothers, both bastards, were tossed aside because her mother remarried and the new husband did not want them. Penelope arranged a place for them to stay and soon the other cast-aside children began to arrive. In Pen's brothers' case, it was jealousy that caused her mother to give them up for her father had strayed, shall we say, and the boys were hard proof of that. She also had a rotten stepfather who wanted nothing to do with them. The other children given into her care were set aside mostly because it soon became clear that they were different. You see our gifts are also our curse."

"I am not sure I understand."

"Wherlockes and Vaughns have a dismal marital history. It appears to be changing, but many marriages ended badly or struggled on in misery. Mothers, or fathers, the ones who were not Wherlockes or Vaughns, walked away more often than not. They leave their children behind with the gifted parent and some even try to disclaim them. They fear what they have spawned and blame the partner who is of our family for what curses the child. Our own mother stayed longer than most, but it might have been best if she had not. She spread her misery to all of us and both feared and loathed her own children. She kept having them, of course, as she was a dutiful wife. Not faithful, but dutiful. In truth, Father was lucky every one of us was a Wherlocke. And I think we are most fortunate our mother did not smother us right after we left her womb. Father grew bitter so, in a way, we lost him too. Long before he died. They both left little behind but debt and scarred children."

"Is that why Argus refuses to marry?"

"Aye. He found little different throughout the clan and decided marriage was not for a Wherlocke. We have recently had three women of the family enter into solid, good marriages, but I think he sees them as an aberration."

"So, he would refuse to marry me even if he really wanted to do so."

Olympia nodded. "He believes he is saving you from the misery of marriage to a Wherlocke."

"What an arse."

Laughing softly, Olympia patted one of Lorelei's clenched fists. "That he is. You will get no argument from me. That does not mean you cannot change his mind on the matter if you wish to. Unless, of course, you only sought a lover." Olympia shrugged when Lorelei cast her a look of disgust.

"I am not fool enough to risk my entire future just because a man kisses me senseless." She sighed. "From almost the first moment I saw him standing in the rose garden, I knew he was the man I wanted. I may be a sheltered country maid, but I have had men court me, have attended balls, house parties, and all of that. Nothing. Not a flicker of interest even though some of the men were nice men, interesting and handsome. I began to think there might be something wrong with me, something lacking inside me."

"And then came Argus."

"Yes, and then came Argus. Perhaps I should have given up when he kept pushing me away."

"Nay. Persistence is what is needed here. But, first, what about Darius and Olwen?"

"They are his sons. My only trouble with all that is that he never told me he had sons. And, yes, a little jealousy." She grimaced when Olympia just stared at her. "As you will. A lot of jealousy. And that is utterly foolish, for I was but a child when he was breeding his sons. It just keeps reminding me that he has been with a lot of women."

"Wherlockes and Vaughns breed handsome devils. It is assured that they will have known a few women ere they reach marrying age. Most men do their utmost to get as much experience in that area as they can."

"I know. I have thirteen brothers. The moment their voices deepen they turn into randy goats." She smiled when Olympia laughed, but soon grew serious again. "So, do his sons have gifts as well?"

"Darius sees, well, we call them auras. Lights and

colors that surround each one of us, with different colors meaning different things. Darius is making a study of them so that he can better understand what he sees. Olwen has visions."

"And those gifts terrified their mothers enough to toss away their own child?"

"Superstition still runs rampant in this land. Darius says that you have a bright, pretty aura."

"Oh." Lorelei did not know what to think of that. "Is that good? It sounds good."

"It is good. He also said that your Max has one just like some soldiers he has seen."

"Ah, that suits. Max is certainly much akin to the major-general of Sundunmoor."

"Do you understand Argus now?"

"He is afraid of marriage."

"In a way. He is afraid that, if he finds a woman he would like to marry, and marries her, that marriage will turn sour. He is afraid of the pain that will bring, although he would never say so. He fears finding love and losing it, finding happiness and watching it twist into bitterness."

"None of which he will say."

"Of course not. Very unmanly."

Lorelei laughed and shook her head. "I do not know what to do."

"You must try to make him see that you truly care for him and that you are neither afraid of what we are nor someone who would ever leave your child. For any reason save death."

"I do not suppose I could just say so," she mumbled, knowing full well that would not work. "Such things are not easy to prove if the one you try to prove them to does not believe you when you say it aloud."

"Nay, but I think you will find a way." She stood up and brushed off her skirts. "I just believed it was time someone told you what makes Argus so set against marriage. As a woman, I knew how easily you might begin to think it was you, and it is not. I have never seen my brother so interested in any woman. Nor so drawn to one that he would break all his rules, such as seducing a virginal duke's daughter."

"I would not say he actually seduced me," Lorelei murmured and then, again, recalled what skill Olympia had. "Sweet heavens," she breathed and felt the heat of a furious blush on her cheeks. "You can read what happened here."

"I can, but I did not. I am able to shield myself from the memories left everywhere and on everything. I have had to learn how to or I would have gone utterly mad by now. No, I know mostly because Iago guessed. Something men can see in other men, I suppose. That and a rather lot of apple-tree leaves Argus brought home on his clothes yesterday."

"You must think I am—"

"In love, and that is what my brother needs. He needs to have someone love him for all that he is. And I want that for him. And here you are. His gift is a frightening one, yet you still love the fool."

Lorelei decided there was no point in trying to deny how she felt. "Actually, his gift does not work on me, or Max."

"Fascinating. And even better. My brother and I are very close. We have had to be if only because we were the two youngest in a large family with a mother who could not stand the sight of us. I know him better than he does himself at times, as he does me. I know he wants what he calls the normal life with a wife who loves him and will stay with him and love the children they will make together."

"As well as those two little idiots who traveled here all alone?" She smiled when Olympia nodded and chuckled.

"Them, too, although I think they will only be a part of whatever life you two might have, for they have built a family with Penelope and the other children she took in. It is a very strong bond. Her husband recognized that and renovated an entire wing for them so they could stay together. Argus loves them and they love him, but Penelope and all those children are their true family and Argus accepts that."

"Yes. They spoke of staying with their father only part of the time because they could not leave the others. I think that tight bond amongst them probably comes from them all having suffered the pain of rejection. They know and understand each other's scars."

"That says it very well." Olympia looked up at the sky. "It grows late. Perhaps you should walk back with me and then Todd can escort you home. You should not be out here all alone."

"Devious," Lorelei said pleasantly as she stood up and brushed off her skirts.

"Yes. I thought it good myself."

Lorelei laughed and walked beside Olympia, a silent watchful Todd falling into step behind them. She would play the game, going along with Olympia as if she just did so because she needed the guard to take her home. From the area within the orchard where she had hidden away, the gatehouse was closer anyway. If Argus wished to speak with her, she would not turn him aside, but, for now, she would not seek him out.

"Ah, Olympia returns and she has brought company," said Iago as he stared out the window.

Argus set aside the papers he had been reading and moved to the window. "Interfering woman."

"Undoubtedly, but, by the look of it, she did it because Lady Lorelei was out wandering about without any guard. It looks as if Todd waits to escort her home." He looked at Argus. "Do you not have a few things to say to her before she leaves?"

"I should leave it as it is," Argus said even as he hurried out of the room to catch Lorelei before she went too far.

He nearly ran right into Olympia as he hurried out the door. Grumbling at her about how she should mind her own business, he stepped around her and went to catch up with Lorelei. He had no idea of what to say to her, knew it would probably be best for both of them if he just allowed her to think him a rutting swine she was better off without, but he could not let her go.

"Lorelei," he said as he caught her by the arm. "Walk with me in the garden for a little while before you go home."

The first thing that entered her mind when he said that was how he had mentioned the old oak in the garden as a perfect place for a tryst. "Why?" she demanded.

Argus smiled in what he hoped was an inviting way, with a hint of apology behind it. "To talk." He tugged on her arm and, after a moment of resistance, she started to walk to the garden with him.

Lorelei glanced behind her and did not see Todd anywhere. Men, she thought, were all allies when it came to matters of romance. The odd one out knew how to play least in sight. Determined not to simply fall into his arms, she moved away from him the moment they entered the garden and sat on a bench, away from the oak tree.

"What did you think we needed to talk about?" she asked, eyeing him with suspicion when he sat down beside her.

"So cold to me," he murmured, "but you have some right to your anger."

Some? she mused. She would like to see how amiable he was if two children suddenly appeared claiming her as their mother. "I believe the fact that you have two children is something you should have told me. At the very least, before we became lovers. It was a great surprise to me when they showed up at my door."

"Aye, I suspect it was. I was little more than a lad who thought himself a man when I became a father, Lorelei. It is difficult to explain because I find it a little embarrassing that I could have been such a cocksure little irritant. Two mistresses, both older than I, but a nice accessory to my manliness during my first year in London. The births of Darius and then Olwen were a shock. Despite my idiocy, I did know to take care because I did not wish to become diseased. I found a way to pay both women a nice sum on a regular basis to care for the children, but as soon as they began to show their Wherlocke heritage, both women wanted nothing to do with them. I took my sons and that nice sum to Penelope."

"At least you saw to their welfare," she said, finding that she did not like the tone of disgust in his voice when he talked about his younger self.

"I tried, but did not keep a close enough eye on matters to realize Penelope was being robbed of most of the funds I and others sent her to care for the children, or to see that heaping that responsibility on such a young girl was very wrong. That has since been sorted out, but, in the years that I continued to live my life as I pleased, albeit with a lot less cockiness and need to show the world I was a man, I lost them."

"No, Argus, you have not lost them, you but share them."

He looked at her. "I suppose that is true, but it is still due to the fact that I was a negligent father who was far too interested in his own life. And, please, do not tell me that I was young, for that is no real excuse. I revealed my Wherlocke blood in my casual neglect of my own offspring."

"Wherlocke blood indeed," she muttered wondering how a grown, intelligent man could be so wrongheaded. "You were an unmarried gentleman and they were not your heirs. Most men would have forgotten them the moment they climbed out of their mothers' beds. You at least saved them from their mothers' fear and the streets. They love you, so you cannot have failed so badly. You will always have to share them though but not because of what you did."

"What do you mean? I left them with Penelope, allowed that young girl to raise them."

"And she was clearly a good choice. You must share them more because of the children that joined them there. Each one of them arrived because they had been rejected by the one person who should have loved them no matter what, their mother. Each time a child arrived those who knew exactly what he was suffering met him and they gathered him into the flock. That is their bond and that is what you share them with.

"It appears that many of the adults in your family have suffered as well, but I doubt it was something that was discussed with the young children. Children understand each other better anyway. So they held on to each other, protected each other, and eased each other's pain. You could have been with them almost all the time and I doubt you could have conquered that bond once it was made. I doubt it will ever break."

He kissed her. "You have a wonderful way of seeing what others cannot, seeing into the heart of it all. You are right. They have a bond nothing will change. I saw it, but I did not look hard enough. The only little girl that is in the group was sheltered and coddled by the children from the moment she arrived. They even stood between her and her mother, who was tossing her into Penelope's lap while calling the poor babe the devil and all manner of nonsense. Penelope told me that they all looked at the woman and told her she could just go away, that Jude was theirs now. I was touched by the tale and proud of the children, but I did not really understand what had happened."

"They claimed her."

"That they did, as the ones who had come before claimed each one that followed."

He put his arm around her, relieved that she did not pull away, did not even tense. What he wanted to do was make love to her, but not because she stirred his desire by simply sitting there smelling so sweet.

He wanted to make sure that he had not lost the passion they had shared. Cautiously he stood up, took her by the hands, and pulled her to her feet.

"You were right to be angry," he said as he took slow steps backward toward the oak tree. "I should have told you before we became lovers. I love my sons, but sometimes I look at them and see that arrogant little fool that I was then and it pains me. It was not something I wanted you to see in me. Now, I wish to apologize to you properly."

Lorelei eyed the oak looming up beside them and shook her head. "If you are leading me behind that tree, I doubt a proper apology is what you intend, you rogue."

He grinned as he pulled her behind the huge trunk, immediately hiding them from the view of anyone in the house. Argus gently pushed her up against the trunk and kissed her. When she slipped her arms around his neck, pressing her soft curves against him, the tight ball of worry that had settled in his stomach from the moment he had seen her with his sons, faded away. Her passion for him still burned hot.

Lorelei briefly wondered if she was giving in too easily, forgiving him too quickly, and then decided she was not. He had spoken of how the boys had come to be, even shared his disgust with the boy he had been back then. It was neither of those things that touched her heart, however. It was his saying that he had not wanted her to see him as the boy he had been back then. He did not want to be diminished in her eyes, and a man did not worry about such things unless the woman and her opinions mattered.

Letting a little gasp of pleasure escape her as he

nuzzled her breasts, she decided it was good to forgive. It also allowed her to begin her campaign to show him that he was loved, loved for all he was, and even for that arrogant man-child he had once been. If Olympia was right, Argus wanted that and she intended to give him so much love that he found himself craving it.

Lorelei basked in the heat of the desire he stirred within her. She only flinched briefly in surprise when he slid his hand between her legs to stroke her. Desire swept away the momentary flare of unease over such a personal touch and she quickly welcomed his touch, welcomed the passion it brewed in her.

"Wrap your legs around my waist, sweetheart," Argus said as he undid his breeches, not surprised that his fingers were clumsy, for he was shaking with the need to be inside her.

"Should we not lie down?" she asked even as she did as he asked.

"Ah, love, you will learn that there are many ways to find the delight we both crave."

When he joined their bodies with one swift thrust, Lorelei decided he was right. Her last clear thought as she drowned in the desire they shared was to wonder exactly how many ways there were.

"I think I should go to the gatehouse and shoot him," said the duke as he watched Lorelei slip up to the house and disappear through one of the lesser-used doors.

"I believe that might upset her, Your Grace," said Max.

"When I decided to just step back and not insist

upon proprieties or traditional wooing, I had hoped this would not happen. Do you have any doubt that he has ruined her?"

"None at all, although I would quibble over the use of the word ruined."

Roland turned around to glare at his butler and best friend. "You saw her. Are you going to try and tell me that she has not been indulging in a very hearty tryst?"

"Not at all."

"I could not deny her the chances to see him. He was the one who put that shine in her eyes. Perhaps that was a mistake."

"Shine, Your Grace?"

"Shine, glow, sparkle." He waved one hand in the air. "Life. Lorelei is three and twenty and has been wooed by some very fine men, yet there was never that glow, that interest that makes the eyes shine. The first time I heard her say his name I saw that shine. At last my daughter had found the right man, the one that made her feel alive."

"He is obviously doing a fine job of it."

"Max! She is his lover. I would be willing to bet on it."

"And I would be a fool to take that bet for I would lose."

"He should be here asking me for her hand in marriage."

"He should, but it will be a while before that happens. The man believes that what he is dooms any marriage he may make. Lady Olympia whispered that to me a day or so after she arrived and quickly saw how the wind was blowing. He has seen nothing but misery in the marriages in his family up until the more recent ones. He thinks of it as the Wherlocke curse. Vaughns, too, I suppose, if what I read was correct. Lorelei has to change his mind."

The duke frowned. "There have been bad marriages in the family?"

"Many of them with wives leaving husbands and husbands leaving wives and none of them taking the children with them or having anything to do with them. If one carefully studies the information you have on them, it is there to see. The gifts they have are passed on to whatever children they have and that appears to be the breaking point in many a marriage."

"Sad, but what does that have to do with him marrying Lorelei?"

"Do you wish to marry again after your experience with your last wife?"

"Damn my eyes, no. So what happens? Do I just sit back until she presents me with a fatherless grandchild?"

"No. He will come to his senses before that happens. I have watched them, Your Grace. The man will probably not admit it, but he is besotted. He may try to leave, but he will be back."

"I hope you are right, Max, because I really do not wish to shoot him. It is messy, it will make Lorelei cry, and I do rather like the fellow even if he is seducing my daughter."

Chapter 14

"Father, Axel and Wolfgang want us to go fishing with them."

Argus looked at his sons and then looked out the window of the parlor that overlooked the front of the gatehouse. The duke, a half a dozen children, and a morose Mr. Pendleton all stood waiting. His sons had been at Sundunmoor for only three days and yet they had already been accepted into the fold. Argus was not sure what to make of that, but could not deny the boys a day of fishing.

"Go on then," he said, "but behave yourselves. Do not repay the duke's kindness with mischief and bad manners."

"I will go with them," said Stefan and followed the boys out.

Argus watched the group walk away. Stefan strode beside the duke, obviously already deep in some discussion with the man. He recalled what Darius had said concerning the duke's aura. The boy had claimed that it made you want to smile. Argus could not argue with that. For all of his eccentricities, the duke was truly a good man, one who cared well for his people and loved his small army of children, his own as well as the ones he had taken in.

He crossed his arms over his chest and frowned. From what Lorelei had told him, two of the duke's three marriages had not been good ones, but the man remained content with his life. Argus could not help but wonder if he could learn a few lessons from that, and then shook his head. The Sunduns did not have to deal with the curse that burdened the Vaughns and the Wherlockes. His children would never tell him that some ghost was seated at the table, or make the vicar take his talk of devils and damnation back to the church and never return, or look at her father and ask why Mother had made love to a man who was not her husband on the settee in the morning room. Olympia tended to jest about that now, but he knew the furious loathing her mother had heaped upon her that day could still sting when it ghosted through her memory.

And just why did reminding himself of all that old misery make him want to go and find Lorelei? he asked himself. The answer quickly came to him. She soothed him, eased the old pains, and made him think, if only for a little while, that he might be able to live a normal life with a loving wife and children. It was a shame that she was the daughter of a duke, a stinking rich duke at that. He was not a good choice for any woman, but certainly not for one who could have any man in the kingdom. Just thinking of Lorelei with another tied his stomach into knots. He really needed to make up his mind about what to do with her, aside from getting her naked, he thought wryly.

"Ah, there you are."

Argus looked at Leopold, but his pleasure over being pulled out of his thoughts faded fast with one look at Leopold's serious expression. "Is there some new trouble?"

Leopold handed him a letter. As Argus read what their cousin Andras Vaughn had written his blood ran cold. Other members of their family were being watched and followed. Someone had already attempted to grab Andras right off the street in front of his home.

"So, even though the one after me still lurks around here, whoever began this now tries to grab someone else. We had considered that, but I had strongly hoped that we would be proved wrong."

"So had I." Leopold glanced over the second letter he held. "There is also some good news. My people believe they now know who is behind this. The man is being watched very carefully."

Argus was not sure how good it could be when Leopold was looking at the letter as if it said that anyone who touched it would contract the pox. "Anyone I know?"

"Sir Sidney Chuffington."

"That little bastard! Now I understand why I was tricked so easily. That is the man I asked to look into whether Cornick could be trusted or not." Argus felt like an utter fool for a moment, and then realized he could not have had any idea, for all he had done was ask the man the government trusted to do what he did best, find information on someone.

"And what he gave you all appeared quite well documented, I suspect. Chuffington was always good with documentation."

"What I do not understand is why he would do this."

"Power. He is close enough to the top and all of its secrets to learn how our gifts can and are used. He wants all that under his fist. Or, from what you told us, he thinks he can take those gifts and use them to get him the power he craves. Who knows, perhaps money and women as well. As I said, he is now being watched very closely. He will not be a problem for long. And we may have finally discovered who Charles Cornick is."

"Do not tell me that the duke has failed to collect information on some family in this country."

Leopold grinned. "Oh, no. The man's papers and books are a treasure, one I have now been given permission to peruse whenever I please. King and country, you know."

"One day you will finally beat that horse to death. So, what have you discovered about Cornick?"

"Your Charles Cornick may actually be William Charles Cornick Wendall the Third."

"Well, no wonder we could not find him. We were using the wrong name. Related to the fool who is letting his fine country house rot while he bleeds his lands and tenants dry?"

"The man's brother. Cornick acts as his brother's steward and is a minor clerk in Chuffington's office, although it seems he has had to retire to the country because of a sick relative. As far as we can tell the Wendall who actually owns that property has no idea what is going on, or what his brother has been doing. He trusts his brother, the fool, and fancies himself a man chosen by God to bring the Bible to the poor pagan natives of the world. At the moment and for the last three months, he has been in Africa. Preaching, I suppose."

"It appears that all this trouble may soon come to

an end." Argus was pleased, so did not understand why his heart felt as if someone's fist was squeezing it.

"Ye-es, and so you can bid adieu to the fair Lorelei and run back to your life as it ever was. Empty."

Argus blinked in surprise at the thread of anger in Leo's voice. "I am not a good choice for Lorelei."

"She plainly disagrees or she would not be slipping over here each night to meet you in the garden."

"You have spied on us?"

"Seen you, no more. Seen the meetings." Leopold shrugged and grinned. "Could not see any more anyway as you always step behind that bloody huge oak tree.'" He quickly grew serious again. "I was not going to say anything for I have no claim to saint-hood, but, curse it, she is a good woman and you are using her in a very shabby way. She has a grand heart and you obviously share a passion that must be as hot as blazes. And lest you have forgotten, she saved your bloody life!"

"I know," Argus said in a quiet voice, guilt a hard knot in his stomach. "I am not good enough for her."

"Bollocks. Because you are a knight and she is the daughter of a duke? Do you truly think that man would care? He would not and well you know it. You are hardly a poor man, either, so that cannot be it. She is not troubled by our gifts, either."

"Not ours, but a woman changes when her child has one, especially one of the stronger ones."

Leopold shook his head. "Argus, you must let go of the past. Have the recent marriages we have seen not shown you that we need not remain shackled by that ugly history? Mayhap we are the ones meant to break that tragic circle of bitterness and rejected children, we who can learn from the mistakes of our forefathers. Greville already has a child who shows signs of being the strongest healer born to our clan in generations, but the man could not love that boy more, nor our Alethea, his wife. Radmoor took in eleven of our children when he married our Penelope. Eleven. And he works hard to learn all he can so that he can help his own children as they grow and help the children Penelope brought with her. It is the same with Colinsmoor and our little Chloe."

"It is still early," Argus said, only to have Leopold silence him with a quick slash of his hand.

"You may knock me down afterward if it suits you, but I will have my say. God's grace, Argus, I would give my eyeteeth to find a woman like Lorelei Sundun. Beautiful, clever, brave, loves children and her family, shows no fear of what we can do, and is obviously a passionate woman. She is risking everything important to a woman of her birthright by what she is doing with you. And if I could get a woman to look at me as she looks at you, I would be a happy man. If you were wise, you would shrug off the chains of the past, grab her, and run as fast as you can to the nearest vicar."

Leopold strode out of the room before Argus could respond, or knock him down. Argus could not believe how angry his cousin had been. He had always thought that Leopold was alone by choice as the man was, as he said, no saint, though he was no great rogue either. Now he had to wonder if Leopold wanted the same thing he did, a normal life with a loving wife and children, but had not been able to find a woman who would accept all that he was. Admittedly, Leopold's ability to sense lies and half-truths was a difficult thing to live with, but he had all the other attributes women looked for in a husband.

He dragged a hand through his hair. He was being besieged by his family, scolded on his behavior and how he was treating Lorelei, and lectured on his wrong-headedness concerning marriage. Even Olympia, who suffered as he had, scorned his opinion that he would only hurt Lorelei if he married her.

Argus went to the window and stared blindly out in the direction the duke had taken the children. Again he thought on how that man had suffered two bad marriages and still enjoyed life. He had had one good one with Lorelei's mother, yet the bitterness that should have bloomed in that last marriage was not there. And the poor man had stepped on that tread-mill when he was still little more than a boy.

While it was true that the duke did not have the curse each Wherlocke and Vaughn did, the many strange gifts that frightened people, he was a bit ec-centric and clearly preferred his country life to the city, apparently a sore point with two of his wives. He also loved his children, who showed no scars from the loss of their mothers. It was something to consider, that perhaps he could build a good life with Lorelei as everyone suggested, just as the duke had built one with his second wife and overcome the bad ones that came before and after.

But, the cold fear of watching Lorelei walk away was still there. He almost laughed, for that one thought told him he was past saving. It was no longer his wife walking away but Lorelei. It was no longer some face-less woman frightened by her own children, but Lorelei. His relatives did not understand, but then they had not seen his father on his knees crying like a broken-hearted child because his wife was unfaithful. They had not seen how his father had turned from a kind, smiling man to a sad and bitter recluse who had no interest in anything but waiting for the undertaker.

The troubling thing was that he did not see himself being saved by leaving her. Argus had the feeling he would find himself in nearly as bad a shape as his father once his enemy was gone and he left Sundunmoor. If he was not allowing vanity to cloud his mind, making him see what he wanted to see, he would have to say that Lorelei cared for him, cared for him deeply. The question was no longer whether or not he could risk a marriage that might make both him and Lorelei miserable in the end, but whether he could leave her without at least taking a chance that they could have a good marriage.

The sound of feet pounding down the stairs pulled him from his thoughts, and he rushed to the door of the parlor. Looking out, he saw Olympia pelting down the stairs, her skirts hiked up to her knees. Leopold and Iago appeared, drawn by the noise as he was.

"Olympia, what is wrong?" he asked as she hit the hall floor hard and fast enough to slide by him.

"The children. Something is threatening the children. How far away is that cursed pond?"

"Not far," Argus said, checking to be sure he still carried his pistol as he followed her out the door.

He could hear Leopold and Iago following him. As they raced by the stable, Wynn and Todd joined them. No one asked any questions. Todd and Wynn just followed as the sturdy, well-trained guards they were, and the rest of them knew that it was useless to ask Olympia to tell them more. She was not a true seer, simply got an occasional glimpse of something. Despite that limitation she had never been wrong, and Argus fought down his fear for the children, all of them, but mostly his sons. Instinct told him they were the ones in the most danger.

Roland sat on the bank of the pond, fishing rod in hand, and enjoyed the warmth of the sun on his face. He occasionally glanced at the boys flanking him and Mr. Pendleton, idly noting that all but Mr. Pendleton looked content. It was a fine summer day, one that demanded people come outside and savor it. Mr. Pendleton was not one who much loved nature.

After a long night of fretting, he had decided just to stand back, remain silent, and let his daughter and Wherlocke sort themselves out. Although he had lived through two miserable marriages and was still content with his life, he knew he did not have the problems Wherlocke and his family did. Not everyone was a rational person, one who thought things out and did not give in to superstition and fear. The man just had to open his eyes and see that Lorelei was one of those people who did think. It was somewhat insulting that the man could even consider that Lorelei would ever leave the man she married, especially when it was for love, or leave her own children, but he could understand the fear when he looked at the marital history of the family.

It had also helped him to understand the man when he had allowed himself to think on his own two bad marriages. The first had actually been the worst, for he had been young, as virginal as his wife, and his first taste of passion, only his own unfortunately,

had left him besotted with his bride. She had been
disgusted and remained disgusted until she died.
Childbirth had appalled her so much that she had
never forgiven the children or him for putting her
through such an ordeal. She had also thought him a
fool for not using his title to its full advantage, not
wielding his power over all, and even for treating his
tenants and workers as if they were actually people. He
still believed her worst sin was demanding that he dismiss Max because the man was, as far as she was concerned, acting far above his station.

His third wife had expected him to become a
London man. At first he had placated her and gone
to the wretched city so that she could parade her title
before all and spend enough to keep the city itself
in clothes. She had whined a lot, too. Whined about
his clothes, his books, his other children, the children she had to bear for him, and on and on until
one day he had ceased to listen. The only good thing
was that she had liked the bedding, but she had obviously liked it enough to try it with others. The final
thin threads of their marriage had snapped when she
had demanded they go to London and he had said
no. Of course, he had said a lot of other things concerning her morals and spendthrift ways, but it was
mostly his refusal to go to London or even fund her
going on her own.

One thing he had learned was that, although it
had all been hard on the children, they had survived
because they had had him and Max. They had been
the anchors in the children's lives. Roland was just
wondering if he should share some of his thoughts
with Sir Argus when a pale-faced Olwen leaping up at
his side startled him.

"We must go," the boy said.

The duke set his fishing rod aside and clasped the boy's hands. Those small hands were like ice. When he looked into Olwen's eyes he saw a look that was not focused, was set on something no one else could see. Roland could not completely repress a tingle of excitement, for he knew he was actually seeing one of the gifts all the Wherlockes and Vaughns had.

"Why, Olwen?" he asked. "Why must we leave here?"

"Danger comes." Olwen's eyes cleared and he stared at the duke in alarm. "Where is Darius?"

Looking around, the duke realized that the boy had wandered off while he had been lost in his thoughts. A glance toward Mr. Pendleton revealed that man discussing the flow of the water in the spring-fed pond with the twins Axel and Wolfgang. Everyone was doing what they had come to the pond to do and no one had yet noticed that Darius had wandered away.

"Pendleton!" he yelled as he leapt to his feet. "We are missing Darius." To his credit the tutor was swiftly on his feet and looking around. "Stefan, do you have any idea where the boy may have wandered off to?"

Stefan stood up and rubbed a hand over his hair. "He was talking about acorns earlier."

The duke looked toward the wood that surrounded nearly a third of the pond. "Did anyone see Darius wander off?" He frowned when only one child, his youngest, pointed to the wood, which was little help except in that it confirmed Stefan's suspicions. "I want everyone to stay close to me, Pendleton, and Stefan. We are going to look for Darius."

They were only a few feet into the trees when a high-pitched cry echoed around them. The duke gave a sharp hand signal to Pendleton to stay with the children, pulled out the pistol he had begun to carry since Lady Olympia's attack, and moved toward the sound. Out of the corner of his eye he saw Stefan moving along at his side, a large, lethal-looking knife in his hand. The boy glanced at him and cocked one brow up in a very adult gesture.

"Cannot shoot," he said in a near whisper.

"Can you use that well?" the duke asked just as quietly.

Stefan just smiled in a way Roland thought would put a chill down any miscreant's spine. He turned his attention to finding out where Darius was. Then the air was filled with a litany of curses, many the duke was unfamiliar with. They were being shouted in both a child's voice and a man's.

He paused as he caught sight of a horse, Stefan keeping pace with him, and then edged closer until he finally saw Darius. The child was being held in a big man's arms and that man was very close to getting on his horse and riding away with the boy. Darius was putting up a furious fight but inflicting injuries that most likely only tried the man's temper. What troubled the duke was that there was no way he could get a clear shot.

A frontal assault, he decided and boldly stepped into the man's view, Stefan right at his side. He noticed that the youth hid his knife down by his side. It occurred to the duke that Stefan might have lived somewhere that did not have the peace of Radmoor. He had what could be considered some of the skills of a London street tough.

"Put the child down, sir," said the duke. "I would prefer not to have to shoot you." The brief flare of amusement on the man's face was an insult, and the duke began to feel his rare but hot temper stir to life. "I will not ask again."

"You shoot at me and you could be hitting this lad," said the man in a thick London accent. "Think you ought to be considering that."

"What I am considering is that you are kidnapping a child in my care and that cannot be allowed. I can see that you find me amusing for some reason but allow me to assure you that the dukes of Sundunmoor have always been expert marksmen."

"If you be the duke then this brat is nothing to you. He is one of them Wherlockes."

"That may be so, but he was still placed in my care. Now, I suggest you put him down."

The man gripped Darius so tightly with one arm the boy could barely breathe and aimed his pistol at the duke. "Never killed me a dook."

He tensed and Roland chanced a quick glance around to see why. His heart nearly stopped as he saw his children and Olwen encircling the area around the man and his mount. Pendleton was there, pale and sweating, but standing straight.

"What did you do, dook, bring out the whole nursery?" the man snapped and held his gun against Darius's head. "You want them to be seeing this lad's head shot off? If not, best be telling them to get back."

The duke felt Stefan press up close behind him as if he was hiding in fear and the youth whispered, "I am going to get him to aim at me. Are you good enough and quick enough to shoot the bastard's gun out of his hand or just his hand?"

He nodded, unable to protest because the man was watching him closely. The duke did not want the youth to take a chance with his life, and not only because he had a mind quicker than any the duke had met in a long time. Sixteen was far too young to die of a bullet to the heart.

"Now," whispered Stefan and he leapt out from behind the duke, his huge knife readied to throw.

The man holding Darius immediately swung his pistol around to aim it at Stefan. Silently praying that nothing went wrong, the duke aimed his pistol at the man's wrist and fired. The scream that split the air made him wince. The man's gun went off, but the shot went wild, spinning off into the air. Darius dropped to the ground the minute the man grabbed at his profusely bleeding wrist and scrambled away. His face twisted into a grimace of pain and fury that made him look less than human, the man then started to run. The moment his back was turned, Stefan threw his knife and it buried itself between the man's shoulders, causing another scream to send the birds flying up in panic.

"He is getting away," said Darius and bolted after the man.

All the other children followed Darius and the duke cursed. With Pendleton and Stefan running apace with him, the duke raced after the young army that had been loosed into the woods. His only comfort was the fact that the man no longer had a weapon, nor the strength to hold one.

"Shots!" cried Olympia as she turned slightly toward the sound.

"You stay here," Argus ordered. "You have no weapon

and we do not know what we are facing. Anyone comes thrashing through those trees, you hide."

He did not wait to see if she obeyed him but ran toward the sound of the shots, the other men right behind him. Then came the sound of a lot of people running toward them, the hoots and cries of children, and a soft low cursing of a man. Argus held up his hand and stopped, his relatives and Leopold's men stepping up in line with him. When the big man stumbled out of the wood, he raised his pistol, but before he could fire it the man fell to his knees, sat there panting for a moment and then collapsed onto his face. Bursting out of the cover of the trees came Darius, Olwen, and half a dozen other children. Mr. Pendleton staggered to a halt, placed his hands on his knees and struggled to catch his breath as the duke and Stefan appeared, the duke still holding his pistol, which Argus suspected was now empty. He recognized the large knife sticking out of the prone man's back as Stefan's.

"Olympia," he called and was not really surprised at how quickly she showed up as he had guessed she would stay close without getting in the way. "Please escort Mr. Pendleton and the duke's children back to the house. Take Todd with you."

"It might be best if your sons go too," the duke said quietly as he glanced at the man on the ground, "for I am not sure but we will have a dead man on our hands soon."

"Darius and Olwen spent their first years in a not so very fine part of London, Your Grace," said Argus. "I fear the sight of the dead is nothing new to them." He walked over to Stefan, who had removed his knife from the man's back so that Leopold could turn him over. "That is Jones," he said and looked at Stefan. "Chances of healing?"

Stefan shook his head. "Mortal. Knife pierced a few important things, but the duke's shot opened his wrist and the blood was pouring out. Steady stream of it as he ran, which just made it flow even faster."

Argus crouched down by the side of the man, whose eyes fluttered open. "Hello, Jones."

"Bastard," Jones said. "Knew you was trouble first time I saw you."

"Where are Cornick and Tucker?"

"Not peachin' on 'em, so stop wasting my dying breath."

"Then answer this, who is the one giving Cornick orders and paying for this hunting of Wherlockes? Have you his name?"

"Chuff something. Cornick just calls him Chuffy." He glanced up at Stefan. "Good toss, lad. Spent some time in my city, I wager. And I demmed well misread the dook. Done in by bloody little nits."

Argus was surprised by how quickly and quietly the man died. He stood up and cursed softly. There had been no time to make him tell them more, to force him to tell where Cornick and Tucker were. The only good thing was that they now had only two men to worry about. The very fact that Cornick and these two men were the only ones hunting him, told Argus that *Chuffy* was not sending any help.

"He did not give you much information, did he?" said the duke. "I should have aimed for the pistol, but I thought shooting his wrist would be a better bet."

"It worked. Unfortunately, he bled to death," said Argus. "But it is one less to worry about. And my thanks for protecting my children."

"Darius was the one the man grabbed," said the duke. "Olwen warned us, so we got to him before the man could get the child on the horse. I have the chilling feeling that the man had been watching us come and go from here for a while, just hoping for some opportunity to get something to use against you. He must have thought God was on his side when young Darius decided to have a wander.

"Now, if you will excuse me, I believe I shall go talk to my children about all manner of things concerning this incident, such as not coming to the rescue when the only place you can reach on your enemy is his knee." He smiled faintly when the men laughed and then patted Darius and Olwen on the head. "I hope you now understand that the danger your father told you about is very real." Both boys nodded and the duke turned to Stefan. "Well done, sir. And perhaps you will wander by soon and we can discuss how you could so easily know that man was dying."

After the duke was gone, Argus looked at the dead Jones one last time and then looked at Stefan. "I am sure you will correct me if I am wrong, but I believe it was the duke's shot that really killed him."

"Most likely, and did so faster," Stefan replied and then quickly told Argus what had happened. "His children did not like him going into danger, I think. He is their lodestone."

"Poor man must have felt his heart stop." Argus shook his head. "Now we just have to tote this corpse somewhere."

"I will fetch his horse," Stefan said.

By the time they returned to the gatehouse, Max was waiting. He and two men took possession of the body, telling him quite nicely that the duke, the magistrate of the area, would tend to the matter. Argus decided that having a duke around could be helpful and then went to find some brandy. He kept an arm around each son's skinny shoulders as he walked, realizing how close he had come to losing one of them. It would be a long time before he forgot it. One glance at the faces of his family told him that his decision would not be argued.

Cornick has to die.

Chapter 15

Lorelei frowned at the note the baker's youngest child had given her. Despite her skill with herbs and salves, she was not often called upon to try and heal anyone. Once a doctor had arrived in the village, the healing skills of the lady of the manor had not been in much demand. The baker claimed the doctor was not to be found, however, and that his eldest son's burns were very bad.

On a normal day, she would collect what she needed and rush off to help, but this was not a normal day. Guards surrounded them as if they were under siege, which she supposed they were in a way, although she was not sure what Cornick and his one remaining henchman could do. However, though the attack on the children three days ago had ended with no one but Cornick's man being hurt, her father had been unsettled by it all. He had had his children with him as well as Argus's boys. Her father even saw Stefan as a child despite how that child had helped him fight the man and put a knife in Jones's back. Now he wanted them all inside, under guard, until Cornick

and his man were caught. Lorelei was a little surprised that her father was not outside marching
around, his pistol in his hand. She had never seen
him so angry.

Yet, the baker was one of Sundunmoor's people.
She could not ignore the cry for help. For a moment
she hesitated, thinking that she should do up her
hair, for it was simply braided and hanging down her
back, and then she shook her head. She had no time
for vanity. Lorelei tucked the message in the hidden
pocket of her gown and went to collect the supplies
she needed to treat a bad burn. And she would take
a very large, armed guard with her even though she
felt certain she would be safe within the village.

To her surprise it was Wynn who stepped up to be
her guard. After she left the baker's message and one
of her own on her father's desk, she found Wynn
waiting by the door when she stepped outside. "I
hope you do not mind walking," she said as she started
off to the village at a brisk pace.

"Like it more than I do riding, m'lady," he drawled.

It was a beautiful day, warm but not too warm, and
sunny. They had been blessed with an unusually fine
span of weather although the farmers were starting
to complain of lack of rain for the crops. Lorelei suspected she would have to bear a lecture from her
father for leaving the house, perhaps even one from
Argus when she met him tonight, but it was still good
to be outside. She hoped the baker's son was not too
badly burned, for that was a very painful injury to
suffer, one that could even scar or maim a person.

Her thoughts drifted to Argus as they too often
did. Although their affair continued, he made no
declarations to her. Lorelei was increasingly afraid

she was about to lose her gamble. She had none of the gifts Argus's family did, but she was also certain this fight with Cornick was rapidly coming to an end. Yet, Argus still gave her no sign that he would stay with her or wanted her to stay with him. It hurt and that pain was increasingly hard to hide.

She had done her best to try to ease the fears Olympia had said afflicted Argus. Lorelei had tried to show him how much she loved him. She had even whispered the words during their lovemaking, but he had never acknowledged them or responded in kind. Another hurt dealt, but she endured.

It was harder to show him that she would never leave, would not walk away from him or any children they had. All she had been able to do was show him how she loved her family and how she accepted his sons. Her jealousy over their conception was gone, or nearly so. She still felt a pinch of it when she feared she would never have his children simply because he would not stay to father them. She endured that, too.

"I am a fool," she muttered.

"Nay, m'lady," said Wynn. "T'other one is though. Lord Starkly had a word with him t'other day but do not think he heeded any of it."

Good God, she thought, did everyone know what was going on between her and Argus? "Um, yes, well. Sometimes a person has to be hit over the head before he gives up a long-held, utterly wrongheaded opinion."

"True. I would not be surprised if one of the others soon tries just that."

It was embarrassing to know that even Wynn was fully aware of what was going on, but she could not fully stop a laugh from escaping. Maybe that was what she needed. From all Olympia had told her there were barely any Vaughns or Wherlockes who had not suffered from parents shackled into a miserable marriage or been deserted by the parent who was not a blood member of the clan. Such troubles left deep scars. If others who had suffered as Argus had talked to him and urged him to shake off his fears, it could help her cause. Right now she would take all the help she could get.

"Ah, there is the baker's shop," she said and started toward the door.

Wynn moved in front of her, stepping inside first and looking around before allowing her inside. Lorelei wondered just how dangerous Leopold's work for the government was that he should have such well-trained guards. As she entered the shop she briefly wondered what had happened to the baker's youngest son, but shook off the concern. Then a chill went down her back as she saw the baker's pale face. He also looked very nervous. Lorelei feared the son's burns could be very bad indeed.

"No sign of the doctor yet, Master Baker?" she asked as she stepped up to him.

"No. No sign of the man."

Master Baker's gaze was darting here and there so much it was starting to make Lorelei nauseous. She had never seen the burly, good-natured man look so nervous and upset. It began to make her uneasy, but she shook that aside. His son was badly injured and the whole village knew that Master Baker was as fond and proud of his boys as any man could be.

"Show me to your boy then, Master Baker, and I will see what I can do for him."

A strangled noise came from the man's throat at the same time that Lorelei heard something heavy hit the floor. She turned to see Wynn on his knees, a knife in his back. Lorelei moved to go to his aid as he slowly fell facedown on the floor, but a hand on her arm yanked her to a halt. She turned to look at her captor and her heart sank so sharply she was compelled to put a hand on her chest. A man she strongly suspected was Charles Cornick stood next to her, his grip on her arm tight to the point of being painful and a look of such smug satisfaction on his narrow face that her palms itched with her inclination to slap it off.

"They have your son, Master Baker?" she asked and saw tears well in his eyes.

"Both of them and me wife."

She patted his arm. "It will be all right."

"For him but not for you."

Lorelei ignored Cornick. "Papa understands the need to protect children."

"How sweet. Now, come with me." Cornick yanked on her arm.

She braced herself and fought against his pull. "I do not think so. You will use me as a weapon against Sir Argus."

"Let me change your mind. Look there and tell me no again." He nodded in the direction of where Wynn had fallen.

She looked and cursed aloud. Out of the corner of her eye she saw the baker's shocked expression and shook her head. Did he expect her to be sweet, perhaps swoon gracefully? The sight before her was enough to make a vicar curse. A big, ugly, and none

too clean man crouched by Wynn, the knife that had
been in Wynn's back now held to his throat.

"Such bravery," she sneered. "Using children and
women to make my baker betray me and now threatening the life of a wounded and unconscious man."

"Damn you, your people done killed Jones," said
the man with the knife.

"I do apologize, but when he tried to steal one of
the children, we did not feel there was time for tea
and talk."

"You best watch yourself, bitch."

"Or what? You will kill me? That has already been
planned, has it not? And you expect me to help bring
another into your trap? I will not do it."

"You do not have to do anything," said Cornick.
"All you need to do is be the bait."

She opened her mouth to scream and he had her
gagged before she could draw breath. Lorelei tried to
struggle free of his hold, but he got her hands tied
behind her back and all she could do was fruitlessly
kick at his legs. That earned her a slap across the face
that nearly knocked her to the floor, all that kept her
on her feet being Cornick's grip on her.

"Listen to me, woman," he hissed into her ear. "I
am a desperate man and it is not wise to push too
hard at a desperate man. You do know what they say
about cornered animals, do you not? Well, I am feeling very cornered now."

"Sir," called the baker, his voice trembling with
fear, "she be the duke's daughter. He will be very
angry if anything happens to her."

"He has a house full of bloody children," Cornick

snapped. "It will probably take him days to know one is missing."

"He will know and right soon, too. He knows all his children, all the others living there, too, and near everybody in the village and on his lands. And what he does not recall, his butler Max does. And he is going to be out for blood when he learns you took his lass."

Lorelei watched Cornick and his man exchange sneers and knew they did not believe a word of the baker's warning. It was interesting to know how well the people knew their duke, she mused, and would have to try and remember to tell him. It would please her father. She refused to even consider the possibility that she would not get free of this man.

"You," Cornick said to the baker, "will wait one full hour before you tell that bastard Wherlocke that one of his men is here and hurt. One full hour and do not think we will not know if you do not do exactly as you are told. Punishment for disobedience will be taken out on that sweet wife of yours."

She subtly shook her head but was not sure if the poor baker knew what she was trying to tell him. He did not know that Cornick and the man Tucker were the only ones threatening him, that the minute they both fled on their mounts, the baker could do as he wished. Glancing at Wynn, she saw a faint flicker of his surprisingly long eyelashes and had a suspicion he was not as hurt as he wanted Cornick to believe.

"Mayhap we should tie the fool up like we did his wife and brats," said Tucker.

"That may be a good idea," agreed Cornick, "but be quick about it. People will start to get curious if he keeps the shop closed, but they can see him in here. Toss him down behind his own counter," he added as Tucker roughly yanked the man around and tied him at the wrists and ankles.

Lorelei winced when Tucker threw the baker on the ground and kicked him with an idle cruelty. He then gagged Master Baker, who was still protesting that he could not help Wynn or his family if he was tied up. It would certainly be enough to get them that hour they wanted, however, an hour to get far away from Argus and any pursuit. No one would wish to break into the shop, and there would be a long time spent talking about what to do and why the baker's shop was closed. Cornick undoubtedly thought that would be good enough.

As he dragged her out the back of the baker's shop she prayed someone, anyone, would find the man. Since Tucker had said they had tied up the baker's family as well, she prayed the baker's wife had a lot of friends who wanted to come round for a gossip, friends who would know the woman should be home and would raise an alarm. She needed someone to know what was happening so that rescue could be planned, because she was certain that, even if he got whatever he wanted, she was going to die.

"Where's my father? I have to see my father," demanded Olwen as he burst into the duke's manor.

Max grabbed the distraught boy by the shoulders just as Darius came running into the house behind Olwen. He could see that Darius was almost as frantic as his brother. Gripping that boy by the arm, Max held them there.

"Take a deep breath and tell me why you need to see Sir Argus immediately," said Max.

"He has to go to the village," said Olwen, gasping slightly as he struggled to calm down. "His lady is in trouble in the village."

"Lady Lorelei is here," said Max.

Olwen shook his head. "Nay, she is in the village and she is in trouble."

Argus hurried out of the parlor, where he and the others had been discussing what they could possibly do next to get Cornick. The man was having his men try to grab people in what appeared to be a completely unplanned way, and yet he kept disappearing. Even Bened had trouble following the trail of the man and his remaining accomplice. Now he could hear that something had upset Olwen and he feared there had been another attempt to kidnap one of his family. He could hear his family and the duke follow him, but Olwen held all his attention.

"Olwen," he said, and the moment Max released the boy he ran to Argus, coming up against him so fast and hard, Argus grunted. "What is it? What has upset you?"

"Your lady is in the village and she is in trouble," replied Olwen. "I saw it. We have to go and get her back."

Argus frowned. "Lady Lorelei had no plans to go to the village."

"Why are you not listening to me?" yelled Olwen. "She is in the village and she needs help. So does the man with the bread."

"The baker," said Max as he stepped up to them.

Argus had not even seen the man leave, but he had obviously gone somewhere and now held two small scraps of paper. He took them from the man's hand and read them before handing them to the duke, a cold knot of fear settling in his stomach. The baker, who was undoubtedly Olwen's bread man, had called Lorelei to the village claiming that his son was badly burned and the doctor could not be found.

"I think we had better go and see if the boy has a right to be upset," said the duke as he marched past Argus and headed out of the house.

Ordering the boys to stay with Max, Argus hurried after the duke, who was already half the way to the stables, Iago, Leopold, Stefan, and Bened hard at his heels. It took him a moment to notice that Wynn was not with their horses, having a comfortable chat with the stable hands as was his habit. "I think she took Wynn with her," he said as he watched the hands rushing to saddle five horses. "So she will be well guarded."

"Then we will find her safe and she can be annoyed at us for racing around and interrupting her healing work." The duke frowned. "The fact that the note said the doctor was not around troubles me. He is almost always around, for those outside the village most often go to him instead of having him ride out to them. There could be a troublesome birth he is attending, I suppose. Mabel Sears was due soon, but she never has trouble, not once with any of her eleven children."

Argus had no answer to that, so he just shrugged. It was a warning sign that all was not right, however. A moment later they were riding to the village. It could have been walked to, but he knew there might be a need to have horses. Better to have them right at hand than lose time by going back to get some.

When they reined in in front of the baker's, Argus knew there was trouble, that Olwen had not been confused by what he had seen. It was almost midday and the baker's shop was locked up tight. There was a small crowd of people gathered at the shop trying to see into the windows. They parted quickly when the duke stepped up to them.

Just as the duke began to ask if anyone had seen anything, a short, plump woman came running out from behind the shop. "I cannot rouse Millie," she cried. "We was to go see the new cloth in the mercantile's and she ain't answering my rap at her door. Ain't seen them lads of hers either and they are near always about."

The duke stared at the door to the shop and then looked at Bened, the largest of the Wherlocke group. "I know one can kick in a door, but I fear I have never learned the art."

"Allow me," said Bened as he walked up to the door, flexed his arms much to the delight of the ladies, and then gave the door one powerful kick.

The moment the now-cracked door opened wide, the duke rushed inside. Argus began to follow but paused next to Bened. "Odd. You did all that muscle flexing of your arms and then used your foot," he drawled.

Bened just grinned and winked before walking into the shop. Then he cursed and hurried over to Wynn, who was groaning and fighting to get up off the floor. The back of his coat was dark with blood.

Since Wynn was still alive, and Bened was seeing to the man, Argus hurried to where the duke had crouched down behind the counter. The duke was releasing the baker from his bonds, and Argus knew before the man even spoke that Cornick had Lorelei.

"They took her, Your Grace," the baker said as the duke helped him to his feet. "I am sorry, Your Grace, but they done tied up my wife and lads and said they would be cutting their throats if I did not do just what they said. What could I do? I do not even know if they left my wife and sons alive."

"They are alive," said Leopold. "Iago and I untied them, and your wife's friend is with them."

The man nodded and wiped the tears from his face before looking toward Wynn. "He's alive, is he? I could hear him moaning but I—"

"Hush, Master Baker," said the duke, patting the man's arm. "Your wife and children are alive, our Wynn is alive, and we will get my daughter back alive. You did what you had to do. You had to save your children. I understand that."

"She said you would, Your Grace," he said. "I need to go an' see them."

"Of course you do. Go on with you. We will deal with the matter now."

The duke watched the men hurry into the back of the shop and then turned to face Argus. "This Cornick must be gotten rid of. He attacks my guests, my children, and now my people. And then he steals my Lolly. No, this is a man who must leave my lands one way or another." He took a deep breath. "We had better get back to the house. Wynn needs care and I believe we will be sent some sort of ransom message soon."

Argus watched as the man made his way through

the growing crowd reassuring everyone. He knew the duke was not as calm as he sounded. He had seen the man's eyes and the promise that Cornick and anyone who had aided him would pay dearly for taking his daughter. The sweet, eccentric duke of Sundunmoor was furious, bloodthirsty furious. Argus felt the same way. He did not think he could stop to comfort worried villagers as the duke was doing. The only thing on his mind at that moment was a blind need to find Cornick and beat him to death.

He did find the strength to stop by Bened, who stood in the doorway of the shop and watched a wagon move slowly toward the duke's palatial home. "You found a ride for Wynn?"

"It was offered," answered Bened. "They all see Wynn as the duke's man for now, and the moment they saw we had a wounded man, several men rushed off to get a wagon for him. They do love their duke. Think I am seeing why. That man is seething, yet he stops to let them know that everything will be all right, accepts the concerns of the silly and the wise, and does not do what he really wants to do."

"And what is that?"

"Same thing I am thinking you want to do, and that is get a horse and go and cut Cornick into ribbons. That sweet duke whom everyone thinks is so eccentric and so lost in his books has his very clever mind set on only one thing now, getting his daughter back and seeing that Cornick is dead."

"Sounds like a very good plan to me."

"It would, but I am hoping our very clever duke friend might be using this show of courtesy and mouthing of meaningless words to calm himself and clear his head. Once he has, he will have all of us beating our heads to come up with a plan that will give him what he wants—Cornick's head on a platter."

"That is exactly what he is doing," said Leopold as he joined them. "You can see the fury he walked out of here with, but now it is not as wild." He looked at Argus. "The baker's family was fine. Scared witless but unharmed save for a few bruises."

"He handed Lorelei over to them," said Argus, knowing the man had no real choice but still angry with the baker for doing it.

"Cornick knew his weakness—his family. I have been listening to the people out there and many have said that the baker worships his little family. What troubles me is how Cornick knew that. Either he or one of his men has been keeping a close eye on the villagers, looking for weaknesses, ones who could be made to do exactly what they asked."

"Disguises?" asked Argus.

"Possibly. He worked in a department that would have had access to many of them, for they liked to have the men make use of them when they went out to ferret out some information. Hellfire, we may have even passed him on the street. Him or one of his men."

"Him. His men are huge thick-necked brutes and would be too easily noticed."

His companions nodded and Argus started for his horse. He could no longer just stand there talking, not in the very place where Lorelei was taken. Argus was a little surprised that the moment the duke knew what had happened he had not just turned around and shot him. Cornick was here because of him, and Lorelei had been put in danger because of him.

He found Darius and Olwen sitting on the wide stone steps of the duke's manor when he rode up.

They both looked hopeful for only a minute and then got a good look at his face. For a moment Argus thought Olwen was going to cry and wondered when his sons had become so attached to Lorelei. He dismounted, sat down between them, and put an arm around each boy.

"I was too late," mumbled Olwen.

"Your warning has given us more time to plan on how to get her back," said Argus.

"Does that man Cornick have her then?" asked Darius.

"I fear so." Fear was not a strong enough word for the emotions tearing through him at the moment, thought Argus. "The duke believes that we will hear something soon, that she has been taken because Cornick wants something from us in return."

"He wants you," Darius said.

"Well, he cannot have you," said Olwen.

"I am not sure what he wants now, lads," Argus said, not telling how much that uncertainty troubled him. "But do not forget that I would not be sitting here now if it was not for that woman. She saved me, took me out of the prison Cornick had stuck me in, tended my wounds, and kept me safely hidden until I could regain my strength. I owe it to her to do all in my power to see that she is returned to her father as safe and unharmed as possible."

"And you must stay safe, too, Father," said Olwen. "We need you to come back safe, too."

"That is my plan, Olwen. Here comes the duke."

"And Olympia and Stefan are coming, too."

The duke reached the steps first and Olwen moved to stand in front of him. "I am sorry, Your Grace," he said. "I was too late with my warning."

"You did your best, lad," the duke said, "and that is all any man can do."

Argus watched Olwen stand up a little straighter and nod. For that he could almost kiss the duke, but suspected all he would get if he got near the man now was a punch to the face. And that would be the least of what he deserved.

Olympia and Stefan were sent off to tend to Wynn. Argus quietly told the boys to go see the Sundun children and then followed the duke inside. Darius and Olwen quietly slipped away to the nursery, a massive room filled to the rafters with toys for all ages. Max waited, and when he saw the look on the duke's face, he patted him on the shoulder and led him into the library. Argus was a little startled when the door was shut, but he shrugged and went into the parlor to wait. It would be a while before Cornick sent word of what he wanted to trade for Lorelei, but Argus doubted it would be too long. It would just feel like it.

Roland slumped down into his chair and stared at his hands. "They took my Lolly, Max. Took my smiling little girl. I cannot bear it."

Max handed him a brandy. "Drink. You will not help her if you grow melancholy. She needs your wits to be sharp and strong."

"Do you think he will hurt her?" asked the duke after a deep drink of brandy.

"I do not know, but I think not. He has kept us running in circles for a long while. There is some intelligence there. It should tell him that, if his grand plans fail, it might be best for him if she remains unharmed. Without her he has no tool to bargain with, no shield to keep him alive until he flees, and nothing for stopping you from hunting him down like a rabid dog."

"And you," the duke said and gave Max a small smile. "He had best be more concerned with what you will do to him."

"Very true. Or Sir Argus."

"No need to look at me like that. I will not shoot the man, although the thought did scurry through my mind for a moment. It was quiet and safe here until he arrived."

"Yes, but we have been long overdue for some trouble. And he did not do anything to the man to cause this trouble—no gambling debts, no seduced wives, just a man who can play tricks on a person's mind making them do what he wants them to do. Of course, it does not work with us for we are all very strong-minded." He folded his arms across his chest. "Are you ready to face them all yet?"

Roland stood up and nodded. "And you feel no need to at least slap Sir Argus around the room a little?"

"A lot, but I have restrained my ire as it should not be directed at him anyway. When the mood strikes me to strike him, I just remind myself that it was your daughter who brought him here. He wanted to go to some relatives."

The duke shook his head. "And instead, his relatives come here. Well, let us go and join the others and pray that Cornick does not make us wait too long."

Chapter 16

"They say they will let her go if you give yourself up to them, Sir Argus."

Argus looked at the duke but could not read the man's expression. The sweet, easily distracted gentleman he had come to know was gone. All softness had faded from the man's eyes. The Duke of Sundunmoor stood before him now.

"Then that is what I will do," he said and not just to please the duke whose daughter was now in danger because of him. He would willingly walk back into Cornick's brutal hands if it could save Lorelei, but he was not sure it would be that simple.

"The father in me aches to tell you to get on your horse and do exactly as this man says. The father in me wants to blame you for the danger my daughter now faces."

"And so you should. These men are my enemies. . . ." He fell silent when the duke held up one elegant, long-fingered hand.

"No. That would be wrong. Once I had my daughter back, the man in me would be appalled that I would so easily exchange one life for another. You did not ask Lorelei to come to your aid. You asked her to send word to your family. That was all. She stepped into this situation of her own free will. She also went to the village of her own free will. Yes, she took a guard with her, but it was still a dangerous thing to do. After all, these men tried to steal Darius while he was with me and ten other people, even if most of the ten were boys. And, I think, the moment she went after you to pull you from your prison, she set herself right in danger's path.

"It is quite noble of you to wish to trade yourself for her, but I believe it would be a useless sacrifice. She knows too much now. She is a threat to him. I do not believe he has any intention of releasing her. He is just using her to protect himself until he can get free, and then he will be rid of her. We must try to plan a rescue that protects her and us, and we have but an hour to do so as it will take close to an hour to get to the meeting place he has chosen. However, we have something on our side."

"What could that be? They hold your daughter. Is that not the winning card?"

"Yes, in many ways it is, but I believe desperation has destroyed a great deal of the cunning they have revealed."

"Indeed," said Leopold. "Telling us where they have been hiding, for one thing, with the choice of meeting place."

"On the far western corner of my lands. A rough area. They are in the woodcutter's cottage there." He sighed. "I suspect poor Old James is dead. If he was not, he would have come here and told me of this danger long ago. But, it is a place well surrounded by trees so that men could get very close before they would be seen. A mistake on their part that I want to make a costly one."

"They have also allowed us time to plan," said Leopold. "They think they have only given us an hour, but they badly misjudged how much attention would be drawn by a shop closed at a time when it should be open. And they did not know about Olwen. So that gave us time and now they have given us a little more. We have the people here familiar with the land and can make the trip to the woodcutter's cottage a little faster than they expect. There is also one thing that Cornick does not know. Chuffington has been arrested. Cornick gains nothing from this folly."

"It might be best if he does not learn that," said Argus. "It could make him desperate."

"True, although I believe he already is. We will keep it in mind, however, because we may find a use for it in bargaining with him. As for desperate? As I just said, I believe he already is. The attack on Olympia, trying to run off with Darius when there were so many others with him?" Leopold shook his head. "Rash, dangerous actions. No real planning to them. In some ways, Cornick is trying to find a way out of a trap he has put himself in. He has to know that simply silencing you will no longer help him because he knows we are here, that you have told all of us everything. He may be fool enough to think Chuffington can still help him, but one would think that he would know differently. After all, he worked for the man for years and Chuffington was never known for his kindness."

"Very true," agreed Argus. "I know of at least one

time where he dithered and calculated until a man was in danger of his life and then he let him die."

"Oh, I think there was more than one time and it might not have been his dithering as much as a calculated way of being rid of someone who outshone him or had more power."

"The man should have been discharged when the first questions were raised," said the duke. "At the very least he should have been moved to a position where nothing he did had an effect upon people's lives."

"He should have been, but his uncle is quite powerful and got him the position," Leopold replied and shrugged. "I fear there are many in the government who got their jobs because some relative made certain they did. Usually they are bunglers. Annoying but harmless, if one is not fool enough to allow them access to any secrets. Chuffington was dangerous."

"Come and look at the map I have set out," said the duke, and he led them all over to a large table. "We need to plan our approach."

The map was enormous and very well drawn. Every rise and fall of the land, every building, was clearly depicted. It was pinned at each corner by a colorful rock. Gifts from the children, Argus thought.

"I began to sketch all the various parts of my lands when I was but sixteen. Max, my heir Theodore, and I would ride to a part of the estate and I would carefully sketch each piece of that plot of land. It took me almost ten years. Then I gave all my sketches to an artist and this is the result." He pointed to a small cottage. "This is new and Lorelei draws the new additions in when she can. I will have to have it painted again soon, for we seem to have gained a number of new tenants and houses." He tapped on another picture of a very small, rough cottage. "This is where James lived. A few trees may have fallen victim to a fierce storm or two since this was done, but it is almost exactly as it is depicted on this map."

Leopold studied the map for several minutes. "I am surprised they settled themselves there. It will be very easy to get very close without being seen."

"I suspect they just saw that it was remote and it only had one occupant," said Argus.

Iago nodded. "Convenience not strategy."

"If they understood strategy, convenience would never have mattered, for the man would have seen the possibilities for an enemy to reach him. Which amongst you is the best shot from a distance?" asked the duke, his gaze still fixed upon the map, but before anyone could reply they were interrupted.

"May we come in?" asked Olympia from the door, Stefan right behind her.

"Of course, m'lady," said the duke and went to take her hand and lead her to the table. "You are looking much better than you did a short while ago."

"Food and drink," replied Stefan. "Fortunately, Wynn's wound was a bad one but a simple one. He will be healing on his own quite quickly now."

The duke shook his head. "We really must talk about that wondrous gift of yours some time, but, now, tell me just how good you are with that knife."

When Stefan just blushed and started to stutter out a humble response, Argus said, "There is none better. He has the eye for putting it just where he wants it. For some reason that eye goes blind when you hand him a gun." He smiled gently at Stefan.

"Is there any objection to his going with us on this venture?"

"None."

"What can I do to help?" asked Olympia.

"Stay here with the children," replied the duke, fixing his gaze back on the map.

When Olympia's eyes widened, Argus noticed that all his cousins echoed the wince he could not hide. Olympia did not like being delegated to the female chores. She did them, but she did not like it when a man ordered her to do so. He glanced at the duke and saw the hint of a smile at the corner of his mouth.

"I can shoot a gun," she said.

"I would prefer it if you did not practice on the children."

Olympia crossed her arms over her chest, and Argus was about to remind her that she was facing a duke, when the duke looked at her, all signs of that touch of humor gone. "Lady Olympia, if I could go to these men and settle this all by myself I would. I do not wish to put anyone else in danger. Since I have seen this lad use that knife and face that brute who tried to steal Darius, I know he has a soldier's instincts and we could have need of the silence of his knife. I will not, however, order a woman into the field."

"But . . ."

"I am the duke and I intend to pull rank on you. You stay here and keep the children safe. Between you and Max and the servants I believe you could hold off an army here."

Argus could see that Olympia really wished to argue, but she saw something in the man's eyes that silenced her. She went and sat down, intending to listen to all their plans, however. Argus fleetingly wondered if he could learn that look. Unfortunately, he would never be able to play the duke with a duke's power.

"Now, who is the best at shooting something from a distance?" the duke asked again.

"Iago actually," replied Leopold. "And Bened"— he nodded at the big man—"is also very good. Nearly as good as Iago."

"Then we should be sure to supply them with rifles."

For a while the duke and Leopold discussed various approaches to the woodcutter's cottage. Argus joined in now and then, but the duke was proving as good at strategy as Leopold. He finally poured himself a drink, sat down next to Iago, and watched the two men argue congenially over which was the best path to take to the cabin.

"There is nothing you need to feel guilty about, you know," Iago said and smiled at the scowl Argus sent him. "Her own father says so."

"That helps only a little. Cornick has taken Lorelei to get to me."

"Mayhap he took her because he thought you would do your best to rescue a duke's daughter."

"No, I think he somehow found out that she meant something to me. What I do not understand is why he is still after me. I am no longer the only one who knows who he is, knows what he has done. Why is he not just getting himself out of the country?"

"Because he has no money," said the duke. "When you go to trade yourself for Lorelei, you are to carry ten thousand pounds with you. A pittance for my daughter's life, but then this man, for all the spying he managed to do, appears to know very little about me."

"Ten thousand pounds?" Olympia shook her head. "Do you actually have that kind of money on hand?"

"Oh, yes, as I need to pay everyone wages, buy supplies, and I had intended to give a generous gift to the new grandchild my eldest daughter just bore. I was thinking I could put some money on top of the bag we take to Cornick and something else beneath, but he will surely look for such a trick and that will only add to the danger."

"Money? This is all for money?"

"I believe that was Cornick's interest from the start. Although, as matters began to go wrong he may have gained a need to make Sir Argus pay for that."

Leopold nodded. "Chuffington undoubtedly offered him money to get Argus. Cornick knows that will be impossible to get now. He needs it, however, to get out of the country and hide." He glanced at the duke. "And he obviously wants to do his hiding in some style."

"It could even have been no more than an afterthought," said the duke. "Best we make our final plans. We can at least be certain to some degree that the man has no one watching us. He only has one man left and will want to keep him close to hand."

"Aye," said Argus. "Cornick will know he will need someone to watch his back even if he manages to get out of this alive. He must know he will never be safe if he harms her."

"No, he will not be. And that is where he made his greatest mistake. He did not study me very carefully or he would know that there is not a place in this world where he can hide safely if he harms my daughter."

It was quietly spoken, only the faintest hint of anger behind the words, but Argus recognized a vow when he heard one.

* * *

Lorelei swallowed a moan as she slowly opened her eyes. Her attempt to escape while they were riding away from the village had earned her a vicious blow and she must have slipped into unconsciousness. Her head was pounding so hard she just wanted to curl up and cry. Her face was throbbing and she was sure it must look as colorful as Olympia's had a few days ago.

One look around was enough to tell her where she was. It was the cottage that belonged to Old James the woodcutter. She recognized the fireplace that was nearly as wide as the room itself and the aging deer-hide rug in front of it. She had not come to visit with her father for years, but she could still recall hearing her father teasing the older man about having a hanging offense on his floor. Even then she had known that Old James had not killed the animal, had just made good use of the dead animal he had found. If she remembered correctly, both her father and Old James had agreed that it had been some pack of dogs that had attacked the buck and, although it had escaped, its wounds had eventually killed it.

She could, however, vividly recall sitting on the floor counting the bite marks still visible on the hide and crying a little over the pain the creature must have suffered. Old James, despite her father's protest, had cut a piece off a branch of the animal's antlers that decorated the wall above that massive fireplace. As he and her father had talked, Old James had made her a pendant of it using a strip of blackened leather, hanging it around her neck when she and her father were ready to leave. In his gruff country voice James had told her to always remember that animals suffer, too, that they knew both pain and fear, but always fight to get up again and go on, just as that wounded buck had. A hard lesson to teach a child, but she still had that crude pendant and every time she saw it lying there amongst her jewels, she recalled the lesson of fight, fall, get up, and go on.

Tears stung her eyes, for she knew Old James would not be getting up and going on. Lorelei was certain these men had murdered the man—Old James would have told her father what was happening if he had gotten away. She wondered where his dog was. James had never been without a dog, always going to pick out the runt or ugly one of a litter when he needed a new dog. *They must have killed the poor animal, too,* she thought.

"Ah, awake now are you?" said Cornick, moving to stand over her where they had obviously simply tossed her onto the floor. "Allow me to help you to a seat."

He grabbed her by the arm, yanked her to her feet, and dragged her over to a chair, shoving her down into it. Lorelei hid her wince over the pain flaring in her bound wrists when they hit the high back of the heavy wooden chair. "You killed James," she said.

"James? Oh, that old man who lived here." Cornick nodded. "We needed his house and he did not appear amenable to sharing. He is out in the wood now. Your lover will soon join him."

Not even by the blink of an eye did Lorelei reveal her unease over the fact that Cornick knew about her and Argus, or had made a very astute guess. She prayed it was the latter. The mere thought that he or one of his brutes had seen her and Argus together made her want to vomit. For a moment she almost gave in to the urge as she eyed his boots but did not really wish to feel the weight of his fist again. She was conscious now and knew it was important that she remain so.

"You believe that Sir Argus will just walk into your grasp, do you?" she asked and knew he had heard the scorn in her voice by the way his eyes narrowed in anger.

"He will trade himself for you, and your loving father will finance my new life with his own money."

"Why should Sir Argus return to your unloving care? And just why do you want him if you are set to run off to a new life?"

"Wherlocke ruined everything. We had a fine plan, but his stubborn refusal to give us what we wanted and then his escape were the beginning of my ruination. He will pay for that and your father will pay for helping him. But he did not help him as much as you did, hmmm?"

"I have no idea what you are referring to." She winced when he grabbed hold of her long braid and pulled on it.

"You are the one who got him out of that house. I saw you. Only a glimpse, but that was enough. Saw that fine arse of yours and this long braid glinting red in the moonlight."

"Mayhap the red was because you got some of Sir Argus's blood in your eye the last time you beat him. Ah, but you did not beat him, did you? You sat and watched while your henchmen did all the work." She bit back a cry of pain when he pulled on her braid so hard tears stung her eyes.

"How did you know where he was? I am curious as to how I stepped wrong."

"He told me."

"Woman, I may have erred in how I played this game and how I secured my prisoner, but I am not an idiot."

She knew the look she gave him clearly expressed her doubt for his fist clenched. She braced herself for a blow, but it did not come. "He *told* me. He appeared in my father's garden and told me of the trouble he was in. Do try to remember, sir, you are dealing with the Wherlockes and their kin."

"But, if he could get out to tell you that he was in trouble, why did he not just leave, run for home?"

"He did not run, *sir.* He escaped. And his body was still held captive. He sent his spirit out to look for aid."

Cornick cursed and tossed her braid aside. "Do not be foolish. No one can do such a thing."

"I should not have thought so, but he did." She shrugged, ignoring the tug of discomfort caused by having her hands bound behind her back for so long. "I suspect he puts himself into some sort of sleep and lets it go. This time it came to me. He told me he was your prisoner and asked me to send word to his family. I did send word but decided that he needed help immediately so I went looking for him myself. I am very good at finding things."

"So you sent word to his family, and that is why this place fairly crawls with Wherlockes and Vaughns."

Lorelei slowly shook her head, but even that added to the throbbing pain in it. Cornick obviously did not believe her. By the look in his eyes as she had told him her tale, he did not want to believe her. There was clearly a point where his fears and superstitions reared up their hoary little heads. She wondered if she could make use of that. Her father liked to say that, if a man allowed fear to control him, he became careless. A few tales about the Wherlockes should do it, and it might help the ones she knew were coming to rescue her. The Wherlockes did not like their secrets told, but she knew, whether she survived or not, these two men were doomed. Even if the miraculous happened and they escaped what was coming for them, her father, the Wherlockes, and the Vaughns would hunt them and put them down like the rabid dogs they were.

"Yes. There is the Lady Olympia, the woman your man tried to drag off. She can go to a place, any place, and see what happened there, read the memory of the event and the people involved as if it was a book. Then, of course, there is the young boy your other man tried to steal. That is Darius and he can see what they call auras, the light and color that surrounds us all but most people cannot see. I suspect yours and Tucker's would be a bit murky. Then there is Lord Sir Leopold and he can tell when a person is lying. You, sir, would probably exhaust him. Then there is the boy who put a knife in the back of your man Jones, a youth of sixteen who is a wondrous healer and, obviously, very skilled with a knife. It is even whispered that the head of that large family, the young Duke of Elderwood, can see right into a man's heart and mind and take out any information he wants."

"Shut her up," snarled Tucker.

"If you are made so uneasy by the gifts the Wherlockes have, why were you so determined to steal one?" she asked.

"It is no *gift* Wherlocke has, but a skill. Just a skill."

"You delude yourself, sir, or you did not take the time to study the man you imprisoned, study him and his family. They do their very best to hold fast to their secrets, as they have been forced to by the ignorance and fear of people, but there is a lot of information on them if one but looks for it. They have more gifts than you can possibly imagine and they will bring every one they have when they come after you for hurting Sir Argus. Now or later."

"You will be quiet now," said Cornick, clenching and unclenching his fists as he glared at her. "The only ones coming here to try and save you are Wherlocke and your father. I will get that bastard, get that money, and leave."

Lorelei noticed that he did not say what would happen to her or her father. She suspected he thought he could just kill them and walk away. For a moment, she thought of explaining to the fool that neither her nor Argus's family would ever allow Cornick to escape justice. Instinct told her that the man would never understand, never believe her. He probably thought some heir would actually be pleased to be rid of the man standing between him and the title, as was the case with others of her class, and would just let the scandal fade away along with the man who helped to make him a duke.

"They should be here soon," said Tucker. "Think they will really come unarmed?"

"Of course they will," said Cornick. "They are honorable gentlemen."

Lorelei did not think she had ever heard those words said so disparagingly.

"That does not mean they will not have one tucked

away on their persons somewhere though," Cornick continued. "But we shall have ours primed, cocked, and ready. They will not be able to pull theirs out of whatever pocket they have stuck it before they are shot dead."

"Have you ever seen Sir Argus or my father draw a pistol?" she asked.

"Woman, Tucker and I will already have our guns aimed at them. We can pull the trigger before they can even reach for their pistols. And I do not concern myself with the duke. Everyone knows he just stays here in the country with his books, breeding like a rabbit. He is no threat. Sir Argus may be, but he will still be at a grave disadvantage. You see, he will be bleeding on the ground before he can even get his finger on the trigger."

"So confident," she murmured. "Mayhap they will just shoot you because they know you have no intention of honoring the deal you brokered."

"Not with you still in my grasp and standing in front of me."

There was really no arguing that, but Lorelei just shrugged, the hint of disdain in the gesture plainly irritating the man. And, despite how good her father was with a pistol, Cornick had some right to his arrogance. There would be that one step farther her father and Argus would have to go before they could shoot their pistols.

"You have no intention of letting any of us walk away from this, do you?"

"You think me no gentleman, that I cannot honor a deal made? They are bringing money and Sir Argus has agreed to take your place as my prisoner. Why should I change such a fine bargain?"

"I have no idea. Actually, I do not believe you ever made the bargain. You just presented it. You sent my father the very demand he expected, knew he would accept, for what choice did he truly have, and never once had any intention of honoring it. Have you considered what will happen if you kill a duke of the realm?"

"Oh, there will be a great scandal, I am certain."

That answered her question nicely, she thought, for he had just admitted to his plans to kill the two men coming to rescue her. Lorelei was certain her father and Argus would be aware of the treachery Cornick might try. Fear for her father and Argus was a hard knot in her stomach, but she refused to let Cornick think, for even a moment, that she doubted her father's or Argus's ability to escape or punish him. She would act as arrogant about his coming downfall as he did about his coming success and pray he was not the one who won that battle.

Cornick took out his watch and looked at it, smiling faintly. "They should be here soon. I suspect a duke is a man who will be punctual. Soon I will be a rich man."

The glance Tucker sent Cornick's way told Lorelei that there was a very good chance Cornick would not live to enjoy the money. Of course, there was a very good chance that it would be Tucker who died, assuming either man survived the confrontation with her father. It was always said that there was no honor amongst thieves. That look Tucker had given his compatriot rather confirmed it.

But, neither of them would have the chance to fight over the money, she told herself firmly. Lorelei refused to let her belief in that waver. Her father might be a very honorable man indeed, but he was far from stupid. He would not honor that agreement any more than Cornick planned to. He would come, he would bring the money and Argus, but she would wager he brought every Wherlocke and Vaughn as well, perhaps even a few of the men from Sundun-moor. Cornick was in for a surprise. Lorelei strongly hoped it was a fatal one.

Chapter 17

The stench of death seeped into the air as Argus and the duke moved silently through the wood toward the woodcutter's cottage. For a moment he hesitated, knowing what was ahead, and not wanting to see it, but then he stiffened his backbone and went on. He grimaced when he found the body of what had once been a man. There had been no attempt to protect his corpse from the scavengers that had obviously found him.

"Ah, damn me, poor Old James," said the duke in a soft voice as he stepped up beside Argus. "The bastards could not even be bothered to protect him from the animals. Old James always feared dying in the woods he so loved and becoming no more than a meal for the carrion. I ought to shoot those men squatting in his cottage just for this alone." He sighed. "I will miss our chess games."

Argus patted the duke on the back and then began moving again. He had not known James but could understand the grief and anger the duke suffered. He had felt its like before. This had been a useless, callous murder of an old man. Cornick and his men had wanted the cottage to hide in so they had killed an old man and thrown him aside like scraps from the table.

It was difficult to hold fast to the stealthy approach. Argus wanted to race to the cottage, kick in the door, and kill both men with his bare hands. The still-sane part of him, the one not driven nearly mad with fear for Lorelei, knew that would be an insane thing to do and would only get him and Lorelei killed. Or, Argus knew, he easily could find himself lying there, bleeding to death, while everyone else rushed in to save his lover. It would undoubtedly look very heroic, he mused, but it would be idiotic.

Once the small cottage was in clear view, the trees thinning out so that the rest of the distance to the building consisted of wide-open space, Argus halted and the duke moved to stand beside him. One more step and both of them would be visible to anyone watching from the cottage. Argus could see his family, mere shadowy forms in the dappled shade of the trees, ready to slip up behind Cornick while he and the duke held the man's attention. There was still a lot of room for disaster to move in, but Argus was as confident of success as he could ever be when Lorelei's life was at stake.

"I pray I was right to say that the man will not kill us immediately," the duke murmured.

"It would greatly surprise me if you proved to be wrong. From what I have observed in the last few hours, our military lost a fine general when you became the heir to a dukedom." He almost smiled when he saw the light hint of a blush tint the man's cheeks.

"It was planned that I would go into the military,

but I am not sure I have the strength for such a life. The strategy is something I can do and enjoy, but I fear my soul, even my mind, would shatter after seeing so many men die. I do not think I would look at the dead and see only brave soldiers who honorably died for king and country."

Argus looked at the man and slowly nodded. "No, mayhap not. You would see sons lost, orphaned children, and the like. Such heart is not a bad thing."

The duke shrugged. "I am what I am." He looked at his watch and then tucked it back into the pocket of his waistcoat. "Best we begin the play. The ease with which that man kills the innocent makes me think it very important that we do not make him wait. And you need not worry that I will see him or his man as someone's son or father. I see both men as naught but vermin that the world will be well rid of. I do not suppose you could use your gift on these men."

"If they have not used the protections they devised when I was their prisoner, I will do so and this will be over quickly and cleanly. At least it will if neither of them are as resistant as others I have met recently. Unfortunately, despite his desperation and the crazed way he has been acting, I believe he will recall what it is I can do. So he and his man will don the protection of tinted spectacles to deaden the power of my gaze and put enough linen in their ears to mute the sound of my voice."

"A shame, for you are right. If they did not, this could all be over quickly. You could just tell them to toss aside their weapons and surrender. Now, it shall be a struggle to keep his attention on us and keep him from shooting any of us until the others can slip up behind him."

There was no argument to make to that statement so Argus simply started walking. He surreptitiously studied the duke as they made their way down a small hill, out of the trees, and into the open, for the man looked a lot different from how he usually did. At the moment, Roland Sundun looked every inch the duke. Between Max and the duke's valet, they had dressed the man with a rich yet subtle elegance that Cornick would recognize right away. All in black save for the crisp white of his shirt and cravat, a faint rim of lace around his wrists appearing at the edge of his coat sleeves, and very subdued silver embroidery on his waistcoat. For once the man's hair was neat, tied back into a precise queue. Argus suddenly realized that the duke was still young enough to be considered a prime marriage prospect, his lean muscular form and handsome looks making him even more so. If the man ever came to London, matchmaking mothers would mob him, especially when it was discovered how rich he was.

Shaking aside that idle thought, Argus studied the cottage they walked toward. Small, sturdy, and well maintained, it was a very fine residence for a woodcutter and his family. The duke treated his people well.

The face in the window to the right of the door was easily recognizable as Tucker's. Argus suspected Cornick was standing back until he was certain it was safe. Cornick was deadly, possessing a cold, murderous heart, but he was also very protective of his person, to a point that bordered closely on cowardice.

"Cornick!" he yelled as he and the duke stopped a few yards from the door.

His body tensed, prepared for a bullet to slam into him, and Argus made certain that his body was placed a little ahead of, and in front of, the duke, ignoring the man's grumbling over such protection. Argus did not believe Cornick would just shoot them, take the money, and run, however. Cornick would want to savor his perceived victory, to boast and strut before them, letting them know that he had power over them. However, Cornick was also desperate and trapped. Argus was counting on the man not knowing just how completely trapped he was.

Lorelei felt as if her heart had just leapt up into her throat when she heard Argus's voice. She could not see out the front window because Tucker's bulk blocked her view, but she was certain Argus was standing out there in front of the house, in the open, a ready and easy target. Guilt soured her stomach, for this was all her fault. She did not know just how she could have refused the baker's plea for help, but she should have taken more guards with her, enough to stop Cornick and Tucker from taking her.

Then her hopes for a rescue were pushed aside by her fear for her father and her lover. She did want to get home safely, but not at the cost of either of their lives. That would be too high a price to pay.

"They be here," said Tucker. "Both the duke and that bastard Wherlocke. Got a nice fat bag with them, too."

"My money," said Cornick and rubbed his hands together. "How very nice." He looked at Lorelei. "You must be so comforted by this touching evidence of their concern for you."

"I will be comforted, sir, when I see your body on the ground with a bullet between your eyes."

"Tsk. Such a crude thing for the daughter of a duke to say," he said absently, revealing that she was no longer of any interest to him. "I wonder just how long I should make them wait. They need to be made to see who is in charge here, of course, but I do not want them to think I have decided to surrender or something equally as foolish."

"Take your time, enjoy the last few moments of your miserable life. Perhaps you should even consider taking this time to try to atone for all your sins. It might delay the devil from pulling you into hell the moment your body hits the ground. Lord Uppington sees a lot of spirits and he claims the ones that belong to the devil rarely linger after death, for the devil is not a patient man." She was pleased to see that both Cornick and Tucker were a little pale. "Some atonement now might give your black souls time to hide."

She forced herself not to flinch when Cornick abruptly bent down and brought his face very close to hers. He was not a particularly handsome man but not unhandsome, either. He could easily disappear into a crowd. She wondered if that was one reason he had become the man he now was. Being ignored or forgotten could twist a man. Why Cornick was what he was did not really matter much, she decided. No matter what her fate, his was written in stone. He would die. There was some comfort to find in that knowledge.

"You will regret those words and soon," he hissed at her. "Death can come easy or hard." He smiled. "Or it can come later, right after Tucker and I cease to enjoy your many charms. It will be a long ocean voyage we will be taking and a little womanly comfort might be nice. And I am sure Tucker would gladly slit your tongue if you were slow to learn to shut up when told to."

The thought of Tucker and Cornick dragging her along with them as they fled the country, forcing her into their beds before they killed her, was terrifying, but Lorelei fought to hide that fear. Cornick was a man who would sniff it out and use it against her. Cruel men such as he was had a true skill at that. It was, in its way, a power of sorts, but she would not allow him to weaken her with his threats. And his threat of rape could be ignored, for she would never allow it. If she could not escape, she would find a way to hurl herself into the water once the ship was out to sea.

"Do you know, I have never understood people who think threatening or hurting ones weaker than themselves is justifiable in any way?" she said, showing him that she knew exactly what game he was playing. "You gain no true power and you certainly gain no respect. The only ones you can truly make fear you are the ones who are weak, or some who are too witless to see what you really are, or utter cowards. Anyone with wit and a spine could beat you. Ah, but I forget. Those are the ones you tie up. Silly me."

Lorelei wondered why he did not hit her. It was obvious that he wanted to and he had not hesitated to do so when she had tried to escape. That could be it, she thought as she watched him bring his fury under control. Cornick needed a real threat to himself or his plans before he could physically strike out. He could shoot people without any hesitation, but actually beating on them with his hands caused him to hesitate. Perhaps he feared getting blood on his fine clothes, she mused. Or ruining his fine manicure.

It made no sense, but she was glad of that hesitancy. She did not wish to be knocked unconscious again, not when her father and Argus were both in danger and she had no idea what their plan was. Lorelei wanted to be fully aware and ready to do whatever she could to help so that they could all get out of this alive. It might be best if she curbed her sharp tongue, but something about Cornick made her every word come out razor sharp. His grand plans to murder people who had never done anything to him were part of what so infuriated her.

"You do not understand who you are dealing with, bitch," he snapped.

"No," she said quietly, never taking her gaze from his face, "I do not. You obviously have money enough to buy yourself fine clothes and have had an education, so why are you doing this? Why steal a man and beat him senseless regularly in a vain attempt to steal his God-given gift? Why do something so certain to get yourself hanged?" She nodded at Tucker. "He I can understand as he has probably done enough to get himself hanged a dozen times, so there was no added risk to this for him. But you are the son of a gentleman, are you not?"

He brushed off his coat and stood up straight. "Of course I am, but I am only the youngest son of a minor baron. I had to work for my coin like some commoner. Uncle thought himself so benevolent when he got me a job in the government. As a lowly clerk! I worked there for years and never got anywhere, was never made anything more than the clerk I started as. They never even noticed the work I did, not even my uncle. Then I was offered a chance to finally rise up in the ranks, to join with a man destined to gain some real power. A lot of power. And money. Wherlocke has destroyed that chance, but you, and your father, will ensure that I do not have to retire from the field as a beggar."

Cornick grabbed her by the arm and yanked her to her feet. "You will not retire from the field, you fool," she snapped. "You will be buried in it."

Out of the corner of her eye Lorelei could see through the small window at the side of the house, and caught a glimpse of movement. There was a plan, she thought with a surge of hope that made her momentarily light-headed, and she became determined to keep Tucker and Cornick's attention fixed on her. She would not be surprised if her father and Argus intended to do the same. If they were truly hoping the others could sneak up behind Cornick and Tucker as she, her father, and Argus kept the men's attention on them, it could prove to be a risky plan. Lorelei prayed hard that it would work.

"Cornick!" bellowed Argus again. "Do we meet now or have you changed your mind?"

Tucker stood up and idly checked his pistol. "I want to shoot that duke. Never killed me one of those before. Damn my eyes, but it would be near to killing the king."

"'Ware, friend, that tastes of treason."

"Just let me kill the duke." Tucker shrugged when Cornick looked hard at him. "I want to."

"Then he is all yours," said Cornick as he also checked his pistol.

Since they had only recently checked the weapons they had been aiming at her father and Argus through the window, Lorelei did not know what they thought had changed with the things, but she decided to test their watchfulness. She took a step away from a distracted Cornick the moment he released her to play with his weapon, but both men glared at her. She doubted she would get very far if she bolted and could not open the door anyway, not with her hands tied behind her back.

To her dismay, the men donned their tinted spectacles and stuck bits of linen in their ears, thus stealing the power of Argus's greatest weapon. Cornick pulled a lethal-looking knife from his boot and pressed it against the small of her back. If there was a plan to save her, Lorelei had the sinking feeling that a very large complication had just been presented.

"Walk in front of me," he ordered. "Show no sign that I have a knife at your back, make no attempt to bolt, or I will have Tucker shoot your father in the gut. Then you can watch him die slowly and in agony."

A whole litany of daring plans went through Lorelei's head as Tucker opened the door. Every one of them ended with her standing over her dying father or lying in a pool of her own blood. Cornick might be a coward, even a fool who took a chance to grab for riches and power without pausing to consider the consequences, but she had been right to think he was very good with a threat. He had sniffed out her fear for the men out there and, probably uncertain of her relationship with Argus, had threatened the other important man in her life. She started to think of ways that she could warn her father and Argus that Cornick had a knife digging into her back hard enough to have already scored her skin.

Argus nearly slumped in relief when he saw Lorelei walk out in front of Cornick, but he knew they were not out of danger yet. A soft curse vilifying Cornick's ancestors escaped the duke at the same time that Argus saw the livid bruising on Lorelei's face. He ached to make Cornick pay dearly for that, to suffer before he died. Lorelei was a great deal smaller and lighter than the man. Argus doubted she presented enough of a threat to Cornick to warrant a hard punch in the face.

"Still beating on people who cannot fight back, Cornick?" Argus knew it was not wise to anger the man, but the smug look on Cornick's face was more than he could stomach.

"I but subdued her when she tried to run away," Cornick replied calmly. "I fear the duke has badly spoiled his child. She does not take orders very well at all. Spare the rod and spoil the child," he intoned piously.

Before Argus could respond, the duke stepped forward and said, "Sir, there is still a chance for you to walk away from this a free man. If you release my daughter unharmed and leave Sundunmoor, leave the country, we will bring no charges against you and there will be no pursuit."

"Papa, he killed James," Lorelei said quietly, knowing it would be a good thing if Cornick did as her father asked, but heartsore that poor James might never get justice.

"James would understand," said her father. "He would want you free."

"You cannot possibly believe I am so stupid as to believe that," said Cornick. "Oh, you may hold to your word on it, but Wherlocke will not. I notice that he does not add his support to your offer by word or movement. His family will most certainly come after me as her ladyship so graciously, and repeatedly, told me."

When her father gave her a gently chiding look, well acquainted with her sharp tongue, she just smiled. Then she winked and was pleased to see the alert look on his face that told her he had understood her signal to keep his attention on her. It was an old trick they had devised to let each other know that something needed to be said that the children should not hear. Over a long, miserable winter they had learned Gaelic from the Gregors and that was now their secret language. It helped to discuss what to do about the twins' latest mischief even when Axel and Wolfgang were in the room, usually awaiting some decision about their punishment. Now she told him about the knife Cornick held against her back.

"What did you just say?" demanded Cornick, pressing a little harder on his knife until it pierced her skin a bit deeper, releasing a little more blood.

"I told him that he was a good man and that I love him dearly," she replied, weighting her voice with every bit of innocence she could put into it, but she could see that Cornick doubted her word. "It was to have been a private moment between father and daughter."

"It does not matter," he said after staring at her for a moment, confident in the fact that Tucker still watched his back.

Lorelei began to wonder if she had been imagining that shadowy movement in the window, for nothing was happening. Her father, Argus, and Cornick traded increasingly vicious quips as they tried to decide how to make the trade Cornick had no intention of honoring anyway. She continued to try to hide the pain she was in as Cornick kept his knife embedded just inside her skin. A faint but growing dampness on her back told her that she was still bleeding, perhaps even more than she had been before. There was a chance, she thought, fighting the urge to try to step away from that knife, that the others saw what Cornick was doing to her and had to move more slowly.

"No, there is no deal to be made, not beyond what I have asked for," snapped Cornick, obviously tired of the game of wit he was playing with her father and Argus. "I hold the power here. I have the winning card. I want that money."

"You do not wish to kill my daughter," her father said, the ring of command and anger behind each word.

"Actually, Your Grace, I think I do. She has a very sharp tongue that fairly begs a man to silence it," Cornick said and smiled. "As you have already remarked upon, I have been forced to discipline her once. I admit to being surprised that you are willing to buy her back."

He is searching for that weak point, Lorelei realized. If her father expressed any affection for her, by word or deed, Cornick would use that to torment him. It did not look as if Cornick would get what he wanted, for her father was looking very ducal, right down to his stony, emotionless expression.

"She is my child," was all her father said in a cold voice.

"Thinking we should be done with all this talking," muttered Tucker.

"Just another moment, Tucker. I am enjoying this. A duke and an arrogant Wherlocke at my mercy." Keeping his gaze fixed unwaveringly on both men before him, Cornick kissed Lorelei's cheek. "And a sweet woman in my arms. It is a moment to savor, one to place firmly in my memory so that I might relive it again from time to time as I spend His Grace's money."

"Enough," snapped Argus. "Take your blood money and release the lady."

"So impatient," murmured Cornick and smiled as he pushed the knife a little deeper into Lorelei's back.

A scream surged up into her throat, but Lorelei swallowed it. *Please, someone kill this man,* she prayed silently, only a little shocked at her own bloodthirsti-ness. Pain spread throughout her body from the point where the knife dug into her flesh almost as quickly as the blood ran from the wound. At the speed she felt it running down from the wound, she would not be surprised if she were soon standing in a pool of it.

The way her father was looking at her told Lorelei that he had guessed that Cornick was not being gentle with the knife he held on her, but she prayed he would believe it a minor nuisance since she neither moved nor cried out. She was not going to give her rescuers any reason to act rashly. They did not need anyone making an openly aggressive move, not with the pistols Cornick and Tucker held steadily aimed at the two men she loved most in the world, especially since she was certain those two men were hiding a pistol or two of their own. It would be a bloodbath.

There was a grunt from the side, right where Tucker stood. Lorelei glanced toward him and watched as the man slowly lowered his pistol, a surprised look on his face. A moment later he sank to his knees.

"Damn idiot," he said to Cornick. "Your need to preen has done got me killed. Stupid sod."

He fell facedown in the dirt. In his back was a large knife. Both her father and Argus moved toward her, but Cornick tensed, his pistol aimed right at her father's head. Lorelei softly moaned as that knife went deeper into her back and wondered why the one who had thrown the knife had not aimed for Cornick. She suspected there was a good reason but wanted his knife out of her back so much she doubted she would care to hear it.

"You have lost this fight, Cornick," said Argus. "We have men all round this place and two have rifles. You do not have a chance of getting out of here alive unless you put that pistol down now and release Lorelei."

She could almost smell the panic that had seized Cornick when Tucker had fallen. He was panting softly as he tried to think of a way to save himself. Lorelei knew when he had decided he could not, for he went very still. Fear crawled up her spine. Every instinct she had told her that Cornick did not intend to die alone.

He could still shoot her father or he could finish shoving that knife into her back, and she did not much like either option. Lorelei wondered if she could move away from him now, but doubted that would save her. He could still kill either her or her father before she took more than a step or two.

"I must say I am shocked that a duke of the realm would break his word," said Cornick.

"I did not give my word," said the duke. "I believe I simply responded that I would meet with you. I do hope you did not kill the boy you used as you killed James."

"Of course not. The boy was no threat. I simply did not pay him as promised. Tucker kindly chased him away." He glanced quickly at Lorelei, but the aim of his pistol did not waver. "I suppose that is another sin I should have atoned for."

"Yes," came a deep voice from behind them that Lorelei recognized as Iago's. "I fear your friend has already met the devil. Do you wish to or will you surrender?"

"Surrender? Oh, yes, that is so tempting. Die now or wait for the hangman."

"Move the weapon," began Iago.

"And so I shall."

Lorelei did not have time to even think of what was coming. Cornick shoved the knife into her and then shot at Argus, who leapt out of the way the moment the man pulled the trigger. As she stood there, pain holding her rigid, several pistols fired at once. She wanted to see who had been hurt but could not move. A moment later she began to sink to the ground. She was on her knees and sliding onto her face when her father reached her.

"Cornick?" she asked.

"Quite dead. I think at least four of us shot him."

"Good."

"Oh, my poor Lolly, what has he done?"

"I fear he may have killed me," she said and let the blackness sweeping over her take her away from the pain.

Chapter 18

Argus rushed to Lorelei's side just as the duke turned her over, tore her cloak off, and revealed the blood-soaked back of her gown. All the strength went out of him and he fell to his knees at her side. She had been stabbed, low on her back, and it was bleeding freely, too freely. Argus stared at the woman lying so still and pale on the ground and called himself a thousand kinds of a fool.

This woman was his life. Knowing that such a loss of blood could be fatal, even if Cornick had not managed to damage anything vital, his mind was suddenly crowded with all he wanted and needed to say to her.

"You knew," he said to the duke, trying and failing to keep the tone of accusation out of his voice. "She told you."

"With that little display of Gaelic, yes, she did." The duke almost smiled as he brushed the hair from Lorelei's white face. "She told me that the bastard held a knife to her back. A little later I suspected he had used it, but only to cause her a little pain, not to kill her. That was foolish of me. He meant to kill us all right from the beginning. He certainly was not about to change his plans much when he knew he was doomed."

"He wanted to make certain you paid for his loss in some way," said Stefan.

"Can you help her?" asked Argus.

"I can slow the bleeding," Stefan said even as he knelt next to the duke. "I cannot close the wound when it is so large and deep. That will require a skilled surgeon."

"She will have one as soon as we can get her home," said the duke. "If you can slow that cursed bleeding we have a chance."

Argus sat back and watched Stefan work. The duke caught the boy when he swayed the moment he finished. Argus moved forward to wrap a bandage around the wound. He could not believe that she had not made a sound, had acted as if all was fine so that they could deal with Cornick.

"It is deep," said Stefan as Iago and Leopold fed him with thick pieces of bread, cheese, and cider, obviously having come prepared in case anyone needed any healing. "I do not think anything inside of her is damaged, but I am still learning. I can ease bleeding, help with a fever, ease pain." He shrugged. "If the doctor stitches her up, then I can help her regain her strength or ease a fever if she suffers one."

Before the duke could do so, Argus wrapped Lorelei in her cloak and picked her up. The duke looked as if he would protest for a moment, but then he just half smiled and shook his head. When Iago and Leopold returned with the horse, having sent a few of the men on ahead to fetch the doctor, Argus discovered that he did not want to let go of Lorelei. Finally recognizing that he would not be able to mount his horse with her still held securely in his arms, he gave her to the duke. He mounted quickly and then held out his arms, taking her into his as gently as he could. As soon as he was holding her again he had felt something ease inside of him.

"Somehow we must ride swiftly yet not so fast that she is bounced around," said the duke as he edged his mount up next to Argus's. "We need to get her to the doctor quickly as the ride will be long and could weaken her, but we need to do it gentle as otherwise the ride could be rough and Stefan says it could easily make her start bleeding again."

Argus glanced back at the bodies of Cornick and Tucker. "What about them? Personally, I would leave them for the carrion."

"As would I if only because of what they did to James. But, I am the magistrate and they must be brought in and everything done properly. Then they can rot for all I care. I will bring James home, too, so that he can be buried next to his wife on the chapel grounds."

"We have other healers, ones with more knowledge and experience," said Argus, already thinking of the ones he could send out an urgent message to if needed.

"So Stefan said. I hope we have no need of them."

The ride was long, each bump and sway alarming Argus. He checked on Lorelei's wound each time she moved, but the bleeding did not start up again, not as badly as it had been back at the woodcutter's cottage. By the time Sundun House came into view,

Argus's whole body ached from all his attempts to make certain Lorelei did not move, that she remained as still as possible in his arms.

He allowed the duke to hold his daughter again, just for the time it took Argus to dismount and hand the reins of his mount to a stable boy. Once on the ground he quickly retrieved Lorelei. Argus knew he was behaving somewhat irrationally, but he feared that if he let her go, she would slip away from him.

"Shot?" asked Olympia as she met him on the stairs and then helped him to Lorelei's bedchamber.

"Stabbed in the back," he answered. "Cornick wanted someone to suffer when he realized he was losing."

"Bastard. He is dead, right?"

"Very dead. We all shot him. The duke, Iago, Leopold, and me. Stefan had already put a knife in the back of Cornick's henchman Tucker and brought him down."

It was not easy for Argus to let go of Lorelei when he reached her bed, either, and he was a little embarrassed about how his arms tightened around her at the mere thought of releasing her from his arms. He knew she had to have her wound tended to properly. Once he put her down on the bed, he left her in the care of Olympia and Vale, and rushed back to the gatehouse. He washed up, changed his clothes, and packed a few things because he had no intention of leaving Sundun House and Lorelei until he was certain that she was healing as she should be.

Then he had some traveling to do, and some work. He needed to report in to the man he worked for in the government, for Cornick was, after all, one of their men. After that he had a great many matters to settle and arrange before he could set his feet on the path he now wanted to travel.

"I think the boy has had an epiphany," murmured Max as he and the duke stood in the doorway of the front parlor and watched Argus run up the stairs, bag in hand.

"He could not let go of her and that had to be a very uncomfortable ride home for him," said the duke. "I do not recall inviting him to move in."

"He is not leaving our Lolly's side until he sees that she is well again."

"You really think he will stay with her now, that this is not just a natural concern for someone he lusts after and likes? I know my Lorelei. She needs him to belong to her and her to him. She needs a good marriage of companionship, lusting, and loyalty. And she truly needs to be loved," he added quietly. "Lolly thrives with love."

"He does, Your Grace. What I saw when he first brought her in the door, poor child all limp and bloodied, was a man terrified of losing someone. A man does not look that afraid unless his heart is caught and held tight. I suspect he had a moment when all he could think of were the things he wanted to say to her and might never be able to now."

"Lorelei will be all right," the duke said, his voice a little sharpened by fear.

Max patted his lifelong friend on the back. "I know. I believe she will be. She is young and strong."

"She will be better," said Olwen as he walked up to the men.

"Have you seen that, young man?" asked the duke.

"I have. She will be very sick, and it will be frightening, but then she will get all better."

"I am pleased you came here to tell me that," said the duke.

"I did not want you to worry, especially since you have been very good to us all."

"And now I shan't worry. Tell me, young Olwen, do you play chess?"

"Aye, Your Grace, I do."

Roland wrapped his arm around the boy's shoulders and smiled at him. "Shall we play a game then?" When the boy nodded, the duke started into the library, calling to Max over his shoulder, "A bit to eat and drink, if you please, and send the doctor to me when he is done examining Lorelei."

Argus confronted the doctor the moment the man stepped out of Lorelei's bedchamber.

"How is she?"

"I was just headed to speak to the duke," the doctor began.

"Speak to me first so that I may go and sit with her. I am the one who carried her all the way here and need to know that she suffered no further injury."

The doctor hesitated a moment and then began, "Whoever stuck her with that knife was either poorly trained with a knife or so well trained he knew exactly where to put it to cause the least amount of damage possible. As far as I can see, nothing on the inside of her was damaged. Bruised a little, but not hurt. She will heal with only a small scar and she needs to rest as much as she can. No heavy foods and plenty to drink. Just watch closely for a fever although Lady Olympia says she can care for that if it comes."

After assuring the doctor that she would be well cared for and he would be called immediately if needed, Argus watched the doctor go down the stairs and then headed for Lorelei's bedchamber. He was a little afraid that the duke would corner him and ask him what he thought he was doing. He and Lorelei were not formally betrothed, yet here he was, in her bedchamber, set to care for her. And he had moved into the house without being invited.

He entered the bedchamber and walked straight to the side of the bed. Lorelei looked so small in the huge bed, her skin so pale it nearly matched the linens. She was settled on her side with pillows at her back to stop her from rolling onto her newly stitched wounds. Argus reached to gently stroke her hair.

"She will recover, Argus," Olympia said as she stood up.

"Did you have a knowing?" he asked as he took the seat by the bed that she had just left.

"Olwen did and hurried up here thinking you might be here. Watch her closely though, for the boy did think she would get very sick before she fully recovers. I told him I would tell you, and then he ran off to tell the duke."

"That will ease the man's mind. He was very concerned. I think his *Lolly* is one of his favorites. It is not because she is his only daughter, either, as he has three others."

"I saw a portrait of his second wife, the one he was happy with, and she looks a lot like the woman, especially that dark red hair. But, I also think they think alike in some ways and she has become mother to many of the boys."

"Are you trying to warn me about something?"

"Mayhap. She is well loved in this house. Just be careful. Now, I am off to get some rest." Olympia kissed him on the cheek, picked up the book she had been reading, and left.

Argus frowned down at Lorelei after the door shut behind Olympia. He knew he was overstepping his bounds by miles, but he had not been secretive about that. If the duke did not like it, Argus knew the man would be right there, telling him ever so nicely to leave. He hoped the man did not do that, for he really did not wish to get in an argument with the Duke of Sundunmoor. Argus had no intention of leaving Lorelei's side, except to preserve her modesty, until he knew she was safe and healthy.

He sat forward and brushed his fingers over her forehead. She had been through an ordeal and that could easily have weakened her as much as the wound itself. The long ride home had surely sapped what strength she had as well. Argus thought all that added up to good odds that she could take a fever, and fevers had killed too many people. His family had been right. He had been about to toss away the best for some twisted idea about cursed marriages.

It was difficult to admit one had been an utter fool, but he did it. He had clung to his belief that marriage to a Wherlocke or Vaughn was much akin to having a curse put on your family. There was no question that his childhood had been miserable, mostly due to his parents' even more miserable marriage. Unfortunately, he had clung to that image of marriage as if it were the only truth instead of looking closely at everything else that was wrong in that marriage.

One of the first and foremost things wrong with his father's marriage was his mother. She had been spoiled, had expected balls, gowns, and a man who would spend hours just telling her how beautiful she was. His father was the second thing wrong because he had married the woman when he had to have guessed at least some of what she was like before he had even proposed. It did not change the fact that his mother had hated and feared the gifts that ran rampant through the whole family. That was something his father should have put to the test before he had put a ring on her finger.

Argus now wondered if too many of his forefathers, and mothers, had never put their spouse to the test before the marriage. Many may have continued to try and keep everything a secret for fear of being told no when they proposed or the fear of never being asked, of dying a spinster. It made an odd sort of sense. It was why so many of the children born on the wrong side of the blanket ended up tossed out. A man did not tell his mistress everything about himself, certainly not something the family was trying to keep as secret as possible, yet when a child was born of the relationship, those gifts could not be hidden from a mother.

It was not a curse upon the Wherlockes or the Vaughns; it was bad choices, secrets, and attempting to hide amongst the people who had no strange gifts as if you were really one of them. Argus shook his head. There were a few good marriages in the clan amongst the previous generation, and he would be willing to bet that it came about in part because the truth was told before the vows were taken.

He did not like to think about how long he had clung to the idea of a curse. It was embarrassing now that he sat and actually thought it out. Worse, he had left Lorelei to think that he saw what they shared as no more than an affair. That was something he would have to deeply apologize for.

It was also embarrassing to think he had to see her on the ground bleeding before he understood what she meant to him. He had even just silently accepted her words of love when they had made love, as if somehow they were his due. Something else he would have to apologize deeply for, as it must have hurt her.

Sitting back and putting his feet up on the bed, Argus watched her sleep. She was beautiful to him in so many ways he feared he might get maudlin if he tried to list them. The biggest thing was that she accepted him for all he was, just as she accepted his family. She even accepted Darius and Olwen. Leopold was right; Iago was right; every one of his family who had talked to him was right. He was an idiot.

Well, no more, he decided. He needed to get a few things sorted out, but then he was coming after Lorelei. Argus thought it a little amusing that after she had given him her innocence and whispered her love several times he was now feeling nervous about trying to offer her his.

A soft moan from the bed tore him from his thoughts and he leaned over her again. Argus cursed when he saw the little flags of red on her cheeks. He touched her forehead and cursed again. The fever was coming on. Stefan had helped ease the bleeding and the pain, but it would take some hard work to banish the fever.

He rang for Vale and ordered the woman to bathe Lorelei's face with a cool cloth. Argus brushed a kiss over Lorelei's forehead and, as he pulled back, was startled to see her eyes open. She gave him a smile that was a weak shadow of the one he loved to see.

"Only the bad men died, right?" she asked.

"Right," he replied. "Everyone else is hale save for you and poor Old James."

"Ah, yes, poor Old James. He was such a nice man. You should probably not get too close to me as I am feeling rather poorly."

"Lorelei, Cornick stuck a knife in your back, remember?"

"Oh, of course. I can feel that wound. No, it is the rest of me that is feeling very poorly. Is that because of the wound? Do I have a fever then?"

There was a slight hint of panic in her weak, husky voice, and he brushed his hand over her hair. "A touch, that is all. I am about to go and find someone to help with that. It came on suddenly, so I suspect it will leave just as suddenly, especially with a little help from my family. Vale is here and she will bathe your face, mayhap your arms too, in cool water and that will make you feel better. As you and Max told me often enough, rest. That is the best cure."

"You will be back?" she asked even as her eyes closed, but her hand tightened around his with a good strong grip.

"Yes, I will be back."

Argus hurried out of the room and ran down the stairs. It was not just the fever that worried Argus, but the fact that Lorelei had it when she had not had any time to regain her strength after such a wound and the blood loss. He intended to go to the duke's library to write a few messages to some of the more experienced healers in his family when he nearly ran into the man.

"There is a visitor for you in the parlor," the duke said and grabbed him by the arm to steer him that way.

"I was going to send out messages for a few of my family."

"Healers?" asked the duke as he stopped abruptly and looked at Argus. "Why the running? She has grown worse?"

"She is already showing signs of a fever. I think it might be because she lost so much blood. Vale is bathing her down with some cool water right now, but I wanted to get one of our stronger healers here as soon as possible."

"Well, first come and see if what you want is already here."

Argus stepped into the parlor behind the duke and nearly cheered when he saw the two people who stood up to bow to the duke as Argus hastily introduced him. "Septimus, Delmar, I am so glad you have come." He glanced at Stefan, who shook his head, then looked back at Septimus. "How did you know?"

"Chloe sent word that you might need us and told us to come here. She was very persistent," said Septimus.

"You know what our trouble is?" asked the duke as he wandered over to look at the food Max had set out for the guests and helped himself to a small cake.

"Someone is hurt and ill," replied Septimus, and then he looked at Argus. "She said we must come and help you or you will be lost, but you look quite hale to me."

"I am, but Lady Lorelei, the duke's daughter, is

not." Argus briefly explained the situation and tried not to flush beneath the intent and slightly amused look Septimus was giving him.

"Then we shall all go and see what we can do. Delmar and I have discovered that, by working together, we can ease a lot of pain and cure serious injuries or disease without hurting ourselves. I think that, together, we ought to be able to suit all her needs."

"Do you mind if I watch?" asked the duke.

Argus noticed the unease Septimus and Delmar could not hide. "It is fine. Truly. The man knows a lot about us and I trust him."

Within moments they were in Lorelei's room and Argus had to stand aside as Stefan, Delmar, and Septimus encircled the bed. He quietly ordered Vale to leave, knowing the woman was the type to become upset by some of the things she might see. Standing beside the duke, Argus watched as his cousins touched Lorelei, stroked her brow, and fought to heal her.

"Knife was dirty," said Delmar.

"Very dirty," agreed Septimus. "Infection has already begun and the fever is because she is fighting it tooth and nail."

"Deep wound, so the infection goes deep, too."

Argus listened to the three talk as they kept their eyes closed and their hands on her. Septimus had clearly been training young Delmar, and that was what Stefan needed. Since they lived in the same house, the youth needed to pick himself up and ask for the training. He suspected he would now, for he had badly wanted to do more for Lorelei.

When they were done, all three looked a little pale as they stood by while the duke went to stroke his daughter's forehead. Argus desperately wanted to do

the same, but knew he had to wait his turn this time.
The soft look on the duke's face as he stroked Lorelei's
hair told him that, for now, the father needed to be
with her.

She was sleeping so peacefully that they all stepped
out of the room to talk only to find the hallway
crowded with boys, a few adult women, and a few girls
who were either just out of the schoolroom or soon
would be. Some standing, some sitting on the floor.
Argus even saw his sons sitting with the twins, Axel
and Wolfgang. The duke just smiled at them all.

"She is much better. These fine young men have
come to help heal her," the duke said and made a
gentle shooing motion with his hands. "No need to
lurk out here. Now I have to get these young men
something to eat and drink for their kindness in
coming all this way to help us." He looked at Aunt
Gretchen. "You know what rooms are empty, do you
not? Or who to ask? We shall need a room for these
fellows."

Aunt Gretchen hurried off to see to the sleeping
arrangements and the others soon dispersed. Argus
decided that Sundun House was like a small village.
He wondered if the duke knew how to say no.

"She is healed now?" asked the duke as they all
went down the stairs to the parlor.

"Not quite, Your Grace," said Septimus. "She is
healing. You may have heard us say that there was
some dirt or the like on the knife he used and that is
now deep in the wound. It and the fever have weakened, retreated a little if you will, but they will try to
come back depending on her state of health before
the attack. We can better judge then how long she
may take to fully recover."

"I suppose it should not surprise me that a man like Cornick did not even keep his weapons clean." The duke shook his head as they all found seats in the parlor, where food and drink awaited the healers. "Eat, eat. I have learned from Stefan that it is needed. So what happens now?"

"We shall keep an eye on her, and at the first sign of the fever returning we will do it again. And again. Until all the poison bleeding into her wound, and through her wound into the rest of her, is gone."

Argus listened to them talk about the wound for a while and then quietly slipped away. He had to be with her, had to watch her, as if his presence would keep the danger of such a wound away. It was foolishness, but it was not something he could fight.

"Your Grace, if you would excuse my impertinence . . ." began Septimus.

"Son, I was a father by the time I was fifteen and have sired seventeen children. I hear impertinence all the time."

"Very well then. How do you feel about Sir Argus and your daughter, Your Grace?"

"Ah, been sent to gather some information, have you?"

"Some. Mostly to heal. It was our cousin Chloe speaking of how Argus would be lost if we did not get down here to heal someone. Watching him look at your daughter made me certain who that someone is, but he is only a knight while she is . . ."

"My daughter. Yes, I am well aware of it. I do not care whom any of my children marry so long as the match is right for them. I do believe Sir Argus is right for Lorelei. She certainly thinks so and that is more important. I think that, somewhere between the kidnapping of my daughter and the knife shoved into her back, your cousin had an epiphany."

"Ah, yes, the marriage-to-a-Wherlocke-or-Vaughn curse. I am pleased that he appears to have shaken that off his shoulders. None of us plan to repeat those mistakes. Secrecy, Your Grace. Many of them did not tell their spouses exactly what they were until they had to explain why the children were so different. It is obvious that those secrets are not hidden here."

"No, I have raised my children to be rational, open-minded, ready for new things. They will be a match as surely as I am a duke."

"And your certainty is such that you allow him to go to her bedchamber?"

"She is three and twenty, and your cousin is the very first man she has ever had any real interest in. Her eyes shine when she speaks his name. A wise man does not get in the way of that shine."

Argus sat down by Lorelei's bed and took her hand in his. She was sleeping peacefully, a hint of healthy color in her cheeks. He kissed her hand, grateful for the sight of her even breathing. The boys would heal her. He knew it might take several times, for fever and infection were tough enemies, but they would do it. Now he had to plan what he needed to do.

"You will heal," he told her. "And we will celebrate your good health in the apple orchard."

"Rogue," she whispered, but her eyes only fluttered for a moment and he knew she was more asleep than awake.

"You inspire me."

"Do I? How lovely. I will have a big scar on my back now."

"I will kiss it." He was pleased to see her sleepy smile. "Rest, Lorelei. Even with healers here to help fight that fever, you will need a lot of rest."

"I know. Thank them for me, please."

"I will, and your father already has."

And that easy acceptance of the fact that his cousins had healed her with their touch was one reason he knew he would be a fool to let her go, no matter how disparate their births and financial situations. When her hand went completely limp in his, Argus knew she had gone back to sleep and tucked her hand under the blanket. The sun shone through the window of her bedchamber, shining on her glorious hair, and he knew he had to do all he could so that he could be privileged to see that sight every morning for the rest of his life.

Chapter 19

"Left? What do you mean he has left?"

Lorelei wondered if she sounded as confused, outraged, and uncertain to Olympia as she did to herself. She was finally feeling almost completely healed after two long weeks. She knew it was only due to the help of Septimus, Delmar, and Stefan that it had taken just two weeks, but she was tired of spending day and night in her bedchamber. She had a lot of guests as everyone in Sundun House and an assortment of Wherlockes and Vaughns meandered in to speak to her, but she was able to walk around now and the man she wanted to walk with was gone. The way he had stayed near her bedside while she was so ill, talking to her, reading to her, and kissing her forehead just before she went to sleep, had made her hopes for the future soar.

And now he was gone, without any explanation. It was as if he saw that she was all healed from the wound his enemy had inflicted upon her and decided his job was done. So he left to go and do whatever it was he did. Yet, why was his family still wandering around? she asked herself.

"You are working yourself up into a state of nerves for nothing," said Olympia. "He had a lot he needed to do because he had sat around here for a fortnight, watching you like a hawk to be sure you healed."

That was true. Almost every time she had opened her eyes he had been there. She had not even seen her father as much as she had seen Argus. Along with the other things he had done for her, he had spoon-fed her, bathed her forehead with cool water, and just kept her company. She did not think she had seen him so much since the first two days when she had rescued him and brought him here to Sundunmoor. She supposed that was why his desertion was such a shock.

No, she told herself firmly, it was not a desertion. He just had things he had to do. Olympia was right. The man had not done the things that earned him a living since the night he had been abducted by Cornick. For all of his reading and being lost in his own little world, her father put a lot of work into keeping them all housed, clothed, and fed. As he liked to say, the wood sprites do not print money, one has to actually do something to get it.

"I am certain I heard him mention that he had some work that he needed to do," said Olympia.

"You are right, for now that I think back, he did mention that. He just did not say what he needed to work on and I think I just assumed he meant around here."

"Oh, no, he is in London."

Lorelei tried to ignore the painful twinge in her heart when Olympia mentioned that. She did not really like to think of Argus in London with all its experienced and beautiful women. A few days there and he would see her for the sheltered little country girl she was. It was too horrible a thought to contemplate, yet, now that it was in her head, she could not shake it out. All she could see in her mind's eye was Argus escorting some fashionable beauty through the streets of the city.

"If you are quite done imagining my brother involved in some sort of orgy with half a dozen London ladies, mayhap we should go for a walk. It will clear the nonsense from your head."

"Half a dozen? Surely you cannot, I mean, with half a dozen?"

Olympia shrugged, stood up, and brushed out her skirts. "I have heard that things can get very wild, very unseemly at an orgy."

"Just how is it that you have heard of orgies when I thought they were only done in Rome or Greece in the ancient days? I read about them in one of Father's books that he thinks are well hidden."

"Everything old becomes new again eventually. And anything old that concerns men slaking their lusts on a bunch of women, will continue to be reborn in one way or another. And it is never one, but always a bunch, for they do have delusions about their stamina."

"Ah, good point. Wicked little rotters," she mumbled as she stood up and was pleased to feel no dizziness. Those boys were true miracle workers. "It would serve men right if women decided they should have themselves an orgy or two."

Olympia paused at the door. "Oh, what a lovely idea."

"I was jesting, using a hypothetical comparison, if you will."

"Still, what an intriguing thought. An orgy for women where the women decide which men may be invited and they are all up for grabs and bound to do as we insist."

Lorelei frowned as she tugged on her boots. "Odd. Just a while ago I would have been plotting away with you, but now it does not hold much interest."

"That is because you are madly in love with my brother."

"I would not say madly," Lorelei protested as she followed Olympia out of the room. "And, well, I have a bit more information now, shall we say, and I am not sure I would like so many seeing me naked. On the other hand, there are some very pretty men. . . . Oh, what am I saying . . . ?" She shook her head. "You can drag me into the most ridiculous, and usually improper, conversations."

"But those are the best kind."

"What are the best kind?" asked Septimus as he stepped out of the parlor just as they were walking toward the steps that led to the front door.

"Improper conversations," replied Olympia.

"Ah, may I join in?"

"You are too young."

"I am as old as Lady Lorelei."

"Women mature faster than men, who stay little boys until they are into their thirties. And then only for a short while as they begin to turn back until they are little boys again by the time they are in their fifties. This is a known fact. So, you may join us during that short interlude when you are a full adult."

Septimus laughed and kissed her cheek. "You are a wretch." He then looked at Lorelei. "Feeling stronger?"

"Much stronger. I needed to get out of that room. I think that, if you had not aided me in healing and I had had to stay abed for the full time, I should be drooling mad by the time I left." She smiled when he laughed.

"So you are going for a walk," he said. "Might I join you for at least part of it?"

"Of course," Lorelei replied, "but why only part of it?"

"I have to go into the village because there is a woman there who is having a difficult birth. Your father asked me to meet him there. I gather the woman is important to him?"

"Papa does not believe we know, but she was his mistress a few years ago."

"So not his child then."

"No. Papa told my older brothers that one must be very careful when bedding the lasses and try to keep his seed from taking root. He then went on and told them the many ways, stressing the one that will also protect them from the pox."

"I cannot believe he would have such a discussion with his sons with you sitting there."

"No, had my ear pressed up against the keyhole. Then Max caught me, so I did not hear any more of it. Max told me later that, since my father understands boys very well, having been one himself, the latter part of the talk is all about the worst of the nasty diseases you can catch if you are not careful." She smiled when Olympia and Septimus laughed. "He must have been very convincing because for several months afterward, all Philip, the heir who is second in line, could talk about was how he was sure he had a calling to serve God and maybe he should join the church. Papa had to inform him that, unless he became a Catholic, that would make little difference as there would be no vows of celibacy. He persisted for a little longer, but then he met the milkmaid."

They stepped outside to a lovely summer day and started walking, talking nonsense most of the way. It lightened Lorelei's spirit, which she suspected was their intent. Although it was somewhat embarrassing to have her feelings read so easily, she was grateful for the company. She just wondered how long Argus intended to be gone but did not want to ask.

"It will be a month tomorrow, Olympia. He is not coming back."

Lorelei wondered if her heart had turned to stone it was so heavy in her chest, but the pain it gave her told her that was not possible. It might be preferable, she thought morosely. There had been no word from Argus either, not even a brief note hoping that her health had continued to improve.

She had failed, she thought as she slumped down in the chair in the morning room. She had tried so hard to make him see that she would love him and never leave him and had failed to win his heart. Obviously, she should never take up gambling, she decided.

"Perhaps you should go for a walk," said Olympia, not even looking up from the intricate embroidery design she was working on. "The rain is gone and the sun is shining. Mayhap that will cheer you."

Lorelei doubted it, but she knew she was poor company at the moment so she left. It did not surprise her to find herself in her special spot in the orchard. Here was where she felt close to Argus, here where they had first made love. She had had such hopes then, such dreams. They were all crumbling to dust, she decided as she sat down and slumped against the tree trunk.

"Lolly!"

She peered through the leaves and caught Darius and Olwen headed her way. That was one thing that had kept her hopes alive. Argus would not leave his children behind, and they showed no inclination to return to Radmoor. The only ones who had left were Iago and Leopold, who had a great deal of work to do, and most of it very secret from what little she could discern. She quickly moved out of her hiding place and waved at the boys.

"You truly like it here?" asked Darius as he frowned and looked around.

Lorelei looked at the place through his eyes. It was a tangle, the trees overgrown and little care taken of the shrubs and grasses that grew up around them. She liked the wildness of the place, however. It was as nature had intended it, compared to the very neat orchard that led up this corner.

"It is mine so, yes, I like it." She smiled at the boys. "Can I help you with something?"

"Your papa said that you used to collect all types of rocks," said Olwen, "and we were wondering if they had been thrown away or if you knew where they had been stored."

"I believe they are in a large blue trunk in the east-wing attics. My name is on it in bright red paint. You are interested in rocks?"

"Some, because I think each one is different, but

Darius is not so sure. I thought the ones you collected would prove I am right."

"I suspect they will. I can come and help you find them, if you want."

"No, it would not be good for you to climb up into the attics and move trunks and such around."

"Oh, I am all healed from the knife wound and quite strong."

"Not that," said Darius. "It could hurt the babe."

"Excuse me?"

Lorelei had heard exactly what the boy had said, but she did not want to believe it. Her mind grasped frantically for some fact that would utterly disprove it and all she got was a reminder of how she had missed her woman's time twice as of today. This could be a disaster.

"A babe, you said?" she asked Darius.

Olwen replied, "Aye, and actually it is two. Just like your papa had twins, so will you. But we will not say anything until you can tell our father."

She talked with them for a little while longer, although she could not recall what she had said. The whole conversation had become a blur of words ever since she had heard the one word—babe. *But it will not be a babe*, she thought as she climbed back into her hidden corner of the orchard. *It will be two.*

At first she tried to deny it by pointing out it had been two beardless boys who had told her she was with child. Her mind refused to stop preying on the matter, however. It reminded her of her nausea in the morning just yesterday. She had thought it was a lingering remnant of her illness, but it fit into the little notch in her mind now labeled baby.

"Oh, I am so doomed," she moaned and flopped

onto her back to stare up at the sun from between the leaves.

Lorelei did not even want to think of what her father would do. He was the sweetest of men, but, as had been proven by all the trouble with Cornick, he could be pushed only so far and then you met the eighth Duke of Sundunmoor and not Roland or Papa. He would never stand for his daughter to bear a child outside of wedlock, not when he probably knew exactly who the father was.

She wanted Argus to be hers more than she wanted her next breath, but she did not want him dragged into her arms. That was what would happen if Max and her father discovered she was carrying Argus's child, or, rather, children. There had to be a way out of this. She had some time before the whole of Sundunmoor would begin to guess her condition, for it was hardly a rare one in the house. If she tried real hard, she told herself, she would find a solution that did not force the man she loved to marry her when he did not want to. That way laid utter disaster. In truth, it would probably prove his theory that marriages in his family were cursed.

Argus straightened his clothes and rapped on the door of the duke's library. He was as nervous as a young boy approaching his first girl. That was ridiculous, but, no matter how many times he told himself that, he remained nervous.

"Well," said the duke as Argus stepped inside in answer to his invite, "you clean up well. Where have you been for a month then? Come." He waved toward the chair in front of his desk. "Sit down, sit down."

"I have been in London for most of this time, Your Grace," he said as the duke poured them both some wine. "There were a few things that needed clearing away concerning that Cornick business. Investigating to be sure everyone involved was rooted out. Only two others and they were very minor players. They will be taking a sojourn in Canada, sent off by their fathers to avoid scandal and, perhaps, knock some sense into them. Fathers both have land there."

"So, it was really just Cornick and Chuffington?"

"And those two brutes from the docks. Seems they had worked for Chuffington before. The man will hang and not just for what happened here. More and more is coming to light to reveal that he had a way of getting rid of those who annoyed him."

The duke shook his head. "And to think he had the resources of the government to aid him in his petty vendettas. I can see why you were away for so long, but your boys had a grand time here."

"I am sure. They have become quite good friends with Wolfgang and Axel, God help us all." He smiled when the duke laughed. "But I was also doing a lot of work in getting my affairs together."

"Going somewhere?"

"I hope not, Your Grace." He set his papers on the duke's desk. "I mean to marry your daughter, but I realize, that as only a knight, I am not of a rank with her. However, I do believe I can support her well."

Roland listened as the younger man talked of property he now owned, his finances and investments, and hinted at his work for the government. He did not tell him that he knew some of that already, for, as soon as he had seen what was developing between his daughter and Sir Argus Wherlocke, he had done his best to find out as much as he could. Having members of the man's family as guests for so long had also helped. He firmly believed you could tell a lot about a man by studying his family.

The older Wherlockes had had a lot of miserable marriages, but so far the younger ones had done much, much better. Roland suspected it was because they learned from the mistakes of the fathers. Deserted or abandoned children littered the landscape of the Wherlocke and Vaughn past, but the boys Argus had sired when he had been not much more than a boy himself were well taken care of and being given all the benefits of their class.

He had also found very few criminals in the family tree and that, considering the gifts they all had, was nearly a miracle. Max had found nothing either, except that they had a very select group of servants, mostly from just two families, and they treated them very well. That was only in the younger man's favor as well.

What he was not hearing was how Sir Argus Wherlocke felt about Lorelei. The girl had been shuffling about the house pretending she was not unhappy and Roland was tired of it. He would not, however, force her to marry a man who did not care for her.

Then something Argus said made him blink in surprise. "You bought the very house where you were kept prisoner?"

"Yes. It was for sale at a very reasonable price. It is actually a very sturdy house, with, as my man puts it, very good bones. It is being repaired, cleaned, and painted as we speak. I thought that Lorelei would like to be close to her family. I also have several relatives within a day's journey from there."

"Not worried about bad memories?"

"No." Argus smiled. "As I am hoping to be living there with a new wife, I suspect I can find ways to push them aside if they intrude. I just do not see them doing so. I associate the bad memories with the men who inflicted the injuries and they are all dead."

The duke leaned forward, resting his elbows on his desk and clasping his hands together. "That is all very impressive, Sir Argus, but, to be blunt, so long as she will not starve, I am not much interested in the financial side of my daughter's future husband. I want her happy. I want her to have children who are happy because their parents are. I want her husband to have true affection for her, for Lorelei needs that."

"I know, Your Grace." Argus cleared his throat, unaccustomed to speaking of his feelings, especially in front of the father of the woman he wanted. "I love your daughter, Your Grace. I fought it, ignored it, and argued it away, but none of that did any good. I love her and I believe she loves me."

"If the amount of sulking she has done in the last few weeks is any indication, then I suspect she does. Now, you being a London man, and clearly no saint, I must ask—what about faithfulness? I know many men think they have some right to have a mistress or two as well as the wife, but that brings only misery or bitterness. I do not think I have seen many couples where both sides are content with it."

"When I take my vows, Your Grace, I will abide by them. If I thought I could not, then I would never take them. Personally, I have never understood men who make a vow to a woman before God, the vicar, and a few hundred guests and then, as soon as the heir is born, go about their business as if they were not married. It is not just the mistress, is it? It is an utter disrespect for the person who just gave you a child. It shows the woman, most clearly, that you married her for her breeding to pass on to your child, her money, or her property."

"That is what is behind many marriages."

"I know, but it also reveals that the man, or woman depending on who breaks those vows, had no intention of honoring his vows or even trying to have a decent marriage. It reveals a deceitful nature and, as I said, disrespect for the woman."

Roland sat back in his seat and looked at the man who would certainly become his son-in-law shortly. "I have always thought the same. Well, there is one last thing."

"And what is that?"

"You have to convince Lorelei and she is not in the best of temper at the moment. A note or letter might have been welcome."

"I told her I had a lot of things that needed to be worked on."

"Day and night for a month?"

Argus grimaced. "There was some traveling to do."

"To your new home barely a day's ride from here?"

"Damn. I did not wish to come back here until I had everything in order, until I could prove that I could give her a good life," Argus said. "She is so high above me in rank that I had to have something to show you that would tell you that I can care for her and any children we have. I had to show her and you that I was not marrying her for anything else but her, as I had all I needed already."

"Argus, and may I call you that now that we are soon to be related by marriage?" When Argus nodded, Roland continued, "My daughter is very similar to her mother, a woman I sorely miss. She thinks too much. I know it is odd to hear this from me, but, while I think on whether there is any sense to the cuckoo laying its eggs in another's nest, Lorelei is thinking, why has he not returned yet, why has he not at least written me? Then they snub you, or sulk alone and think the worst things about you. Last thing I heard was that you were at some orgy with a half-dozen females." He grinned when Argus choked on his wine. "You can blame that on your sister, who seems quite fond of conversations about utterly irrelevant things. But, back to what my child is now thinking. London is full of beautiful women, she thinks. All those beautiful women, will naturally want you because you are not here. Are you beginning to understand?"

"Very much so. I have left her uncertain of me and that cannot continue. As I said, I but wished to have everything in order when we had this talk. I believe I can get her to understand the importance of that, at least the importance of it for me."

"I certainly understand." He smiled at Argus. "It will help your cause a great deal if you utter some pretty words. Lorelei is sharp of wit, but she is also very soft of heart. Do not think I mean that she will be ever demanding flatteries and assurances. But, right now, with you having been gone for a month with no word, she is not sure of herself as a woman and not sure of you.

"Lorelei never showed an interest in any man until you. She was polite to, danced with, and even kissed a few, but there was no real interest. I saw the interest in you from the first moment she spoke your name. It sounds foolish, but there was a shine in her eyes when she spoke of you. I stepped back and let matters take their course. Do not think I did not notice what went on. I chose not to interfere. Max also chose not to interfere. So not only do you have to deal with a woman who might be irritated that you disappeared for a month, but also you have one who, I believe, finally thought of herself as a woman, and now she is questioning that. So"—he waved a hand at Argus—"go and fix it."

"Now I am duly intimidated," said Argus as he stood up. "May I leave these papers here?"

"Of course. Big wedding or small wedding? In other words, quick or slow?"

"I am sure you will understand if I say I prefer quick. I have been without her for a month. But I will bow to what she wishes."

The moment Argus was gone Roland rang for Max and smiled when the man entered only a moment later, revealing that he had probably been listening at the door. "So, he is back." He patted the papers on his desk. "Brought everything to show he can support her well and has even bought a place not far from here—the very one he was held prisoner in. Now he just has to convince her."

"I think she ought to make him suffer some. He should have at least written a letter or two."

"Max, you are one of the few men I know who enjoys writing letters. But, yes, he should have to grovel a bit if only because he did not reassure her before he left. I think we may be having a wedding very soon."

"Oh? Why do you think that?"

"Heard his sons talking as they headed for the attics in the east wing. One reason I was so pleased the fellow came back and acted like the gentleman he is."

"Your Grace?"

"It seems my daughter who is not yet married is presenting young Darius and Olwen with twin siblings in less than eight months." He laughed and poured Max a drink when the man sank down into the chair. "Do not worry, Max. Our Lolly will be fine. But, most important of all, she will be happy. The young fool loves her."

"I heard. It is past time he recognized it."

"At least he has, Max. And he will be making my child a very happy woman." He held up his own drink, clinked his glass against Max's in a silent toast, and drank to the future of his favorite daughter.

Chapter 20

"I will not cry anymore," said Lorelei as she stared up at the sunny sky through the leaves of her favorite tree.

It was a foolish promise because she suspected she would break it before the day ended. Night was the worst time for trying to hold to such a vow. She would lie in her bed painfully alone, aching for Sir Argus Wherlocke, needing his warmth at her side. Then the regrets and the questions would begin, pounding in her head and stealing her sleep. Regrets for the loss of something so wonderful, something she needed so badly, and questions about why she had failed to make him love her. The answers brought the bitter taste of failure, and then she would cry. She always cried. It was beginning to make her very angry.

Perhaps it is the anger I should cling to, she thought. Anger was so much sweeter than regret and failure. Anger did not cause people to look at her with pity or try to talk to her, cheer her, or encourage her. Anger would make people leave her alone and, at this moment, she rather liked the idea of being alone in her misery.

For a moment, she tried to convince herself that Argus was just acting like a man, that he did not like writing and had not given any thought to how much time had passed. It did not work, just as it had not worked for the last fortnight. Olympia could convince her for a short time that Argus would be back, but the moment she left or even just stopped speaking, the doubt was back.

"And I am so weary of doubting," she muttered.

Now she had to concern herself with the fact that she was carrying Argus's child. *Children,* she corrected and nearly groaned. It was no true surprise that she was carrying twins as her father had produced several sets of them. Without the father of her children standing by her side, however, she was both saddened and alarmed by the news that she would soon be a mother.

There would be no salvaging her reputation then. For once, Vale would be correct to say her reputation was utterly destroyed. The rest of her days would be spent as the ruined daughter of the duke, the daughter who was remaining appropriately secluded and living off his largesse. Lorelei did not even want to consider how her children would suffer for being born on the wrong side of the blanket. Being the grandsons of the duke, and she knew her father would not hesitate to recognize them as such, would not really save her children from the scorn and unkind whispers that would follow them all their lives.

That was, of course, if her father was not hanged for killing Sir Argus Wherlocke. Lorelei grimaced at the mere thought of her father's fury. There might be some disappointment revealed for the way she had behaved, but she knew most of her father's anger was going to fall on Argus's head. The hurt part of her wanted that, but her heart did not want the man it loved hurt. Certainly not by the other man she loved dearly.

The sweet song of a robin drew her attention from her dark thoughts, and she studied the little bird with its bright breast for a moment. Birds did not have trouble with men. They found a mate in the spring, raised their family, and then, next spring, found another. So beautifully simplistic. Lorelei wished people could be that way, but people had hearts that got in the way of such rational simplicity. They made rules and laws, and had morals, or at least pretended to. They also did not have to worry about the trouble their father might get into if he decided honor demanded he shoot the rogue who despoiled his daughter.

"Do you know, Master Robin, mayhap the solution to my trouble is to load Papa's pistols and shoot the miserable, rutting swine myself?"

Argus frowned as he heard Lorelei discuss his murder at her hands with, if he was not mistaken, a bird. This did not bode well for his carefully planned talk of marriage. Her father was right. He would have to try and soothe a lot of troubled waters.

"It is good of a daughter to want to take such a burden off a father's hands," he said as he slipped into her hiding place. "I, on the other hand, would like it if you gave the miserable rutting swine a chance to explain himself."

Lorelei looked at the man she loved and had the

strongest urge to get up and kick him. Several times. Her heart leapt with joy, but her mind demanded some answers. For all the time he had been at Sundunmoor she had been the one in pursuit, although she liked to think she had been subtle about it. She would not leap into his arms now, not after a month with no word, and show him just how delighted her heart was to have him back before he had even attempted to apologize for his neglect.

"Have you come by to collect your family?" she asked as she sat up, frowning when he sat down right next to her without being invited to.

"I did not know they were still here."

Oddly enough, his apparent ignorance of his family's presence pleased her, if only because it proved they were not the reason he was back at Sundunmoor. "They have not left. Oh, Iago and Leopold did, but your sister, Septimus, Delmar, and your sons are still here. Bened was until yestereve, but that was because he was entertaining the widow Morris. Obviously, the entertaining has ended."

"Bened? Huh. I had not seen him as a man for the ladies."

"Perhaps it runs in the blood."

Lorelei wanted to kick herself now. There had been unmistakable jealousy behind those words. There was the touch of a gleam of amusement in his eyes, but he had the sense not to smile. Lorelei had to fight hard to cling to a sense of anger and outrage over being ignored for so long just to smother the blush that threatened to bloom on her cheeks.

"It may, but most Wherlockes and Vaughns cast such reckless behavior aside when they meet the woman they are fated for."

Argus thought that a nice, romantic statement, but the woman he loved eyed him with suspicion. He cautiously reached out and took her hands in his. He wanted to take her fully into his arms, but, although she did not yank her hands free of his, she sat tense and unwelcoming as she watched him.

"Lorelei, I told you I had matters that needed attending to," he said.

"Yes, although you never did tell me what they were before you left so abruptly."

"I needed to go and see the man I work for in the government to settle the last of that business with Cornick. There were questions to be answered and more men to arrest. Then I set about the business of settling my own affairs."

"Your business," she said, reminding herself that a man had to do something to earn his money, even if all it consisted of was collecting rents and seeing that the harvest was good.

"Yes, my business. To sort out my finances and set them in order, to see that the house in London is soon to be ready to be lived in, and to find myself a house in the country. I bought that deserted manor I spent so much time in as Cornick's guest."

"You did what? Why would you want to buy that place unless it was to burn it to the ground?"

"The house did nothing to me. Cornick was the cause of my misery there. It is a good house, solid, sturdy, and with some very fine lands attached, lands that can be made profitable. The man who owned it, Cornick's brother, was more than happy to have it taken off his hands. I could have played on his belief that it was a weight, producing little income, but I fear I looked at the fool and was sorry that he had been cursed with such a brother, one who had now thoroughly blackened the family name. We agreed to a price that was both fair to him and affordable for me. I have been having it repaired for a fortnight now and it is nearly ready to be lived in."

Lorelei was not sure she could abide him living so close at hand if he did not want her to live with him. Yet, she also could not believe he would be so cruel. A little spark of hope bloomed in her heart and refused to be vanquished by the hard cold fact that he had not yet mentioned what, if anything, he intended to do with her now that he had so nicely sorted out his lands and finances.

"So you will be close at hand," she said.

"Lorelei, I did all this for one reason. I wanted to show your father that I could care for you, financially, as you ought to be cared for. I wanted him to see that, although I am not as highborn as you, I can both support you and house you in a fine manner."

"Argus, I cannot be your mistress."

She halted when he placed one long finger against her lips. He looked both dismayed and a little irritated. Lorelei was not sure, but she had the distinct feeling that he was insulted but did not blame her for the insult.

"I would never ask you to come and live with me at Tandem House to be my mistress. I would never shame you so before your family, many of whom live close at hand, although the way I have behaved since meeting you undoubtedly allows you to think I could do so. I am bungling this, but my hope is that you will come to live there with me as my wife."

It was what she had wanted from the start. Lorelei knew that her heart was dancing in her chest in utter joy, for it beat so hard she was amazed he showed no sign of hearing it, but her mind forced her to hesitate. Where were the words of caring, the words of love and passion? He spoke of housing her, of having enough money to please her father despite the fact that society would see him as reaching very high above his station for a wife.

Did he not know that such things did not matter to her? Or to her father? He had spent a lot of time with them all and should know what was important to her family, yet his words were all of practical matters. Unfortunately, she did not know how to get him to tell her what she needed to know, to let her see what was in his heart.

"Ah, you hesitate," Argus murmured and sighed. "I have made you angry. Lorelei, I did all that for me, not you. I did it all because I had to face your father with a full purse and property. I knew you would not care, and in many ways, knew your father would not care. *I* cared. *I* needed to prove to myself that I could care for you as you should be cared for.

"It is not just that your father is a duke and I am a knight, or that you would be a prize for men far higher placed than I. It is just that I did not want you to think I was asking you to be mine for any reason other than that I want you as my wife."

"Why?"

"What?"

"Why do you want me to be your wife?"

Argus stared at her. There was a hint of anxiousness in her voice and her face. He realized that she wanted to hear more than words concerning the state of his purse and his lands. Slowly he pulled her into his arms, ignoring the tension in her body.

"You are the only one I want to be my wife. That is the whole reason I went away to do those things. I erred in becoming so intent on that business that I never thought to send word to you, to let you know that you were still in my thoughts."

"It would have been nice to hear what you were doing from time to time," she said as she leaned her cheek against his chest, savoring the sound of the steady beat of his heart.

"I realize that, now that I have been made aware of how much time has passed, of how you may have thought yourself deserted." He placed his hands on either side of her face and turned it up to his. "I worked to get back here, worked unceasingly. I but ask that you forgive a man his pride, a pride that demanded I come to you with such things as money and lands."

"Argus." She blushed, the words she wanted to say sticking in her throat, and then stiffened her spine. "I appreciate the fact that you wish to keep me well housed and clothed, but I need more. I have offered you more a time or two, but you never responded, never indicated that it was what you wanted. But, you see, it is not only what I wish to give, it is what I need to get in return."

"Oh, I heard you whisper those beautiful words and I have held them close, greedily hoarding them, but I did not see myself as worthy of holding you for longer than a short time. Then I almost lost you, watched you lying there bleeding and knew there were words I needed to say to you, words I might never have the chance to say. It was then that I decided that I would get all I needed to present myself to your father as a good match. Mayhap not as high a standing as he could demand for you, but still a good match who could support you without trouble."

"So you waited until I healed and then left, never hinting that you intended to return and marry me?"

"Perhaps not the most well-thought-out plan of action," he muttered and then brushed a kiss over her lips, his whole body aching to take more. "I want you as my wife. I want to wake up beside you every morning. I want to make love to you every night. Name any way a man can want to hold fast to one woman and that is the way I want you. You are my sun, Lorelei," he said quietly. "I can see a future now and it holds only you. I love you." He frowned when tears filled her eyes.

"Oh, do not fret," she said and gently patted his cheek. "I but cry a little because I have wished to hear you say that for so very long."

Argus kissed her as he had been wanting to since he had first set eyes on her, devouring her mouth and reveling in the sweet heat of her kiss. The way her passion rose to meet his eased the last of his fears that he might not win her for his own. He had acted with unhesitating determination to get all he believed he needed to win her father's approval, but he admitted to himself now, that he had always been a little uncertain that he would be able to win hers.

"You truly love me?" asked Lorelei as she pushed against his chest until he was sprawled out beneath her. "Are you certain, Argus, for I ask a lot of the man I love aside from his saying he loves me."

Since Lorelei was busy taking his clothes off, Argus was not sure he had the wit to have any long, serious conversation with her. His body was almost embarrassingly eager for a taste of the desire it had been denied for too long. "What do you wish, my love? You have my devotion."

"And your passion."

"Oh, aye, you most definitely have that," he muttered as he unlaced her dress.

"And your respect." She scrambled out of his reach just long enough to pull his boots of and toss them aside.

"Always." He pulled her gown off over her head and threw it to the side, noting that the fine silk caught firmly on a bramble bush and thinking how that could cause them a problem later. Then he did the same to her shift.

"And your fidelity."

He realized that they were both naked. His thoughts immediately turned to all the things he wished to do to her beautiful skin, to her full breasts with their taut, inviting nipples, and to the downy, heated place between her slender thighs. She sat astride him and slowly unpinned her hair, the long thick locks falling down until they brushed against his thighs. He knew she had no idea of how beautiful she was.

"Always," he whispered as he slid his hands up her rib cage and over her breasts, teasing the nipples to an increased hardness with the tips of his fingers.

Lorelei placed her hands on his shoulders and stared into his eyes. "I mean it, Argus. I know how men think. Well, men outside of my family. They see naught wrong with a mistress or some tavern maid as a little treat when the mood strikes. I confess to you now that that would break my heart, crush me in a way I do not wish to think about."

"And you have no need to consider it. I will be faithful. My family may have a long history of disastrous marriages, but hardly any were destroyed because one of my family betrayed the marital bed. I would never ask you to marry me if I thought I might waver in that, might not love you enough to want no other." He frowned when she just smiled and kissed him. "You have not yet answered my proposal."

"No." Lorelei began to kiss her way down his strong chest, savoring the taste of him, the scent of his body filling her head and rousing her desire. "I believe I need to reacquaint myself with all the reasons why it might be best if I do marry you, the man I love and have thought of unceasingly for the last month. Not always in the kindest of terms."

Argus started to reply to that, only to have the words stick in his throat and come out as a growl when Lorelei nipped the inside of each of his thighs. He shuddered when she slowly dragged her tongue up the length of his manhood. Burying his fingers in her hair, he wildly wondered if this was her way of accepting his proposal. Then she took him into her mouth and he lost all ability to think clearly.

When he reached the point where he knew he could take no more, no matter how much he wanted to, he grabbed her under her arms and dragged her up until she straddled his body. Watching as she took him into her body, her glorious hair curling around her slim body as she lowered herself down on him, Argus did not think he had ever seen anything as beautiful or as arousing. He grasped her by the hips and aided her in moving as his body now demanded her to move, taking them both to the heights with a speed that was both exhilarating and disappointing, for he did not want the pleasure to end.

Lorelei slumped in his arms, her body still shivering from the force of the pleasure they had just shared. She sighed with regret when nature ended the closeness of their embrace, and Argus slipped free of her. Then again, she mused with a smile, people would not get much accomplished in life if nature did not put a stop to such delight once in a while.

Argus stroked her back, content to have her back in his arms, but his mind was demanding that he push her for a firm acceptance of his proposal. "Lorelei, you have not agreed to marry me yet."

"Ah, just let me affirm a few things," she said and setting her elbows on the ground on either side of his head, she propped her chin in her hands and kissed the tip of his nose. "I love you and you love me." She decided she really liked the way his eyes shone when she told him she loved him.

"Yes, very good reasons to get married."

"Especially considering that we have just proved that we share a very fine passion."

"And one I cannot wait to savor in the comfort of a bed," he drawled.

"And you have said you will be faithful as I intend to be faithful to you."

He grunted, not liking even the idea that she should be anything else but utterly faithful to him in word and deed. And in where she looked and what she thought. And, he decided, there should be no more talk of improper things like orgies with his irrepressible sister.

"Yes, we will be unfashionably faithful to each other."

"And we shall have children, correct? You do wish to have children with me, do you not?"

"Of course I do, but I do not demand that you give me a house full of them. You decide how many you wish."

"Oh, that is very fine of you to say, Argus. You shall have to tell me how one goes about ensuring they only have the exact number of children one chooses to have. A good time for that would be right after I finish having these."

He blinked and slowly sat up with her still in his arms. "I beg your pardon?"

Lorelei looped her arms around his neck. He looked so beautifully stunned. She smiled and brushed a kiss over his lips.

"The children I will give you in eight months, perhaps less. And 'ere you remark on the fact that I said children and not child, I have it on good authority that I shall bless you with twins."

Argus set her aside and scrambled for their clothes. "And you let me make love to you right out here, on the hard ground, and with a rough greed?"

"I do believe I was none too gentle with you either."

"I am not the one carrying two babes." He frowned as he started to assist her in getting dressed, fighting her obvious reluctance. "How do you know it will be two?"

"Darius and Olwen told me so." Her voice muffled by the dress he was yanking on over her head, she explained about the rocks, the trunk, and the attic. "Are you not pleased?" she asked when she could finally see him and saw him frowning at her.

"When did you plan to tell me?"

"What do you think I was out here talking to the birds about? As I just said, I only just found out myself and that had me thinking very hard."

"About shooting me."

Lorelei flung her arms around his neck and kissed his chin. "Have we not settled why I was thinking that? Why I was not sure if I should marry you?"

"God's tears, you would actually have refused my proposal if I had not said the right things?"

"Perhaps. For a little while in the hope that you would say what I needed eventually. Argus, there is no sense in going on and on about what I might or might not have done. I do not know and I am very glad that I shall not have to face that decision. I was sure that I wanted a father for my children and I wanted a willing one, not one dragged before a vicar by the ear or with a gun pressed to his head. I have that, do I not?"

"You do." He kissed her, trying to convey all the love he felt for her, and all the joy that suddenly filled him at the thought of the children she would soon give him. "Aye, my sweet Lorelei, you do."

"Then why are we sitting here with all our clothes back on?"

He grinned. "I thought we might wander back to the house and allow your father and the rest of the family congratulate us on our engagement."

"They are not going anywhere." She tried to pull him down to the ground. "They can wait. I have not seen you for a month."

"Ah, my sweet eager love, how I would enjoy giving you what we both want." He stood up and pulled her to her feet. "But, I do believe we need to plan a wedding. A very quick wedding."

Lorelei was not pleased to leave the shade of the trees, to leave the privacy she knew would be very difficult to find once they told everyone of their engagement, but Argus was right. They needed to plan the wedding and it needed to be a quick one. When they reached the house and stepped inside to find both her and his family filling the entry hall, she laughed. She could foresee a grand life ahead for her and Argus, one filled to the rafters with love and family. As she accepted the hugs and congratulations of everyone gathered there, she winked at Argus and was pleased when he smiled back at her.

A few moments later Argus managed to grasp a brief moment with Lorelei with no one standing right at hand. "I have a feeling I will be allowed to see very little of you for the next three weeks."

She stood up on her tiptoes and kissed him. "But then I will be all yours, Argus, and you will be all mine. Is that not wonderful?"

Argus looked down into her smiling face and felt himself smile back in a besotted way that would have shocked his friends and family. "Aye, my love, it is wonderful."

Epilogue

One year later

"Greetings, Max."

Max stepped up to Lorelei and carefully looked over the child she held in her arms, touching the child's thick raven curls with a gentle hand. He did the same with the child held by the gently rounded nurse standing beside Lorelei.

"M'lady. Sir," he said and bowed, and then he looked at Lorelei and nodded. "Well done, m'lady. Well done, indeed."

Lorelei looked at Argus, her smile so wide and bright he wondered if it hurt. She had been nervous for the entire journey to Sundunmoor and he had not understood why. Her father had written every week since the twins had been born, wondering when he would be able to see his new grandsons. He could not believe she feared her father would be disappointed in her children. Now he began to understand. It was not her father she was worried about, for even Lorelei at her most doubtful had never, and would never, doubt that man's love or acceptance. There was a little girl inside his wife who had still been anxious to win Max's approval of, as she liked to tell him, the nearest thing to a miracle she has ever accomplished.

"I got a nod, Argus," she said.

"As you well deserve, my love," he replied and kissed her forehead.

"Where are my grandsons?" demanded Roland as he hurried over to them and stopped to stare at the babies. "Oh, they are fine, healthy lads, Lolly. Fine healthy lads." He held out his arms. "May I hold one? Aunt Gretchen twisted her ankle last week and cannot rush here as she wishes, so I thought I would take one of the babes to the parlor."

Lorelei placed her firstborn son in her father's arms and watched as he walked away, silently counting the steps he took. At number five, her second-born son started to fuss. Miss Jones began to follow her father, careful to keep exactly five steps behind him, even closer if she could. Finally her father stopped and looked at the woman.

"They cannot be separated, can they?" he said. "You are the nurse?"

Miss Jones blushed and curtseyed. "I am Miss Jones, yes, Your Grace. And, no, Your Grace. No more than five paces, or one or the other begins to fuss."

Lorelei watched her father look at the plump woman she had hired to help her with the twins and knew what he saw. He saw a not-plain-but-not-beautiful woman who was still young in his eyes, but definitely considered a spinster by the rest of the world. A woman with wide brown eyes and wild reddish brown hair who had so much kindness in it glowed in her face. For just a moment, Lorelei saw the look of a man's interest in her father's eyes, a shine. Then he grinned and she tensed.

"Only five paces, is it?"

It did not surprise her when her father hastily trotted down the hall, putting at least ten paces between him and Miss Jones. The whimpering began but did not last long, for Miss Jones chased after the duke until she stood within the distance acceptable to her sons. Then her father trotted away again. Lorelei watched the pair disappear down the hall and looked at Max to find the man smiling faintly.

"I believe you will end up with the older Miss Pugh, m'lady," he said.

Lorelei sighed. "Are you sure, Max?"

"Oh, very sure, m'lady. I did heed Lady Olympia's words but still needed to see for myself. I have. I saw that gleam he so loves to talk about seeing in your eyes."

"Damnation," she muttered and ignored Max's repressive frown. "I like Miss Pugh, do not think I do not, but I did not wish to be changing nurses so soon."

"Do you not wish your father to find a little happiness in his declining years?" asked Argus, all too aware of Olympia's prediction that the Duke of Sundunmoor was soon going to shock the world by marrying the nurse to his daughter's new sons.

Lorelei gave him a half smile. "Well said and the words even made me feel the pinch of guilt for about a heartbeat. I just did not wish to lose one servant I was almost accustomed to and have to start all over again, but if Max says it will happen, then it will." She cocked her head. "Ah, the thunder of the approaching herd of family."

She laughed as her family soon surrounded her and Argus. The moment she told them where the babies had gone, they all raced off to find her father and Miss Jones. Lorelei looked at her husband and Max, who were both frowning at her, and shrugged.

"That was most unfair, m'lady," said Max as, after ensuring that the footman had taken their coats and hats, he began to lead them to the parlor.

"A prize is always appreciated more if it is hard won, Max," she said piously.

"You also know that your father will now hear them all coming and work even harder to elude them."

"With dear Miss Jones desperately trying to always stay just five paces behind or closer, no matter where Papa goes or how fast he runs," she said and grinned.

Max paused in opening the door to the parlor and looked at Lorelei. "You did see the glow. I had wondered."

"I saw the glow."

"I am pleased you recognized it."

Lorelei looked up at Argus and smiled. "How could I not, Max? I see it every time I look in a mirror. I just pray that Papa will find as much happiness with Miss Jones as I have with my husband."

"It is, of course, not seemly for you to attempt to take a hand in matchmaking when it concerns your own father."

"Why not? He is too young to lurk about here all alone and, once Olympia told me there was to be a match between Papa and Miss Jones, I will confess that I could see it. They are perfect for each other."

"Which they should be allowed to discover for themselves just as His Grace and I allowed you to discover your love for yourself."

"Oh. So you think I should not have tried interfering in any way?" She shrugged. "Oh, do not fret so, Max. It will not hurt anything."

"Of course not. I am certain you know best, m'lady." Opening the door, Max bowed and then ushered them inside the room where Aunt Gretchen waited. "As you await your father's return, m'lady, do enjoy your visit with your aunt. She has some lovely scarves made in a stunning new shade that she is most anxious to gift you with."

The door shut behind her and Lorelei looked at the yarn her aunt was merrily knitting away with. Every so often Gretchen came up with a color that was just not going to please anyone but herself. This was definitely one of them. An odd shade that reminded her of rotten fruit. Max had always warned her when her aunt had such a horrid color so that she could avoid being gifted with anything the woman made in it. He had clearly neglected to do so this time and Lorelei knew it had been on purpose. She looked up at Argus, who grinned.

"My love, I do believe Max won that round."

ABOUT THE AUTHOR

Hannah Howell is an award-winning author who lives with her family in Massachusetts. She is the author of over thirty Zebra historical romances and is currently working on a new historical romance featuring the Murrays, HIGHLAND AVENGER, coming in December 2011! Hannah loves hearing from readers and you may visit her website: www.hannahhowell.com.